WHAT READERS A

*T*IME ANL ~ ~~~~~

BOOK 1

"A unique premise ... sort of a Back to the Future meets virtual reality, with a little dash of Seventh Heaven thrown in. Abby and Merrideth are wonderfully developed characters, and I loved watching them bond over the history behind the house and its previous inhabitants."
—Tiffany A. Harkleroad, "Tiffany's Bookshelf
Amazon Top 1000 Reviewer/Vine Voice

"What if you could have a God's-eye view of your own life, running it forward and backward in time, viewing it from different points-of-view? How might that affect your understanding of events, especially the ones that disappoint you? Abby and Meredith have that kind of view of the life of Charlotte Miles, the girl who lived in their house one hundred and fifty years before, and it leads them into new understanding of their own lives and God's not-always-comfortable way of caring for them."
—Leanne Hardy, author of *Crossovers*

Time Travel without the SciFi! McCullough complains of history textbooks that are boring and poorly written, unimaginative, creating a distaste on the part of students for history. He states, "....there's no end of wonderful books to read. Give them good books!...Go where things happened. Feel what it was like in the snow at Valley Forge." Thank you, Deborah Heal, for such a book. Kids would devour history if they were required to read books like this... I thoroughly enjoyed this story and look forward to the next two in the series. 5 out of 5 stars.

—Mary L. Hamilton

Highly recommended for YA and Adult book clubs! A story crossing three genres! Time and Again is an unparalleled story of Fantasy, Sci-Fi and Historical fiction all into on one extraordinary tale! Deborah Heal has successfully created a unique story that YA and Adults will both enjoy. The characters seem so real the reader will feel he/she knows them. The addition of characters and intrigue steadily builds until the very end... The descriptiveness is complete so the picture of the background scenery is vivid in one's mind. 5 out of 5 stars.

—LA Wonder

"The characters are likable and I cared about them—those in the here and now, and those from the past. The two main characters are able to watch history unfold, literally before their own eyes with a neat modern twist, while it shapes (as history should) their own lives. It's a great book for teens and adults."

—Susan S., Amazon reviewer

"An easy flowing book where the characters and town came to life. It was one of those books for me that was hard to put down, "just one more page" type books. It is so special to watch Merredith as she comes out of her shell and the friendship they give to Michael. The history they learn as they go back in time was put in such a way that I found myself sitting there `watching' the Douglas/Lincoln debate, seeing the difference in the candidates clothing and speeches from the author's description. Deborah's writing brought out the emotions for me as well....whether a smile or tears. Much of the story was built on true facts. I'm looking forward to the next book, *Unclaimed Legacy*.

—Jutzie (Top 1000 Reviewer)

Wonderful insight into God's view. Besides providing a great insight into some of the issues and realities of slavery, this book does something even more important. It gives a very useful insight into God's view, which is outside time, and how "all things work together for good for those who love and fear God" works. This is cleverly done through the time travel computer and is a wonderful lesson for people struggling to understand why things have happened. 5 out of 5 stars.

—Craeg Grace

"The story's 21st-century realism, its time travel via desk-top computer, and its embedded Civil War-era story appeal to a broad range of interests. Positive character formation, an appreciation for the past, and recognition of God's hand in our daily lives make this book a great read."

—Philippians 4:8 reviewer

Written with authentic, detailed research and faithfulness to the era, Deborah Heal's book, *Time and Again*, brings alive the pre-Civil War year of 1854, Abraham Lincoln's run for government office, the Underground Railroad and the brutal, harsh realities of slavery... The subtle Christian faith message in this story is in no way preachy or overwhelming because Deborah presents the life lessons the main characters learn in a way that's natural, believable and relevant. Mysteries are solved, truths are revealed, and Merrideth learns she can trust God and "all things work together for good for them that love God."... Engaging and entertaining, this book is appropriate for ...young adults and adult readers alike. What I want to know now is how I can get my hands on that computer program so I can go back in time too! 5 out of 5 stars

—Paula McGrew

"This was one of the most original and enjoyable novels I have read in a long time. I usually read suspense, but didn't miss the "action" because the characters kept me interested in their historical discoveries. Heal is a gifted writer. I am delighted to add her to my favorite authors list, and have already downloaded the second in this series."

—Cheryl Colwell, author of *The Secrets of the Montebellis*

Read to the final full stop and be amazed! There are many wonderful things about this book, like an insight into the lives of people helping slaves, fascinating insights into history...but the most amazing is understanding the verse "All things work together for good to them that love God, to them who are the called according to his purpose" (Rom 8:28). This is one of the most powerful ways I have read where this is made real. We can't see life from God's eternal perspective, but through the clever use of a time travel computer Deborah lets us in a sense experience life as God does… I recommend is reading to the final full stop, because in true brilliance the real power and message is all finally revealed at the very end. I highly recommend this to all readers, but especially to teenagers or anyone trying to understand why problems and other horrible things have happened in your life. See how God may be seeing things...it's way different to how we do, and it's because he loves us! 5 out of 5 stars.

—Malo Bel, author of *Four Given*

TIME AND AGAIN

"For I know the plans I have for you," declares the LORD, "plans to prosper you and not to harm you, plans to give you hope and a future."

Jeremiah 29:11

TIME AND AGAIN

BOOK 1

DEBORAH HEAL

WRITE BRAIN BOOKS

www.deborahheal.com

Time and Again

This is a work of fiction. Any references to real people, events, institutions, or locales are intended solely to give a sense of authenticity. While every effort was made to be historically accurate, it should be remembered that these references are used fictitiously.

Scripture quotations are from the Holy Bible, King James Version, except for Jeremiah 29:11, which is from the NIV
Photograph: "Heal Farm House" by Robert Heal

ISBN: 978-1482627213
ISBN: 1482627213
Literature & Fiction: Religious Inspirational: Historical
Fiction: Mystery/Detective: Historical

Also available as an e-Book.Other works by Deborah Heal:
Unclaimed Legacy (book 2)
Every Hill and Mountain (book 3)
Once Again: A Novella (book 4

IN MEMORY

To Ruth Fite, my eighth grade English teacher, whose words next to the star at the top of my story opened my eyes to the possibilities:

"Be sure to give me a copy of your first book!!"

CHAPTER 1

Abby had at first considered volunteering at St. Louis Children's Hospital for her required Ambassador College service project so that she could "contribute to the community while also enlarging her horizons." But her roommate, Kate, reminded her of her tendency to faint at the sight of blood. Several of her classmates chose to build homes for disadvantaged families with Habitat for Humanity. But since she had never actually used a hammer before, much less a power saw, being a "companion and tutor to an economically disadvantaged adolescent" had seemed like a much better choice. After all, it would be good practice for when she became a teacher after she graduated.

After packing up her dorm room for the summer and saying goodbye to Kate, Abby left Chicago and drove south six and a half hours, following the directions her client's mom had given, through terrain foreign to her city-girl eyes. Just after the sign that said Brighton, Illinois—

population 1,750—she turned onto Miles Station Road. It got narrower and bumpier with each mile until there were no more houses, only cornfields and the occasional tree.

Then, in the last bit of daylight, she crossed the railroad tracks she had been told to watch for and pulled up to the house where she would be spending the summer.

Kate had teased her about being a "governess" and warned her to watch out for dark, brooding men skulking about. Now, getting slowly out of her little blue car, she thought maybe Kate was more right about the Jane Eyre bit than she knew.

The two-story house standing in the gloomy shade of several huge oak trees had once been white but had obviously not seen a paintbrush in about a million years. One faded blue shutter hung at a drunken angle, squeaking as it shifted in the wind. There were no shrubs to soften the foundation, just some scrubby grass struggling to survive in the shade.

Service Project, she reminded herself firmly and knocked on the door. It opened and a smiling woman with an outstretched hand said, "You must be Abby. I'm Pat. Come on in."

She shook Pat's hand, relieved to see her friendly and pleasantly ordinary face. She didn't look at all like the sort of housekeepers in gothic novels.

"Hi, Abby Thomas."

Pat held the door wide, and Abby stepped into a sparsely furnished entry hall.

"I'm sorry everything is still such a mess around here. I haven't had much time to get moved in, much less begin fixing things up." Her words bounced off the bare wood floors and tall ceiling.

Pat turned toward the staircase behind her and called,

"Merrideth! Come on down. Abby is here."

"I can't wait to meet Merrideth."

"She'll be right down."

But there was no answering call from upstairs— no happy cry, no sound of eager, hurrying feet. Her young charge was apparently not as anxious to meet as she was. Pat called for Merrideth again, and when there was no answer turned to Abby and said, "How was your trip?"

"It was nice. I've never been this far out into the country before."

Still no Merrideth.

Pat glanced over her shoulder. "I'll go see what's keeping her." She pointed to a door opening off the hall. "Just make yourself at home in the living room."

The room where she was to attempt this was huge, or appeared so because it was nearly as empty as the hall, the only furniture a sofa and a television set. The gold floral wallpaper was faded and loose in some places. The floor was of rough wooden planks, bare of any rugs. Abby sat on the sofa for a while and then remembered she had promised to call home. She dug in her purse for her cell phone. No bars.

A whispered argument was raging upstairs. She strained to hear. It sounded as if Pat might be losing. She thought about going back to the car for her suitcases— and to try for better phone reception—but then she heard footsteps, thankfully two sets of them, coming down the stairs.

The girl came no farther than the doorway and stood there scowling at a chocolate-colored cat in her arms.

Abby approached her with caution. "Hi, Merrideth," she said, extending her hand. "I'm Abby." She lowered it when the girl continued stroking the cat.

Pat removed the blue baseball cap her daughter was

wearing and smoothed away a strand of hair that covered her eyes. "Say hi to Abby, Merrideth." The girl raised her eyes to glare at her mother and at last gave Abby a quick look and a mumbled greeting.

Merrideth had obviously not been blessed with her mother's good looks. Her face was round and pudgy, her eyes small and squinty. It was impossible to tell their color because her greasy bangs had fallen into them again.

On the phone Pat had said that Merrideth was "plump," and maybe could she help her with her diet? Fat was the word that came to Abby, even though she was ashamed of herself for thinking it. She had always considered herself a loving and accepting person, and she did feel pity for the sullen girl before her. But distaste was warring with compassion and about to win.

Abby reached out a hand again, this time to pet the cat. "Your cat is very pretty. What's its name?"

"She's not an it. She's a she."

Pat laughed a little and looked anxiously for Abby's reaction to this additional bit of rudeness.

Abby stroked the cat's head, and it began to purr politely. "What's her name?"

"Kit Kat. It's my favorite."

"Your favorite cat?"

"No. My favorite food."

"Why don't we help you with your stuff, Abby, before it gets too dark. Merrideth, would you like to help?"

Merrideth apparently wouldn't, because she left, still clutching Kit Kat. Pat helped Abby carry her things up the stairs and down the hall. She stopped at the last door on the left. "I figured you'd use this room for lessons."

A state-of-the-art computer and printer sat looking out of place on a scarred old oak table. It seemed an expensive purchase for someone who qualified for her school's tutoring program.

On the monitor, colorful images of beautiful homes scrolled by in a slide show, one the Frank Lloyd Wright home her brother had taken her to see in Chicago. The only other furniture in the room was a wheeled secretary's chair and a couple of mismatched straight-backed chairs.

"You're probably wondering how I can afford such an expensive computer," Pat said with a glance.

Abby tried to think of something besides, "Yes, I was wondering if you're ripping off Ambassador College." She couldn't come up with anything both polite and honest, so she mumbled, "Uh..." instead.

"It's from Merrideth's dad. He feels guilty about what he did—and about the fact he never visits her. It was probably bought with....Well, anyway, I didn't buy it. Just so you know."

"It looks like a good one."

"He put a gazillion computer games on that thing, but she's always playing with that house program. It doesn't seem like something a kid would be interested in," she said with a short laugh. "But I'm just the mom. What do I know? I just wish she'd remember to turn it off when she's through."

Pat went to the computer and began shutting it down. When the monitor blinked out she said, "Now, let's get you settled in. You're just across the hall."

After the barrenness of the downstairs, Abby was relieved to see the bedroom had the usual complement of furniture. Pat had obviously worked hard to make it cozy. The bed was covered with a pretty comforter in shades of rose and sea foam green. And it came decorated with its own sleeping cat, this one tan and white.

"It's a beautiful room."

"I'm glad you like it. The bathroom is next door."

Merrideth, her blue baseball cap back in place, appeared in the doorway, still carrying the purring Kit Kat. "There you are, Chippy!" She dropped the cat in her arms and went to scoop up the unsuspecting cat on the bed. "I've been searching everywhere for you."

Pat turned to Abby with a rueful grin. "Feel free to banish the cats from your room if you'd rather not have them underfoot."

"That's all right. I like cats." She stroked Chippy's warm golden back. "I can see why you named your other cat Kit Kat, Merrideth. But why is this one Chippy?"

"It's short for potato chip."

"That reminds me," Pat said suddenly. "I need to check on dinner. I'll leave you two to get acquainted."

Abby opened her suitcase and began taking clothes from it. Merrideth seemed intrigued in spite of herself, probably only sticking around out of curiosity. Personally, she was already exhausted from the effort of getting acquainted. Merrideth, making no effort at conversation, pulled a Kit Kat candy bar out of her pocket and watched her unpack.

Kate had said sarcastically that tutoring sounded like "a ton of fun," and Abby had reminded her that service projects are not done for the fun of it. She reminded herself now.

"So how do you like your new neighborhood?"

Merrideth contemplated the Kit Kat under her left arm and the Kit Kat in her right hand. "I don't know," she said, putting down the feline version in favor of the candy.

"Have you met any new friends yet?"

"No." She unwrapped the candy bar and dropped the paper onto the dresser.

"I'm sure there are other kids around." It was such a

lame thing to say that she expected Merrideth to flee in disgust.

"Yeah, but the only ones I've seen were wearing red baseball caps."

"So what's wrong with that?"

"They're not Cubs fans. That's what."

"Well, even though we're in Illinois, we're closer to St. Louis than to Chicago. You're in Cardinal territory now."

"That figures. This is such a stupid place."

When Merrideth glanced away, Abby whisked her bright red Cardinals shirt out of the suitcase and hid it in the bottom dresser drawer. Wearing it would not win her any points with Merrideth.

"Anyway, I'm getting out of this dump soon. My dad said I can come visit him this summer any time I want."

Abby took a stack of underclothes out of the second suitcase and put them in the top drawer. "That will be nice."

"So I wouldn't unpack everything if I were you."

Abby hid a smile. "I think I'll go ahead and unpack my underwear just in case." She laid her Bible on the nightstand.

"So, are you religious or something?"

"Something."

Abby took her cell phone out and flipped it open. Still no bars. She'd have to e-mail her friends later.

Merrideth sneered. "My phone's way better than that Quasar."

"You have your own phone? I had to wait until I was eighteen."

"Yeah," she said, pulling it out of her pocket. "My dad got me this Rhapsody II before I left Chicago. He said Rhapsody II is way better than Quasar. My dad said I can call him any time I want to."

"You have a great computer too."

"Of course I do. My dad bought it for me last year. Mom won't let me use her laptop. She says it's for her stupid business."

"You want to go play around on the computer then?"

"No."

Abby pulled her softball and glove out of her suitcase. "Do you want to play catch?"

"No."

Pulling her sketchpad out, she said, "Do you like to draw?"

"No."

"What do you want to do, Merrideth?"

"There is nothing around this stupid place, not like Chicago."

"That's true, there's no place like Chicago. I love going to college there. But we'll find neat places to go and things to do around here." She hoped.

Abby finally got a good look at Merrideth's eyes— which were actually a nice shade of brown—when she used them to shoot daggers at her.

"I'm eleven and a half, and I don't need a babysitter!" She stormed out of the room.

"Well, that was a good start," Abby muttered under her breath. It was going to be a long summer.

Delicious smells were in the air, and Abby followed her nose to the kitchen. It had to have been remodeled since the house was built back whenever, but it definitely needed a new look. The chrome-edged countertops looked like something from the 1950s, the avocado appliances were pure 1970s, and the cabinets were thick with who knew how many layers of yellowed white paint.

Pat was easing lasagna oozing with melted cheese

onto three blue plates.

"That looks and smells wonderful—just like my mom's."

"Homemade lasagna?" Pat said with a laugh. "Right. The kind that comes fresh from the deli. Would you mind telling Merrideth dinner is ready? Maybe she'll come if you ask her."

Abby frowned in confusion. "Sure," she said, wondering why anyone would have to be coaxed to come eat lasagna.

She found Merrideth in the living room watching some new reality show about supermodels. It didn't seem like a wise choice for an impressionable pre-teen.

"Your mom said to tell you dinner is ready."

"I'm watching TV, in case you didn't notice," Merrideth said without looking up.

"It's lasagna, and it smells great," Abby said pleasantly.

Merrideth turned at last and stared unblinking at Abby. "I'm not hungry."

Abby shrugged. She must not like lasagna as much as her mother thought.

Pat's embarrassment was obvious when Abby reported Merrideth's response. "Don't mind Merrideth. She'll warm up to you. I'll fix her a snack later."

And that would explain why Merrideth wasn't hungry for dinner. That and Kit Kat bars.

"As I said before, we moved from Chicago when Merrideth's school was out." Pat paused and set her glass of iced tea down. "Guess you're wondering why we would move into this run-down old place out in the middle of nowhere?"

"Well," Abby said, passing the salad bowl, "it does seem like a big change from the city."

"You see, I inherited this house from my great aunt. She died in February and left it to me in her will. Then when I found out my husband…when he got involved with…. Well, I won't go into that. Let's just say I was lucky to have this chance to start over."

"Merrideth said she's going to go visit her dad."

Pat glanced at the living room door and lowered her voice. "That's not going to happen, not if I can help it." She sighed and turned back to Abby. "I shouldn't have said that. Please don't say anything to Merrideth. I'm waiting for the right time to tell her."

"Okay." Abby studied her lasagna. She didn't know what to say. She realized suddenly that she had never actually talked to a divorced person before. Some of her high school classmates had suffered through the trauma of divorce, but she hadn't thought of it from the parents' perspective before.

"Anyway," Pat continued briskly, "I've always wanted to live in a big old house. I'd love to restore it to its former glory. I can already see the way it should look. Of course, I realize there's lots to do. For one thing, as you probably can tell, it isn't air-conditioned. To be honest, I don't have the money, at least not yet. Obviously, if I did, I'd pay you."

"Don't worry about that. I volunteered for this. I'm majoring in elementary education. Tutoring will be good teaching experience. And my parents live just over in St. Louis, so I can pop over and see them too."

"Then I'll try not to feel bad." Pat's smile left her face and she rubbed her forehead as if she had a headache. "When my husband and I—well, I've been a little distracted. Actually, a lot distracted. I'm ashamed to say that I didn't notice for quite some time that Merrideth was having trouble in school. It was gradual at first, and then her grades started dropping like a rock. I never expected it since she's so smart."

"What does she need help with most?"

"Everything, actually. You know, math, English, history. I talked to her new principal and thankfully, she's not going to hold Merrideth back a grade. She can transfer right into sixth grade. That is, if she works over the summer to catch up."

"I'm sure she'll be fine by the time school starts this fall." Abby wasn't sure of any such thing, but it seemed like the kindest thing to say to a woman with a headache. She would do her best, but wouldn't most of it depend on how committed Merrideth was? And she had a bad feeling about that.

"I've been swamped with my new job, and I will be all summer. So I didn't know when I was going to get the time to work with her. Then I just happened to see a brochure about your college's tutoring program. I was so relieved."

"And here I am, at your service. We could get started first thing tomorrow. You said you had books for me to use?"

Pat stood and started stacking their dishes. "I'll show you right after I clean up the kitchen."

"I'll help you."

"That's so sweet of you. I just know you're going to be good for Merrideth. She hasn't had much of a chance to meet friends."

Abby took the salad bowl to the counter. "Then I hope I can be Merrideth's first new friend." If she'd let her. "By the way, Pat, I'm having trouble using my cell phone—"

"Oh. Sorry, I forgot to tell you. Cell phone reception is really iffy out here. Feel free to use our home phone to call out."

"Thanks, I want to call my parents tonight to let them know I arrived safe and sound."

Abby carried the stack of textbooks she had been given, with the phone balanced on top, and plopped onto her bed. She had blinked in surprise when Pat first put the books into her arms. They were shabby and torn and smelled strongly of mildew. But knowing how tight money was, she hadn't commented. Where on earth had she gotten them? A yard sale maybe?

She thumbed through the math book. It was as bad as she had imagined: copyright 1984 with black-and-white photos of dorky kids. The English book was even worse: 539 pages of wall-to-wall text with only a few lame illustrations to break the monotony. It looked boring even to her, and she loved English.

She couldn't wait to hear what Merrideth would say when she got a look at the books.

Not bothering to open the other books, she stacked them all on the nightstand and picked up the phone. Her mom answered on the second ring. She didn't say she had worried about her, but Abby knew she always did.

"Wait, your dad wants to hear all about this, too. I'll get him on the extension."

Abby reassured her dad that she'd had no trouble on the trip downstate. She had not run out of gas, been approached by axe murderers posing as hitchhikers, or had any breakdowns. Furthermore, she had found the address with no trouble. And she reassured her mom that even though it was a creepy house in a creepy neighborhood, Pat seemed like a really nice woman.

"Except she spoils the girl rotten, so Merrideth's a little brat—well not so little. And she smells bad, too."

"Really? What kind of woman doesn't bathe?"

"Not her. Merrideth, the daughter. And worst of all, she's a Cubs fan."

"Now that's the first thing you said that has me worried," her dad said with a chuckle.

"Very funny. You should see the books I have to work with. I don't know how I'm supposed to help her without some decent materials."

Her dad chuckled. "Sounds like you've got your work cut out for you."

"This is going to be harder than I thought," Abby said.

"Maybe God put you there to bring a little discipline to her life," her mother said. "And if God put you there— and He did—He'll show you what to do."

Later, when she turned out the nightstand lamp, she was astonished at how dark the room was. She couldn't tell where the darkness of the walls met the darkness of the night sky in the window. There were no stars out and no streetlights. And no street noises intruded either. The bed was the right degree of softness, the sheets were cool and crisp, and she was wearing her favorite comfy nightshirt with the Ambassador College logo on the front. Perfect sleeping conditions.

But it was a long time before she felt herself drifting off. And when a tiny electronic beeping sound punctuated the silence she was instantly fully awake again. A blue glow, which in the absolute darkness seemed ridiculously intrusive, was streaming through the large crack under her door. Even though the light looked like something from a sci-fi movie about invading aliens, it was probably just Merrideth playing on the computer across the hall. Knowing that didn't make it any easier to get back to sleep, and so Abby pulled back the covers and got up.

The door to her room creaked horribly as she opened

it. She hadn't noticed it earlier in the light of day. Did doors creak only at night?

Both Pat and Merrideth's doors were closed, and the only light was the blue one coming from the open door of the computer room. Merrideth wasn't there, but the slide show of houses was going again. When she touched the mouse, it stopped and the words *Beautiful Houses: Take a Virtual Tour* were superimposed on an image of a contemporary glass and stone mansion.

Abby shut down the program and computer, and the room went black. Fortunately, she didn't run into anything as she stumbled her way in the dark back to her bed.

CHAPTER 2

Sunlight pierced her closed eyelids, and a fly kept buzzing around her face. When it decided to land and walk around on her lip, she pulled her arm out from under the sheet and swatted at it. Kit Kat, lounging comfortably by her side, meowed at the sudden movement and jumped off the bed. Too early, Abby thought and turned over with a groan.

It had taken a long time to fall asleep, and when she finally did, the sound of passing trains awakened her several times. And once she dreamed that the blue light had come back on.

Now, there was only the pleasant sound of leaves rustling in the early morning breeze, mixed with a wonderful birdsong, one that had a dozen different melodies and seemed to come from just outside her window. At about the same time, the sound of voices—a combination of cartoon and human—began to register. Tweety Bird and Sylvester were at it as usual, and so were

Pat and Merrideth.

"I tawt I taw a putty tat."

"It's summertime, Mom. Remember? School's over."

"But, honey, you know you're behind."

"I deed, I deed tee a putty tat!"

"If you'll do your schoolwork," Pat pleaded desperately, "I'll bring you home a nice treat. All right?"

Abby couldn't entirely make out Merrideth's reply, but she thought she heard something about Kit Kats, and then the front door thunked shut.

Abby's eyes flew open and she looked at the clock. Oversleeping on her first day on the job sure wasn't a good way to impress the boss.

She slipped out of bed and went to the window to check out the day. Her room faced east and the view was of the backyard and a weathered barn framed by flowering trees. Halfway between it and the house was an old well covered with warped wooden planks. Some kind of blooming vine twined up the iron pump handle.

She was about to turn away when the barn door opened and a small boy came out carrying a black cat and stood there in the morning sun as if he owned the place.

"Hi there!" Abby called.

Startled, the boy glanced up, trying to see where the voice came from. The cat began to hiss and struggle, and then springing from his arms, raced back to the barn. The boy took off just as quickly in the opposite direction.

"Hey, don't be afraid."

But the boy continued running and was soon out of sight behind the stand of trees at the edge of the yard.

She yawned and headed for the shower. It was time for the rookie teacher to prepare for battle.

As hot as it was already, shorts and a T-shirt would be nice, but instead she chose a loose-fitting white cotton dress, because it looked more mature. She wanted every weapon she could find to fortify her position with her student.

After toweling her hair a bit, she combed and scrunched it. If she left it down it would dry in a riot of brown curls. Instead, she pulled it to the top of her head and fastened it with a clip. It would be cooler off her neck, and more importantly, it might make her seem more teacher-ish.

With the hairstyle and the dress, Abby was as ready to face Merrideth as she ever would be.

"There are definitely kids in this neighborhood," she said cheerfully as she entered the living room. "At least one, anyway."

Merrideth didn't reply. She was sprawled across the sofa in her pajamas. Her hair hung in limp, dull strands, even worse than the night before. Abby leaned against the doorway and waited. Merrideth continued to focus on the TV.

Finally, Abby went to stand in front of it. "Hi, Merrideth. What's on?"

"Duh. Cartoons."

"Did your mom leave for work?"

"Yeah."

"Should I make you breakfast?"

"Already ate."

"Okay, then."

Abby found every evidence of that when she entered the kitchen. Three tiny, individual-sized boxes of Sugar Puffs lay empty on the table alongside a jug of milk getting warmer by the minute. A bowl of Sugar Puffs was glued to the table in a sticky puddle of milk and sugar, which Kit Kat and Chippy were helpfully lapping up.

Abby shooed them away and took the dishes to the

sink. Remembering there was no dishwasher, she resolved to have more appreciation for the conveniences she usually took for granted.

When she had her own breakfast of scrambled eggs and toast ready, she sat at the kitchen table to eat. The morning sun was streaming in the window, which like all those in the house, was very large, nearly reaching the ten-foot ceiling. Its fluted and elegant wooden trim was covered with the same thick, yellowed paint of the cabinets. A window like that, she thought, was just begging to be refinished. The sill—maybe ten inches deep—would be perfect for pots of bright flowers.

When she got back to the living room, Merrideth was still draped over the sofa, having gone from cartoons to game shows. Kit Kat, purring loudly, seemed enthralled with the TV, but Chippy was on the windowsill thinking private cat thoughts.

"Merrideth, can we turn this off and talk now?"

"I'm watching this."

"But it's time to begin your lessons. So, what's your favorite subject? I thought we'd start with math."

"I hate math."

"Okay, how about English?"

"I hate English, too."

She'd heard Granddad say a dozen times, "You can lead a horse to water, but you can't make him drink." But what if you couldn't even lead the horse to the water? It was time to improvise.

"You won't get the Kit Kat bars your mom is bringing home if you don't do your work."

"Oh, all right!" Merrideth hauled herself out of the sofa and stomped over to the TV to turn it off.

That was easy, she thought. Who said bribery was a crime? "Good. Let's work at the kitchen table."

Merrideth underlined the verb twice and looked up from the book with satisfaction. "You're wrong." She said, sneering. "Not every sentence has a subject. This one doesn't."

"Let's see." Abby looked over Merrideth's shoulder at the sentence in question: *Pride goes before a fall.* "Yes, it does. Look closer."

"You said that the subject is always a noun or pronoun. And this one doesn't have a noun or pronoun, so it doesn't have a subject."

"The subject is *pride.*"

"That's not a noun."

"Sure it is. It's what's doing the action of the verb *go,*" Abby explained.

"You obviously don't know what you're talking about." Merrideth angrily swiped her bangs out of her eyes. "*Fall* is the verb."

"No, it's a noun. It's the object of the preposition *before.* Haven't you had prepositions yet?"

"Sure I have. But a noun is a person, place, or thing." Merrideth pounded the table in frustration.

"Person, place, thing—or idea. A noun isn't always something you can see or touch. It can be intangible."

Merrideth frowned, but didn't argue.

"And there's another noun in that sentence. I'll give you a clue. The articles *a, an,* and *the* always signal a noun is coming."

"*Fall?* But that's an action word, a verb." Merrideth let her pencil drop from her hand and tugged at her hair.

Abby felt like tugging her hair too. "In this case, no one fell. It's the hypothetical idea of falling, a noun."

The English lesson went from bad to worse, frustrating both of them. Abby gave up trying to explain gerunds after a heated discussion that lasted fifteen minutes and got nowhere. The final straw for Merrideth came with the sentence, *You will need hiking boots for this vacation.* She confidently marked *hiking* as the verb of the sentence and closed the book.

"There," she said. "Can I go now?"

"Wait a minute. *Hiking* isn't the verb."

"Yes it is. It's definitely an action word."

"Yes, but it—"

"Don't tell me it's another one of those gerund things!"

"No…." Abby didn't have the heart to bring up participles. "We'll discuss it after lunch. I think we need a break."

But after lunch, Abby couldn't face another English lesson and gave Merrideth the afternoon off. Merrideth spent the time glued to the TV, but Abby sequestered herself in her room with the English textbook and wondered what in the world she should do next.

Pat struggled through the door at five o'clock, carrying her purse, laptop, and several plastic grocery bags.

"I'm home."

"Here, let me help," Abby said, taking two of the bags from her.

Merrideth tried to look in the bags her mother still held. "Did you bring me a treat?"

"Of course I did. I promised you I would." Pat clutched the bags close and asked Abby, "Did she do her work?"

"Yes, we worked on grammar today."

"Honey, I'm so proud of you." She pulled out a twelve-pack of Kit Kat bars. Merrideth snatched it from her, and having obtained her reward, headed toward the living room.

"Just one for now," Pat called. "I don't want you to

spoil your appetite. I brought home fried chicken, and I know you love it."

Pat was pleased that Merrideth came to the table for dinner—although she didn't touch the slaw and took only a few bites from her drumstick. And she was happy with the upbeat—if edited—report Abby gave of Merrideth's progress with English. Merrideth frowned and said nothing.

"That's great!" Pat said. "You'll be caught up in no time."

Abby wanted to ask her more about Merrideth, especially that bit about her being really bright. But she didn't want to talk in front of her student. Pat chattered happily through the rest of dinner about how well her job was going, describing the office she had been assigned and talking about several promising contacts she had made for possible real estate deals.

Merrideth wore her frown all through dinner, and spoke only when spoken to, although Abby didn't figure it had anything to with that old-fashioned rule about kids being seen and not heard. And afterwards, when Abby suggested Merrideth help her wash the dishes Merrideth didn't answer at all, just shuffled out of the kitchen, presumably to go watch more TV.

Pat seemed to take her behavior as normal, but Abby could barely resist the urge to go haul her back and hand her a dishtowel. When she was little, Abby had sworn to her parents that when she had children of her own, she would never spank them. Now, she wondered if she had been a little hasty in taking that option off the table.

Once Merrideth left the kitchen Abby expected the conversation to turn again to the topic of her academic progress. And she would have the opportunity to ask more about Merrideth's ability and background. But Pat began a long, detailed story about a family who might be looking for a realtor since they were rumored to be moving away from the area.

Then, when they finished the dishes, Pat dried her hands and said, "I'm going to my office to make some phone calls. I want to follow up on it before some other realtor swoops in. Why don't you girls play a game or something?"

Abby didn't see Merrideth in the living room. And the door to her room stood open so it was easy to see she wasn't there either. She should probably try harder to find her. But the thought of enduring Merrideth's surly attitude through whatever games adolescents played—assuming she could even talk her into playing one—was more than she could face at the moment. And so she settled into her room with the books Pat had provided. After all, a good teacher must make lesson plans.

She picked up the math book and thumbed through the musty pages. It wasn't her best subject. English was, and considering how well that had gone—well, she'd better postpone math until Merrideth was in a better mood. History might be easier to handle.

She got caught up in the history books. They were a lot more interesting than their boring, moldy covers had indicated. She jotted down some notes to herself and felt pretty good about how she would handle the lesson for the next day.

She flipped open her phone. Still no bars. The clock said 11:23. More time had passed than she realized, which often happened when she was reading. And something was nagging at her and had been for the past hour. The house was too quiet. She had not heard Pat come out of her room or Merrideth come up to bed.

When she stepped out into the hall, she saw that

Merrideth's door was still open, the room dark. A light came from under Pat's door, and she was talking softly on the phone.

Across the hall, the computer was on again. The *Beautiful Houses* program was back up, the houses scrolling by across the screen. She must have been so zoned out that she hadn't heard Merrideth come up.

She went in and sat down at the computer. If Merrideth liked architecture and beautiful houses that would be at least one thing they had in common. Maybe they could take a look at it sometime after their lessons. She closed the program. Besides *Beautiful Houses*, the computer was, as Pat had said, loaded with lots of games and educational programs. Merrideth's dad had obviously spared no expense.

But right now, all she was interested in was reconnecting with the outside world. She logged onto Yahoo and checked her e-mail. After only one day away, there was a ridiculous number of messages waiting for her, including one from a college friend bewailing his troubles fixing the muffler on his car and asking how her tutoring was going.

And Kate had sent one of her typical rambling messages. As usual, it was mostly about her boyfriend Ryan, who was "so sweet." The rest was about her upcoming trip to Europe, which was going to be "awesome," ending with a plaintive, "Why don't you answer your phone?"

Abby sent off quick replies to everyone, explaining that she would have poor phone service for the summer and they should e-mail her instead.

She shut down the computer and went into the hall. As she passed Pat's door, she heard her still talking on the phone. She didn't linger to eavesdrop, but it didn't sound much like a business conversation.

She could hear the television and started down the stairs, determined to make Merrideth turn it off and go to bed. The stairs creaked and the only light came from somewhere far away. She should never have let Kate talk her into watching that marathon of horror movies, especially the one about the babysitter dismembered by chainsaw-wielding crazies.

But when she reached the living room, she saw it was inhabited by neither psychopath nor even angry pre-teen girl, just Chippy and Kit Kat, who were playing a rousing game of hide and seek under the sofa.

When she silenced the TV, she heard a noise coming from outside the front door that sounded a lot like shoes scuffling across the wooden porch. Knowing she was lit up like an actor on a stage for anyone looking in from the darkness, she scrabbled to find the light switch and flipped it off. Then, flattening herself against the front door, she turned the deadbolt. After she had resumed breathing, and a minute had gone by with no further sounds, she leaned over and cautiously peeked out the door's side window.

There was Merrideth, her phone in hand, calmly sitting on the porch step.

Abby tore open the door. "What are you doing out here alone this time of night?"

"Relax. This isn't the city."

"Maybe not, but you never know what might happen."

"Don't worry. Nothing ever happens here. This place is completely dead, which is why my stupid phone still doesn't have any bars."

Even a Rhapsody II? Abby knew she was being snarky, if only inside her head. She tamped down her impatience and said, "Well, come inside. You should be in bed."

"I can go to bed any time I want, especially in summer. Mom doesn't care."

"Well, I care. Kids your age need at least nine hours of sleep. Sleep deprivation causes—"

"How do know so much about it?"

"My mom's a pediatrician. She was always harping on it when I was growing up. When I was your age, I had to be in bed by nine o'clock. Even in the summer."

"Well, my mom lets me do whatever I want. My mom loves me."

"I'm sure she does, but please come in now."

"Whatever. I can't call my dad anyway."

Pat's room was dark and quiet when they went past it. But the blue light was on again in the computer room. Pat must have decided, for some strange reason, to play on the computer before she went to sleep.

"Go on to bed. I'll shut it down."

Merrideth just frowned and said, "Whatever," before closing herself in her bedroom.

CHAPTER 3

"No." Merrideth yawned. "It's too boring."

"Well, we could try math or—" Abby began.

"I hate math."

"—we could go back to English."

"No way." Merrideth, dressed in pink shorts and an oversized T-shirt with a photo of a cat on the front, lay on the sofa with Chippy under her arm.

"In that case, we're back to my first choice—history," Abby said firmly. Merrideth sighed but didn't answer. "So let's get started. We don't even have to go up to the school room—"

"It's a computer room, not a school room."

"Okay, fine. Let's just work in the kitchen."

Merrideth didn't move.

Abby's first inclination was to say, "I'll tell your mom," but she restrained herself because she was pretty sure it wasn't something a professional teacher would say. But she had no problem resorting to bribery again so she said, "You won't get your treat tonight."

Merrideth looked up and smiled smugly at her. "I still have some Kit Kats left over from yesterday." She turned back to watching Sponge Bob.

It might be helpful if Pat could hear the lecture that Abby was starting to form in her head: "The Supply and Demand Theory as Applied to Kit Kat Bars." But lecturing one's client wasn't exactly the kind of behavior that would result in good relations and a glowing report to her college supervisor. And she was counting on a strong recommendation for her resume from her supervisor.

Apparently, she would have to rely on her persuasive abilities alone. Abandoning any hope of getting Merrideth to the kitchen table, Abby nudged Kit Kat from her customary spot on the windowsill and settled comfortably there with one of the history books Pat had given her. Grumbling in complaint, Kit Kat padded away in a huff.

Merrideth lethargically played with her hair as she stared, seemingly entranced, at the TV.

Having a voracious appetite for learning herself, it was hard to understand how a person could be as resistant to learning as Merrideth was. Abby remembered her professor's opinion on the subject, that a desire to learn is one of the things that distinguishes man from other animals. And when that desire is completely gone, that person has become something less than human. Based on his theory, Merrideth had already passed the couch potato stage and was well on the way to becoming a real slug.

"This should be interesting," Abby said, thumbing through the book. She saw Merrideth grimace and quickly added, "It's a little different, The History of Illinois." She paused to examine a page of black and white illustrations and thought of all the unfortunate students who might have perked up had they been in color.

"Okay, for fifty points, what's the state bird of Illinois?"

Watching Sponge Bob with exaggerated interest, Merrideth didn't answer.

"It's the cardinal," Abby said patiently. "How about the state tree?"

Merrideth rolled her eyes wearily and said, "White oak. The state flower is the violet. The state animal is the white-tailed deer. The state mineral is fluorite. The state prairie grass is big bluestem. The state slogan is 'Land of Lincoln' and the state nickname is the 'Prairie State.' Oh, and I forgot—the state fossil is the tully monster."

"What's a tully monster?" Abby asked in surprise.

"A soft-bodied marine animal. Any more questions?"

"Of course, you know the state capital is—"

"The first capital was Kaskaskia, but it kept getting flooded so they moved it to Vandalia, but people up North complained so they moved it to Springfield because it was near the center of the state. Illinois became a state in 1818. Now can I get back to my show?"

She might claim not to have a favorite subject, but Merrideth was sure good at state history. "Let me find something more challenging," Abby said, flipping through the book. Then she got caught up in what she was reading, and for a while the only sound came from a commercial about the latest Barbie. Astronaut Barbie came with her own space suit, complete with air tank and helmet, other accessories sold separately.

At last Abby looked up from the book and said, "I bet you don't know where the first battle of the Civil War was fought."

"Well, it wasn't in Illinois," Merrideth said with a snort. "I think it was South Carolina."

"You're right, Fort Sumter. But in a way, the first

battle happened nearly twenty-five years before that in Illinois, not far from here. As a matter of fact, the battle occurred in Alton, where your mom's real estate office is. That's only about fifteen miles from here."

Merrideth didn't answer.

"Listen to what it says here."

Elijah Parish Lovejoy published an anti-slavery paper in Alton. Although Illinois was a free state, it bordered the slave states of Missouri, Kentucky, and Ohio. Many Alton citizens were pro-slavery and didn't like what Lovejoy published.

Three different times, Lovejoy's presses were ripped apart and thrown into the Mississippi River. But it didn't stop him. Each time, he purchased a new press and kept on writing against slavery.

In 1837, the fourth press arrived by steamboat in the night and was secretly stored in a warehouse until it could be installed at the newspaper office. But word got out and a mob gathered, demanding Lovejoy turn over the press. When Lovejoy and his friends refused, the mob shot and killed him, torched the warehouse, and destroyed the press.

The story of Lovejoy and the abolitionists is the story of the enduring vigil for freedom of thought, speech, and the press. The mob action at Alton was the first, but unrecorded, battle of the Civil War.

"Well, did you know that?"

Merrideth looked up innocently. "Were you talking to me?"

Abby slapped the book shut and, leaving the window seat, marched over to stand in front of the TV.

"Hey, I can't see!"

Abby closed her eyes, cleared her throat, and counted to ten. She didn't know whether to laugh or cry. At last she said, "Okay, you win. I give up ... for today. But how about this? Instead of lessons, let's go exploring. We could look in the barn. Or we could go for a walk around the neighborhood."

Merrideth snorted rudely. "Have you seen this neighborhood—all six houses?"

"No, I only saw your house when I drove up. Why don't you show me?"

"Because it's stupid and hick and boring. That's why."

Abby sat down on the arm of the sofa. Merrideth pulled away and sat at the opposite end. Abby didn't delude herself that it was to make room for her to sit beside her. No doubt she wanted to avoid touching her.

"I bet it's not so bad. Or we could drive into town and visit the library."

"That's a little too much excitement for me," Merrideth said, still staring at the TV.

"You might be surprised how interesting a library can be."

"Go ahead. My favorite cooking show is just coming on."

"Or you could show me around the house. That would be a history lesson in itself."

"Why do you care about this stupid old house?"

"I love old houses. I got that from my dad—he's a history teacher. How old is this house, do you know?"

"How should I know? Who cares anyway?"

"It's got to be really old. It would be fun to explore the attic. There's probably some really cool stuff up there."

"Mom already looked, and there isn't nothing up there."

"Anything," Abby corrected automatically.

She gave it one more attempt. "Just imagine all the living that has gone on in a house this old."

Merrideth merely stretched and said nothing, seemingly entranced by Paula Deen's instructions on how to make a hash brown casserole.

Abby conceded defeat on round one, but surely she could think of something that would get through to an eleven-year-old child. Hopefully, before the summer was over and she had to submit a report to her college supervisor.

Meanwhile, she wouldn't mind exploring on her own. Actually, she was relieved Merrideth wouldn't come along. Keeping her patience was tiring.

The only thing of interest in the living room was a set of sliding doors, heavy and darkly varnished. It took a bit of muscle, but Abby was able to drag them open. Inside was just another disappointingly empty room.

"I guess this was the dining room," she said over her shoulder. Merrideth didn't comment. "Because, see, it leads right into the kitchen," she said, opening the door on the opposite wall. "This little room between it and the kitchen was the pantry." Merrideth didn't respond, but Abby knew from the sound of channel surfing that she was still there.

She stepped into the pantry and flipped the wall switch. Nothing. Enough sunlight coming from the kitchen revealed dark varnished shelves and cabinets covering the walls.

And there was another door. It was warped and difficult to open, but she scraped it across the floorboards far enough to look in. She let out a little grunt of excitement. "Come look, Merrideth. I found another set of stairs." Still no answer.

She peered into the gloomy stairwell. "They're so steep and narrow, it's a wonder they didn't fall and break their necks," she muttered.

Not wanting to do so herself, she closed the door, promising herself she would explore the staircase and what lay beyond it with a flashlight when she had seen the rest of the downstairs.

Other than that, everything was straightforward and rather ordinary, no secret doorways or trapdoors. So far, Merrideth was right—it was a rather boring house.

There was always a chance there were interesting things upstairs she hadn't noticed yet. But it was time to stop indulging her curiosity and get back to doing her job.

When she arrived back in the living room, Montel Williams was interviewing four skinhead neo-Nazis. Kit Kat and Chippy were still there, both asleep on the windowsill, unconcerned with the argument raging, but Merrideth was gone. Then Abby saw her through the front window and realized she had walked out to the mailbox.

She opened the door and stepped out onto the porch. The yard was so different from her first impression the evening before. The brooding quality was gone, and now she saw that the oak trees she had found sinister at dusk were in the morning light a positive force, like sentinels casting their protective shade on the old house. The quietness—broken only by that strange birdsong again—was unfamiliar, but nice.

There were no ornamental plants, unless the prairie grasses and wildflowers that grew in profusion on the road banks counted. Straight ahead a short distance away on the other side of the lane, the railroad tracks lay shining in the sun. She couldn't see what was on the other side of them, for the embankment on which the tracks ran was several feet higher than the road.

No other houses were visible from the porch, but she knew there must be more behind the trees that blocked her view to the south. To the north they were hemmed in by a field of tall, green corn.

She sat down on the top step of the front porch and waited for Merrideth. "Get any mail today?"

"Why would you, on your second day here?" Frowning, Merrideth started back up the sidewalk, hugging several white envelopes and a small plain package to her chest.

"No, I mean did you get any mail?"

"Just this," Merrideth said, holding up the package.

"I was wondering if you ever get any letters from your friends back in Chicago."

"I got one from Amber last week, but no one else. My dad never writes. He calls me, though— sometimes— and sends me stuff." She shook the package and sat down next to Abby. "Here," she said with a sour smile. "You did get something."

The something was a postcard from Kate, and Abby smiled at the picture on the front. Corn stood tall and green in a huge field. The banner at the top read Springfield—Corn Capital of the World. On the back Kate had written in her usual tiny but neat handwriting:

Dear Abby,

Sure wish I could have talked you into coming with me to Europe! You should have gotten an extension on your service project like I did. Anyway, I promised you postcards, so here's the first... from my hometown! Hope you're having fun in your neck of the woods (or cornfield). Gotta go. I'm late leaving for the airport.

Love, Kate

"What's so funny?" Merrideth asked as she opened her package.

"It's just my goofy college roommate. What did your

dad send you?"

Merrideth peeled away the tissue paper and something pink, orange, and spandex slipped out. "He wants me to start an exercise class so I can get skinny," she said, holding the workout clothes up for Abby to see. "As if. Here, why don't you try it on? It will fit you."

She was searching for something to say when she noticed the name printed on the package. "So your dad calls you 'Merri'? That's cute."

"I hate it. It's so cheesy. And it's not like it fits or anything."

"Well, maybe you ought to be. Merry, I mean."

"I don't exactly have much to be happy about, you know."

"Well, you know what they say, 'A merry heart doeth good like medicine.'"

"No one I know ever says that."

"It's from the Bible. My roommate always quotes it. By the way, when she gets back from Europe, she's going to come visit me here. I'd like for her to meet you."

"No thanks."

Abby felt a flash of irritation. "Why not? She's nice and you'd like her."

"But she won't like me. People don't, you know."

"Well, she will. I would think since you're so bored—"

"Here comes the train."

At first they could only hear it and feel the vibrations as it rumbled toward them from the north. Then an Amtrak with four passenger cars passed the screen of trees.

"I wonder if it's going to Chicago," Abby said.

Merrideth scowled at the train, but with interest. She was probably wishing she was on it.

The train was nearly even with them before they noticed the small figure crouching on the tracks to their right. "Oh, dear God! It's a little boy," Abby cried, springing up from the porch steps. And then the train was thundering past, blocking their view.

CHAPTER 4

In stark terror, Abby began to run, praying that he would be all right, hoping ambulances came this far into the country. When the train was past the boy was gone.

She was breathing hard when she reached the tracks. To her relief, they looked normal, not covered in gore as she had expected them to be. She stumbled over the gravel, steel, and timber of the tracks and saw the boy sitting calmly in the grass on the other side of the embankment. Sunlight sparkled on his shaggy but glossy, black hair. He was studying something in his hand.

"Are you all right?" Abby asked. He looked up in surprise, and she saw that he was the boy she had seen coming out of the barn. His eyes were a deep brown and freckles nearly covered his nose. She judged by his missing front teeth that he was about six.

She heard a noise behind her. Surprisingly, Merrideth had followed and was huffing and puffing her way over the embankment. "Hey, little boy, don't you know...it's dangerous...to play...on the tracks?"

"Yes," Abby said. "You scared us to death. We thought the train hit you."

Eyes shining, the boy held out a rather grimy hand with a complete lack of concern.

Abby took the shiny piece of copper that had borne Lincoln's profile before the train had flattened it. She shuddered and handed the penny back. "It was a very dangerous thing to do, you know."

The boy spoke, obviously explaining something about the penny and the track, but Abby had no idea what he was actually saying. Whatever it was, it sounded as if all the beginning consonants were missing.

"I think we should call the police," Merrideth said. "What's your name?"

He answered politely and even repeated it slowly and patiently when Abby asked him to, but neither she nor Merrideth could understand what his name was.

Merrideth darted a look at her. "Where do you live, little boy?"

Wordlessly, he pointed to the south and then descended to the road and began to walk that way. His grass-stained jeans didn't cover his ankles. The logo on his ragged T-shirt was too faded to read but involved beer.

"We'd better go talk to his mother," Abby said.

"He's retarded, isn't he?" Merrideth whispered.

"Maybe. But maybe he just has a speech impediment." Abby planned to lecture her later on the inappropriateness of the word "retarded," but for now, she was just happy that Merrideth was making conversation.

After they got past the trees at the edge of Merrideth's yard, Abby realized that they weren't nearly as isolated as she had first thought. Several neat, well-kept mobile homes sat on either side of the road as it ran alongside the tracks to the south. But then they came to one that looked abandoned. The grass was overgrown, and a shed lay in ruins, nearly hidden by tall weeds.

"I told you it's a stupid neighborhood," Merrideth said between breaths.

"Shh. He probably lives in one of these trailers." Abby frowned, but she couldn't think of anything positive to say either. "You know it's pretty amazing that anyone lives way out here, besides farmers, that is. I mean, why should these houses be clustered here anyway?"

"Who knows?" Merrideth said, running a little to keep up.

The boy continued on down the road, glancing back once in a while to be sure they followed. When they approached the last trailer, a rather rusty one, the boy slowed and allowed them to catch up with him. Merrideth was just about to ask him how much farther to his house when a dog suddenly rushed at them, barking furiously.

Merrideth shrieked and Abby felt her heart stutter and plummet to her stomach. The boy said something reassuring, which Abby interpreted, after a moment, as, "Don't worry! He's chained to the front porch."

Abby and Merrideth panted in unison.

"My heart is pounding!" Merrideth said. "He scared me to death."

"Me too! I nearly wet my pants."

Merrideth giggled and Abby was surprised. Apparently, it was a bonding moment.

"He just don't like new people," the boy seemed to say. The black dog, medium-sized but very muscular, stopped barking and began to wag his tail furiously as he came near. When he patted its head, the dog added worshipful whimpering.

"Is that a pit bull?" Merrideth said, keeping her distance.

"Maybe part pit bull, but my sister-in-law Meg—she's a dog trainer—says that pit bulls aren't any more dangerous than any other kind of dog. Unless they've been trained to be mean." Abby leaned down to pet the dog.

"Yeah? Well, how do we know whether that one has been or not?"

The boy said something more and motioned them forward.

Abby pulled her hand back. "Well, I think we had better be going."

She and Merrideth decided to walk in the middle of the road to avoid any other unpleasant surprises. It seemed unlikely that a car would come by anytime soon. They crisscrossed the road whenever the boy's eye caught something of interest—a stick or rock here, a wild flower there.

"What I want to know is, are we about to the kid's house or not?" Merrideth's upper lip was sweaty, and her hair worse than ever.

"We haven't walked that far. Besides, what's your hurry? We've got all afternoon."

"Maybe you do, but I'm expecting an important call anytime now. From Chicago."

"Oh. Well, I promise we won't stay long. But we need to let his mother know what he was doing."

They came to a small white house with green shutters. Next to it was a late model car, its front end jacked up and its hood open.

"Look at that!" Abby said. "A silver Camaro, just like my brother's. It's an awesome car. The engine is a 6.2 liter V8 and—"

She was just about to run a hand over its sleek side

when a stream of foul oaths came from beneath the car. She jerked her hand back in shock and saw at nearly the same moment that a man's legs and booted feet were sticking out from under it.

"I didn't hurt your car," she said indignantly.

"Sorry, ma'am," came a muffled voice. "I wasn't cussing at you. It's this d—it's this stupid transmission."

"Oh." she said. The little boy shook his head and put his finger to his lips. "He don't like people botherin' him when he's working." At least that's what Abby thought he said.

"Oh," she said again. "Sorry."

As they walked on, Merrideth rolled her eyes. "Are you a flippin' expert on every subject?"

"No, of course not," Abby said. "My uncle Peter is the mechanical one in the family. He taught me how to do simple auto repairs. Well, actually, he taught my cousins and my brothers and they taught me. Alex and Aaron didn't want me going away to college without knowing a few things about Skippy."

"Who's Skippy?"

"That's my car, nothing as cool as a Camaro."

The boy said something she didn't understand until she had him repeat it.

Abby laughed. "Yes, I do talk an awful lot. I get carried away sometimes. My brothers call me Blabby Abby."

The boy pointed and said something about his house, so they continued to follow him down the lane.

His house was the oddest one Abby had ever seen. It would have been impossibly tiny, but someone had added a lean-to, which now sagged from one side of the building. The whole house was brown—brown shingles, brown siding, even brown window frames. Curtains, which should have made it look homey, somehow didn't.

"It looks like a bathroom at a state park," Merrideth whispered.

After indicating that this was indeed where he lived, the boy showed no more interest, and did not suggest going inside. He said something about "Mrs. Somebody," "nice," and "house," and began to walk away.

Abby called out, but the boy kept going. "Maybe he's afraid he'll be spanked for playing on the tracks," Abby said. "But I'll have to let his parents know."

She knocked on the brown door, lightly at first, and then louder, but no one came. She didn't have the guts to interrupt the man working on the car again. They might as well follow the boy.

The road came to an end at a barbed wire fence enclosing a pasture. The last house was small and covered in ugly gray asphalt shingle siding, but it was neat and well kept. The name on the mailbox said "Arnold."

A woman was chopping energetically at the grass growing alongside the front sidewalk. The boy ran ahead to talk to her. From a distance, Abby had thought her no more than middle-aged, but when they reached the edge of her yard, she saw that, although she was tall and sturdy, Mrs. Arnold was quite old.

She was not dressed like any old person Abby had ever met. On her head, the woman wore a large sunbonnet over her gray hair, which was encased in a hairnet that peeked from under it in places. She wore a faded calico apron over a faded and shapeless calico dress and men's lace-up work boots over bagging socks.

Mrs. Arnold stopped chopping at the grass and leaned against her garden hoe. "Good afternoon to you. Must be the new folks up to the big house."

"Hi," Abby said, shading her eyes from the sun. Mrs.

Arnold smiled warmly at Merrideth. "Your Aunt Ruth was my best friend, God rest her soul."

"Mom said she was my great-aunt," Merrideth said, maintaining the bored look she had perfected. At least she hadn't rolled her eyes.

"Well, now won't that be fun for you to have some nice young people to play with, Michael?"

The boy grinned, and Abby turned to him and said, "Oh. Michael. That's your name."

"He can't talk proper, you know," Mrs. Arnold said.

"I wanted to talk to his mother. I knocked, but no one answered."

"Oh, she's in there."

Abby was going to ask more about that when Mrs. Arnold suddenly cried, "Well come on then," as if she were reluctantly giving in to their repeated pleading. "My garden's this a way." Picking up her hoe, she began to shuffle away.

Abby glanced at Merrideth whose look said, what did I tell you? Merrideth began humming the Mr. Rogers' theme song, "It's a Beautiful Day in the Neighborhood."

Michael opened a squeaky gate and Abby and Merrideth followed the old woman, who, using her hoe like a cane, started down a shady little path covered in wood chips. Ferns, violets, and hostas grew luxuriantly under a large maple tree.

"This is amazing!" Abby said.

A black and white cat sat among the green ferns, meowing as they passed.

"That's Spooky," Mrs. Arnold said. "Best mouser ever."

Past the tree, the path took them back into the sunlight and masses of colorful blooming plants. Abby recognized a few of them—gladiolas, hollyhocks, coneflowers, and phlox. Their combined sweet scents flavored the air. A flowerbed made from an old tractor tire contained petunias and marigolds in colors that clashed but somehow looked just right. Here and there, vegetables grew among the flowers along with other plants that most people would call weeds.

Even Merrideth seemed fascinated. "Look at all the butterflies!" She smiled when a monarch landed on her arm.

A bird, perched on the roof of a small garden shed, was singing the same crazy song Abby had heard from her bedroom window. First it sounded like a cardinal, then a robin, next a blue jay and then other birds she didn't recognize.

"It's that ol' Mr. Mockingbird," Mrs. Arnold said as if she could read her mind. "He sings nice, but he tries to scare away all my other birds, even the bluebirds, and Heaven knows how ornery they are."

Some of the beds were edged with curious glass domes that in the sunlight appeared to be lit up like little lanterns in shades of blue and green. Mrs. Arnold explained they were electric insulators left behind when the power lines were modernized back in the 1930s.

They came to a rosebush loaded with deep red blooms. Abby leaned over to sniff. "Ahh, so sweet!"

"Now Mrs. Miles, she was the one who could grow roses. Her trellises were just covered in pretty pink roses all summer."

"My granddad's a rose expert," Abby said. "He's the rosarian at the St. Louis botanical gardens."

"Ruth's husband was a Rotarian. Helped a lot of folks during the big flood down in Alton. The Rotary Club still meets every Wednesday at Sal's Place in Brighton."

Abby smiled but didn't try to explain the difference

between a rosarian and a Rotarian.

Mrs. Arnold breathed deeply in satisfaction. "Turned ninety-two in May, and I still do it all myself. People say my garden is the nicest one in Miles Station. 'Course my house isn't near as nice as the colonel's. Doesn't have the soul like Colonel Miles' old house has either." Mrs. Arnold looked off to the distance as if she had forgotten they were there.

"Who is Colonel Miles?" Merrideth asked.

Mrs. Arnold's gaze snapped back to them. "Why, he's the one this whole town was named after, honey. It was him that built the big house you're living in. They say it was him that got the railroad to go through here down to Alton."

Abby was puzzled. "What town do you mean, Mrs. Arnold?"

"This town, honey—Miles Station." Mrs. Arnold leaned on her hoe and was silent for a moment. Propping her chin on her ancient, spotted hands, she said, "Well, I reckon it's not much of a town anymore. But farmers used to come for miles around to shop and have their grain milled into flour in the colonel's steam mill."

Abby wanted to ask Mrs. Arnold more about the town, but she turned away suddenly and called out, "Michael, you stop trying to catch my squirrels, boy, or I'll tan your hide."

He turned and smiled, unafraid of her threat. The squirrel wasn't afraid either, and went back to eating from an ear of dried corn wired to a post.

"Take them around and show them my pretty fish." Mrs. Arnold had found more weeds and was happily chopping away again.

Michael led them down the path as it continued its way around to the other side of the house. A bluebird was splashing and preening in a makeshift birdbath made from an upturned garbage can lid. The bird darted away in a flash of blue fire as they approached.

Dozens of Evening in Paris perfume bottles, in another shade of deep blue, were wired to fence posts, for no apparent reason other than to add color. The path took them to another shady, ferny spot where water was trickling over pink sparkly rocks into a child's blue Disney wading pool.

The goldfish didn't seem to mind their humble abode, or that the pennies that dotted the bottom of the pool didn't quite cover the cartoon image of Snow White.

In spite of its oddities, the garden was appealing and restful, and they stayed there for a while before returning to the front yard. Mrs. Arnold was wrestling with a garden hose that didn't want to unwind properly.

"I hate this cantankerous old thing!" She stared at the sky as if to see if any rain clouds had happened to arrive. "Lord, if you would send us some rain, I wouldn't have to water my hydrangeas."

"We could help with that," Abby offered.

"That's all right. You all go on now."

Abby tried again before they left to ask her more about the vanished town, but Mrs. Arnold was no longer in the mood for polite conversation.

"I ain't got time for gabbing. Got work to do," she said, wiping her face with her apron. "You've got work to do, too. You find the soul of that old house and you'll find….Well, Charlotte will show you."

Merrideth tugged on Abby's sleeve and whispered, "Come on. She's a crazy old woman. Let's go home. I've got to be there for my phone call."

Abby said goodbye and Michael waved from across the garden where he was trying to catch a butterfly. The old lady didn't watch them leave, just kept muttering as she wrestled with the hose.

When they had passed Michael's house, Abby stopped suddenly and turned back to look. "Of course!" she said. "I should have realized. That answers our question."

"What's our question?" Merrideth asked.

"Why his house looks like a bathroom at a state park."

"Okay, I give up. Why?"

"Because what Michael is living in is the old train depot—the Miles Station depot."

Merrideth didn't respond. She was already huffing and puffing.

CHAPTER 5

Merrideth raced to the answering machine in the kitchen as soon as they got home. There were no flashing lights, which meant zero messages. Shoulders slumped, she kept her back to Abby.

"Whew!" Abby lifted her damp hair off her neck. "I'm going to take a shower."

Merrideth looked in the living room before turning toward the stairs. "Kit Kat, Chippy, where are you?" The cats came galloping down the stairs, and Merrideth scooped them up and went to the living room.

Abby followed her. "Man, I sure am hot and sweaty," she hinted. "I can't wait to get in that shower. But I will if you want to go first."

"I'm going to watch TV." Merrideth flopped onto the sofa. The cats squirmed and tried to get away.

"I must smell like a pig," Abby continued. "I'm going to use some of my new kiwi-scented shampoo. I have plenty if you want to borrow some."

"No thanks. I hate washing my hair."

Well, she had tried. So much for the I'm-an-older-girl-and-you-should-let-me-be-your-role- model ploy. There was always the bribery technique, but wouldn't offering more Kit Kat bars be contributing to the obesity of a minor? Couldn't she smell herself? Maybe not. She should just say it. But how could you tell another human being, "You stink. Really bad. You should take a shower. Right away. And again tomorrow and the next day. And by the way, get that cat fur off your sweaty arms."

It wasn't her job, was it? After all, she had come here to teach English and math, not personal hygiene. Abby sighed. Feeling like a coward, she left her student and started up the stairs.

Knowing she was just going to get hot again, Abby resumed her exploration of the house after she had showered. At least it would be clean sweat. She had hoped that after the moment of bonding she had sensed earlier, she would be able to coax Merrideth to come along. But she was "too tired" and besides, her "favorite TV show" was on. So Abby continued on alone.

The first thing she checked out was the dark pantry staircase. She came prepared this time with the high-powered flashlight her dad had given her as she left home for college. "Jesus is the light of the world," he had said with a chuckle. "But this will come in handy, too."

The stairs were thick with dust and cobwebs. Pat's great-aunt Ruth had undoubtedly been too frail to climb them in her later years. When Abby got to the top she tried the door, but it wouldn't budge. Whether it was locked or just stuck, there was no use expending all her energy shoving at it. She would have to try it from the other side. She closed her eyes and pictured the layout of the upper floor. If she had it right, the empty room next to hers was on the other side of the door.

She went cautiously back down the narrow steps to the pantry and then up the main staircase to the second floor. She knew there weren't any extraneous doors in her room. And since Pat and Merrideth's doors were open, she poked her head in each of them long enough to see there were none there either. Nor was there much else. She felt a pang of something like guilt. Pat had not expended as much effort redecorating them as she had the room she'd given Abby.

Just as she had figured, the spare room did have an extra door. Just not the right one. When she opened it, sauna-like air—black, hot, and dry—rushed at her face. The stairwell was dark, the wooden steps narrow and dusty. But they led up, apparently to the attic, not down to the pantry. She closed the door, determined to explore that another time.

There were no other doors in the room, not even a closet. But there was a beat up old cedar wardrobe. She smiled, hoping against hope, as she always did whenever she saw one, that it would lead to Narnia. As usual, it didn't. There were only a few tangled wire hangers and a safety pin.

But what if the secret was behind the wardrobe, not in it? She went to the side of it and shoved until she got it away from the wall enough to see that her theory was correct. A small door was built into the wall behind it. She pushed the wardrobe until it was out of the way.

The lock turned easily and the door only squeaked a little when she opened it. She could see all the way to the pantry below and hear Merrideth's TV program loud and clear.

It was only a little mystery solved, but she was pleased. She called out, but Merrideth didn't hear her, or pretended not to.

"Hey, Merrideth, let's play on your computer."

And Merrideth, moving surprisingly fast, came pounding up the stairs. "Don't touch it. It's mine. My dad bought it for me."

"I didn't touch your computer." Abby followed Merrideth into the room. "Well, I e-mailed a few friends last night. Sorry, I should have asked first."

Merrideth took the seat in front of the computer, and Abby sat down next to her. Kit Kat appeared suddenly and jumped onto her lap.

"My dad got me lots of games," Merrideth said, pointing to the icons dotting the screen. "They cost a lot of money."

"That's for sure. What do you like best?"

"This one, I guess." Merrideth clicked on the Bubble Town icon and the screen filled with colorful little bubble faces.

"That's a good one," Abby said, setting the cat back on the floor next to Chippy, who had just joined them. "Kate and I used to get so caught up playing it that we would almost forget to go to class. But there are also a lot of educational programs here we could use for our studies. You have a cool multi-media encyclopedia and dictionary."

"Boring," Merrideth replied without taking her eyes off the screen. She used the mouse to shoot a group of smiling pink faces, which disappeared with sighs and giggles. Next she aimed at some smirking green faces.

"And a typing tutor program."

"Already know how to type."

"How about Music Appreciation?"

Merrideth rolled her eyes. "Please," she said, dragging out the word sarcastically. "All educational games are stupid and boring."

"Well, that one about architecture is educational and you like it."

Merrideth turned to stare blankly at her.

"You know, *Beautiful Houses*," Abby explained. "Your mom said you always play that."

"I don't play that," she said, brushing her bangs out of her eyes. "But it's always showing up on the screen."

"Let's take a look at it," Abby said.

Merrideth grudgingly minimized her Bubble Town game in progress and clicked on the *Beautiful Houses* icon. Immediately, the program flared to life. It featured homes of every type, from Beverly Hills mansions to thatched cottages in Ireland.

"If you could have your dream house, what would it be?"

"I don't know, but it wouldn't be anything like this dump," Merrideth said.

Abby picked up Chippy to make her quit pawing her shoelaces. "Once your mom gets this place fixed up, it will be great."

"But it will still be in Nowhereville."

"Well, I think it's time I explored the kitchen," Abby said. "Your mom would probably appreciate a hot dinner when she gets home from work."

"Something smells delicious," Pat called when she got home that evening.

Abby popped her head out of the kitchen. "Hi. I hope you like stir-fry. It's a variation Mom and I invented."

"That sounds wonderful, but I never intended for you to have to cook," Pat said with a small frown.

"That's okay. I like to cook."

Pat laid her purse on the hall table. "Where's Merrideth? I don't hear the TV."

"She's upstairs on the computer."

They heard her clomping down the stairs, and then she arrived breathless at the kitchen door. "You won't believe what I just found on my computer." Then seeing Pat, she said, "Oh, hi, Mom. Abby, you gotta come see. This house," she said, gesturing expansively, "is on my computer."

"Just a minute, Merrideth," Abby said. "I'm forgetting the stir part of stir-fry." She hurried back to the kitchen with Pat and Merrideth trailing after her.

"Mom, you won't believe how weird this neighborhood is! There's a crazy old woman who lives down the road, and she has a really strange garden. It's kind of pretty. And there's this retarded boy that lives in an old train depot."

"So you went exploring the neighborhood."

"Yeah. There's nothing else to do," Merrideth said.

Abby hid a smile at the way she suddenly remembered to make her voice sound bored.

"I'm not sure Michael is mentally handicapped, Merrideth. And Mrs. Arnold isn't crazy—just kind of eccentric...and very old."

"Whatever."

"Maybe you could go visit her sometime, Pat. She was friends with your Great Aunt Ruth."

"I've been planning to, and I will." Pat sighed. "As soon as I get the time."

"You forgot to tell your mom the best part, Merrideth."

"What? You mean the part where we almost had a heart attack because we thought Michael had been run over by a train. Or do you mean the part where we almost got attacked by a pit bull?"

"No, what Mrs. Arnold told us about. That this used to be a regular town. It was named after a man called Colonel Miles, and this was his house," Abby explained.

"Well, how about that," Pat said. "This must have been an important house. You would never know it from seeing it as it is now."

"Mrs. Arnold said this house has a soul," Abby said, grinning.

"Maybe it does." Smiling, Pat stroked the faded wallpaper. "Like they always say—if only these walls could talk."

"Yeah, and there used to be trellises on the front porch," Merrideth added. "With pink roses growing up them. There's a picture of it on the computer upstairs."

"What do you mean?" Pat said.

"I found it on that program, *Beautiful Houses*. That's what I was trying to tell you."

Abby smiled kindly at Merrideth and then told Pat, "The program features houses from around the world. She must have found one in the style of this house."

"*She* is standing right here. And *she* found *this* house, not one like it." Merrideth stormed off.

Abby's bedroom was on the uncomfortable side of warm. But even so, in a way she was glad the house had no air conditioner. It was sort of nice to lie there listening to the natural sounds of the night. Crickets chirped enthusiastically. And down the road, the pit bull barked twice, and was silent. The curtains fluttered, and that soft sound blended with the creaks and murmurs of the old house.

Other people on long-ago nights had slept here. Perhaps the crickets wouldn't have seemed so loud for them, for there would have been other, town sounds—horses' hooves, wagon wheels, church bells, the depot whistle, low voices, footsteps on board walks. Abby wondered what Colonel Miles and his family had been like.

She didn't realize she had fallen asleep until she started awake at the sound of footsteps, quiet and careful, in the hall. Merrideth, going down the hall to the bathroom? But then came ten tiny beeps. Someone was using the phone just outside her room. She didn't mean to eavesdrop, but the house was quiet and Merrideth's voice was clear.

"Hi, Dad. It's me. Sorry, I didn't know it was so late. I waited and waited, but you didn't call…. I don't know. Okay, I guess…. Yeah. Say hi to Sylvia too I guess…. Yeah. She got here two days ago. And she's not a babysitter… But exercise is so boring and… Dad, you don't understand. There aren't any health clubs around here. This is Hicksville and… I told you she's not my babysitter…. She knows about a lot of stuff, but why should I spend my summer studying? I bet all my friends at home are hanging out and doing fun stuff…. Yeah, all right, but when can I come stay with you?"

The hall was silent as Merrideth listened to her father's explanations. At last, she replied, her voice small and resigned, "Oh. Well, bye."

Abby heard the phone settle into its cradle, and Merrideth's footsteps—more a shuffle than a stealthy tiptoe this time—and then a door closing. Poor kid. It must be tough to be so far away from her dad. Merrideth had refused to talk to her all evening, and Abby had finally left her to her game of Bubble Town.

She turned over and tried to get sleepy again. Just as she felt herself floating away, the blue light was back, insistently streaming into her room again. Funny, she hadn't heard Merrideth come back.

She got out of bed and went to check the computer across the hall. Yep, the houses were doing their slide show again. Why was it so difficult for Merrideth to admit she liked an educational game?

CHAPTER 6

"What do you know? Actual traffic." Merrideth stared out the front window where she sat supposedly reading. "That silver Camaro we saw just went by. Funny, he doesn't look like the kind of guy who would say the words we heard coming from under that car."

From the other windowsill in the living room, having gotten there before Kit Kat, Abby looked up from her Bible. "Okay, enough excitement. Time to get back to your reading." For about the millionth time.

"I don't know why we have to waste time reading. I want to use my computer."

"Quit acting like I'm torturing you." She took several calming breaths. "Merrideth, if the only thing I accomplish this summer is to get you to read a book, I'll feel like I've been a success." Although it was unlikely her college supervisor would agree.

"Yeah, yeah, yeah. I already heard this."

Abby was just ready to resort to bribery again, when

Merrideth picked her book up. She had brought along Jacob Have I Loved because it had been one of her favorites when she was about Merrideth's age. She turned back to her Bible reading for the day in Romans eight, and pondered the meaning of verse eighteen. She heard Merrideth turning pages but carefully kept her eyes on her own reading.

"There, I finished chapter one," Merrideth said with satisfaction. "Nineteen more chapters to go. That's 202 more pages."

"Sorry, reading time is not over."

"But this is boring."

"Maybe it seems boring to you because you haven't gotten past the author's introduction. It's not the most exciting part, but you have to read it before you get to the action."

Merrideth sighed dramatically, and even without looking, Abby knew she was rolling her eyes. She went back to Romans, and soon she heard Merrideth flipping pages.

"But I don't get it. Who's Jacob? I looked through the whole book, and there are no characters named Jacob."

"It's an allusion to Jacob and Esau in the Bible."

Merrideth dropped the book as if it were contaminated. "I'm not reading a religious book."

Abby's eyes widened in surprise. Before she could think of what to say, Merrideth asked, "Who were Jacob and Esau?"

"They were the twin sons of Isaac. 'Jacob have I loved' is a quote. God said it when he blessed Jacob. He went on to say, 'Esau have I hated.' The author wants you to think about that while you're reading the book."

"Does it have anything to do with Caroline and Louise?"

"They're twins, aren't they?"

Merrideth found her place and began to read again. Abby breathed easier. After a while, she closed her Bible, leaned back against the side of the window, and smiled at the sound of Merrideth steadily turning pages.

Abby went to the window and looked out. Merrideth didn't seem to notice, even when the mail carrier's mini-truck stopped at the mailbox in front. After it had gone around the bend, Abby saw Michael scuffling along down the dusty road. He was carrying something covered in what looked like foil that sparkled in the sunlight.

Three boys came out of the trees and joined him on the road. It was nice to see that Michael had other friends his age to play with. Then, one of his erstwhile friends shoved him and Michael almost fell. Now that they were closer, she realized that what she had taken for friendly smiles were not that at all. Another boy grabbed whatever it was Michael was carrying, while the third began gleefully pounding on his arm.

Abby tugged at the window, but it was heavy and swollen shut. Anger gave her added strength, and suddenly the window flew up. The boys were chanting, "Michael is a retard. Tardo, tardo. Michael is a retard."

Fury bubbled up in her throat and she couldn't speak. At last, she sputtered, "Stop that. You, stop that," and ran to the front door.

Frowning, Merrideth put her book down and followed after Abby.

The three tormentors were gathered around what turned out to be a plate of cookies Michael had been carrying, and they were stuffing them in their mouths as fast as they could. Seeing Michael's avenging angels come barreling out the front door, the boys dropped the plate and made a hasty retreat. Abby shouted for them to stop, but they kept going, one boy turning to grin at her.

"He's just a little kid," Merrideth shouted to their backs. "Why don't you pick on someone your own size?"

"Actually, they are his size, Merrideth. But I just can't understand how boys that little can be so mean."

"Girls are just as bad," Merrideth said. "They think they're so special, so above everyone else. They think they can call you anything they want. It's their right in this world to put you down, as if you didn't already know you're a loser. They just can't be happy until they make you cry."

Abby blinked and looked closely at Merrideth. Her face was red and she looked close to tears.

Merrideth knelt beside Michael, who was valiantly trying to wipe the dirt off the two remaining cookies. "Good for you. They didn't make you cry, did they, Michael?"

He held out the plate to Abby. "Mrs. Arnold made these cookies for you."

The pink glass plate looked like an antique, its delicate beauty now marred by a large chip. The cookies were heart-shaped and frosted in pink to match the plate. They would have been pretty except for the gravel and dirt embedded in the icing.

"They look delicious," Abby said. "But, how are you?" Lifting his shirtsleeve, she gasped at the condition of his skinny arm. The bully's punches had left red marks, but worse than that were the bruises, ranging from purple to a sickly green, indicating that persecution from his peers was a longtime sport in the neighborhood.

In spite of the rule about picking on someone your own size, Abby felt a strong urge to take off down the road after the little thugs who had hurt Michael. Then a picture of herself sitting in a jail cell wearing an orange jumpsuit popped into her head, and she tamped down her rage. She smiled at Michael. "Well," she said as calmly as she could manage. "We just finished with reading time and need a break."

Merrideth reached into her pocket and pulled out a Kit Kat bar. Handing it to him, she said, "Here. Sorry, it's a little squishy."

"Thanks," he said, quickly tearing the wrapper back. "It's not too 'quishy."

Abby laughed. "I'm ready to explore the attic, Michael, and since you're so brave, would you like to come with me?"

The little boy's eyes sparkled. "Sure," he said, wiping his hands on his jeans.

"Merrideth, are you coming?"

"Oh, I guess," she said with what seemed like feigned reluctance.

"Okay, my intrepid explorers. Follow me. I know a shortcut." They went into the house, and Abby led them to the door she'd found in the pantry. "Be careful. It's steep. This is the staircase the maid would have used to get back and forth from her bedroom and the kitchen."

Kit Kat appeared beside them. "Look, Merrideth, she wants to be an explorer too," Michael said, grinning.

Merrideth smiled and picked up the cat.

"Everyone hold onto the handrail," Abby said.

Merrideth chuckled. "Except you, Kit Kat."

They clomped up the dark stairs and assembled in the spare bedroom. Neither the cat nor Michael had any comments, but both looked excited by the adventure. Grinning, Abby went to the attic door and opened it.

As before, dry, hot air rushed out of the black stairwell. Kit Kat began to struggle in Merrideth's arms and let out a shriek that raised the hair on Abby's neck.

Even though she held her firmly, Merrideth couldn't prevent the squirming cat from launching out of her arms. She landed with a thump that echoed around them and then padded quickly up the stairs. They couldn't see her in the darkness until she turned and her eyes glowed back at them, as if to say, "Ha! I beat you to the top."

Abby went first, and then Merrideth, panting a little from the exertion. Michael brought up the rear.

When Abby reached the top she ran her hand cautiously up and down the rough, unfinished wall. "There must be a light switch here somewhere." Kit Kat purred and began winding herself around Abby's legs. It wasn't helping.

"You should have brought your flashlight," Merrideth said.

"How about if you—?"

"Don't even think about it. I'm not going all the way back downstairs."

"Wait a minute. I bet there's one of those pull chains." Abby took a cautious step into the dark attic, then two more, her hands blindly batting the air. At the same time that her right hand finally found the chain, something spidery brushed against her face.

"It's in my hair!" Abby squeaked.

Then the light was on, dim and yellow, from a bulb swinging crazily from the rafters, and she realized that she had been attacked by a mesh vegetable bag hanging overhead. Dry flakes fluttered down onto her face, and she brushed them away.

"Onions." Abby chuckled. "Your Aunt Ruth must have hung onions from her garden here to dry. My granddad does that."

"Maybe that's to scare the ghosts away," Merrideth said. "The way you screamed I thought you must have run into one."

"You're thinking of garlic, and I'm pretty sure it only works with vampires."

The attic was disappointingly ordinary. There were no treasure chests, dead bodies, or ghosts. National Geographics filled a dozen large boxes in the center of the room, and stacks of Time Magazine leaned crookedly against the wall under the sloping roofline.

"Some people just can't bear to throw away anything with glossy pages." Abby spotted a small, toppled mountain of brown grocery bags, each filled with yellowed Brighton Gazettes. "Or even newspapers—dusty, faded newspapers."

"I told you there wasn't anything up here but junk. Mom already looked." Merrideth wiped her hands on her shorts and sat down on an orange crate.

"And here I thought we were going to have a Nancy Drew sort of summer."

"More like a bored-out-of-our-skulls sort of summer."

"I hate to admit it, but I guess you're right. This really is a boring attic."

Merrideth sneezed twice and rubbed her eyes with the tail of her shirt. "You'd think that since we're forced to live in this horrible house, we would at least get to have a ghost or two."

Michael laid aside the wooden cane he was brandishing like a sword and went to check out a large cardboard box. Inside was a jumble of old toys. He took out a scratched and dented metal dump truck and gave it a push, seeming to admire the tracks it made on the dusty floor.

"See! You never know what you'll find," Abby said with a smile. Judging from Michael's enthusiasm for the beat-up old truck, he probably had few toys of his own.

"Where do you put the batteries?" Merrideth said, kneeling beside him.

"I'm sure when that truck was made, little boys used their own power and imagination to run it." Abby laughed to herself. She was starting to sound like her granddad. Obviously, there was nothing interesting here. Maybe they should go on down so Merrideth could get started on some math lessons.

She noticed a thick black book sticking out from between two boxes of magazines, and when she tugged it out saw the words Macoupin County Historical Society imprinted on the cover. Fine slanted handwriting filled the ledger's pages. She thumbed through it, scanning the words:

Twelve members present...coffee and cake served...meeting opened with a reading of the minutes...a raffle will be held to raise money to repair the museum roof....

"Let's get out of here," Merrideth said. "I'm hot."

Abby started to put the ledger back, and a sheet of paper slipped out and fluttered to the floor. She laughed. "I'm thinking Nancy Drew again."

Merrideth snorted. "Don't tell me. It's a secret treasure map, right?"

Abby squinted to read what was written on the paper. "Actually, it is. Sort of. Let's take it downstairs where the light is better and I'll show you."

"It's a plat map of Miles Station," Abby explained, carefully spreading the brittle paper on the kitchen table. "And see the date?" She pointed to the print at the bottom of the map, Survey by Charles Bilbruck, 1859.

Merrideth frowned. "What's a plat map?"

"Every county keeps plat books with maps of every

square inch of land. The land is divided into townships, which are divided into sections, which are divided into lots."

"I don't know how you can get so excited about a map," Merrideth said.

"I love maps. See. Here's the railroad. And here's Miles Station Road. These little black squares are buildings. Looks like there were lots of stores along Railroad Street. And see, Michael, here's your house." She pointed to the little building labeled Depot.

Michael got up from where he had been busy building roads of his own with the dented red dump truck and came and looked over Abby's shoulder.

"So what about this house?" Merrideth asked.

Abby rotated the map to the left and squinted. "There it is." She pointed to the owner's name under the little black square: Col. Jonathan Miles. "And guess what? The lane out in front of the house is labeled Maple Street. And see all these other streets—Walnut, Poplar, Chestnut, McPherson—and here's Lincoln Street." Mrs. Arnold was right. Miles Station had been a thriving little town.

CHAPTER 7

The weather seemed uncommonly hot and humid for June, especially for seven in the morning, but Abby wondered if that was just because it was the first time she had ever lived without air conditioning. In any case, her hair was a frizzy mess, and Merrideth's was positively limp and sticking to her sweaty face even though she had heard her tell her mom she had washed it—swore she had washed it.

"You sure have a lot of makeup stuff," Merrideth said, pointing to Abby's cosmetic case on the vanity counter.

"It takes a lot to get me so beautiful," she joked. Leaning closer to the mirror to apply her mascara, she nearly missed the anguish that rose in Merrideth's eyes and then was gone.

"Okay," she said briskly as she gathered up her things. "Before we get to our lessons, I thought we could take Mrs. Arnold's plate back to her while it's still cool—well, relatively cool."

"Anything to stall is okay with me," Merrideth said. "Maybe she'd like to see the plat map."

"That's a nice idea."

"Whatever."

The walk didn't seem nearly as long now that they were a bit more familiar with the neighborhood. The pit bull recognized them and only gave a token bark or two before wagging his tail in friendship. The homes along the way, including Michael's, were quiet. But then they got to Mrs. Arnold's house and heard singing.

Abby lifted the latch on the gate, and they followed the path around to the east side of the house. She stopped and turned to Merrideth. "Shh." Bathed in the morning sun, Mrs. Arnold was tending her garden and singing, in a surprisingly clear and steady voice, an old hymn Abby vaguely recognized.

Unaware of their presence, Mrs. Arnold sang joyously that Jesus was coming again on "some golden daybreak," on which "sorrows would cease," and "all will be peace." On that "glorious morning" even school days would be over.

Merrideth whispered a heartfelt "amen."

Suddenly seeming to sense them there, Mrs. Arnold stopped singing and straightened. "Oh, I'm so glad you came. Look!" She held out a small red tomato for them to see. "First ripe tomato and it's not even July."

Abby smiled and said, "You sure are a good gardener."

"I know it's a sin to be proud." Mrs. Arnold did not look overly contrite. "But I surely do like to get the first red tomato in Miles Station."

There was no sense reminding her she was the only one in the neighborhood who grew tomatoes. "We've come to bring your plate back," Abby said, "and to thank you for the cookies." She held the pink plate out. "But I'm so sorry. There's a chip on it."

A frown glimmered and was gone, and then Mrs. Arnold smiled. "Oh, that's right. Michael told me how those little pirates stole the cookies. Don't worry about that old plate, or the cookies either. Come on. I've got more in the kitchen."

Mrs. Arnold wrestled the warped back door open, and they followed her into a kitchen every bit as odd and beautiful as her garden.

Abby's senses went on overload. A green parakeet shrieked along with a cuckoo clock sounding the hour. The sweet vanilla smell of just-baked cookies was overlaid with the floral scent from perhaps a dozen vases of gladiolas adorning every flat surface. Every vertical space was covered with framed photographs, pictorial calendars—including one ten years old—newspaper clippings, and shelves of ceramic animals of every species known to man—and some not.

Mrs. Arnold gestured toward the metal dinette table in the center of the room. "Sit down and make yourself at home. I'll get the cookies." Skirting Spooky's food bowl and her work boots sitting on a newspaper, she went to the counter. She set the tomato on the windowsill above the sink, washed her hands, and then took out another pink plate from the cupboard.

Merrideth sat down at the dinette table.

"We can't stay long, Merrideth. We've got to get back to our studies."

"Hey, I need to rest."

Abby sighed and sat down too.

Mrs. Arnold filled the plate with pink sugar cookies from a cooling rack on the counter and took them to the table. "Help yourself. I'll pour us some iced tea."

Abby had never had cookies and iced tea at eight o'clock in the morning, but then why not? She moved a vase of gladiolas a safer distance from the edge of the table and laid the plat map down. "We brought something to show you, Mrs. Arnold."

The old woman sank into her chair with a grunt and adjusted her glasses on her nose. "What have you got there?" She brought the map close to her face and squinted in concentration.

"It's a map of Miles Station. We found it in the attic." Abby picked up a cookie and took a bite. "This is great."

"Yeah," Merrideth mumbled around a mouthful of cookie.

Mrs. Arnold handed the map back to Abby. "Tell me what it says."

"The print's faded, and pretty small in the first place."

Mrs. Arnold looked embarrassed, and Abby experienced a moment of shock when she realized she couldn't read.

"Didn't get to go to school much."

Abby put the map down in front of her and explained that the little squares represented houses and stores, and the lines were streets.

"Yes," Mrs. Arnold said excitedly, "there used to be houses and stores everywhere. Show me which one of those lines is Maple Street."

When Abby pointed it out on the map, Mrs. Arnold smiled. "There's the colonel's house and the blacksmith's and depot. And there," she said, cackling with delight, "that's where my house is, right there on Maple Street."

"It says Miles' Mercantile," Abby said.

"Yep, this here house is built where the Mercantile used to stand. My husband found all manner of antiqueytype stuff when they dug the basement for this house."

Mrs. Arnold leaned heavily on the table to stand and then went to a shelf by the back door and took down a globe-shaped glass jar on a battered black metal base. "Like this jelly bean machine." She set it on the table before them. *Jelly Beans* was printed in a fancy script across the glass, and on the base, in smaller gold print, Wm. Shrafft & Sons, Boston.

"It still works too. You just turn the crank and jellybeans come out. Well, they would if I hadn't eaten them all. The colonel used to bring jellybeans home from the mercantile for Charlotte because she was so partial to 'em. She used to watch for him at the front window. She was the prettiest little thing. Of course the colonel also had two sons, but he always said—"

"But Mrs. Arnold, you said...I'm confused," Merrideth said. Mrs. Arnold was back to peering at the map in fascination and didn't seem to hear her.

"When was all that, Mrs. Arnold?" Abby asked. "When you were a little girl?"

She looked up at them, eyes clouded with confusion. "No, that was the olden days."

"But how do you know so much about it?" Abby asked.

"Oh, don't mind me. I'm just a mixed up old woman. Probably Ruth told me about the colonel." Mrs. Arnold's supply of hospitality had apparently run out. She rose from the table again, and so of course Abby and Merrideth did too.

"Thanks for the cookies," Abby said. "I'm sure you want to get back to your garden, and we need to get back to work too."

Mrs. Arnold's smile was back. "You're welcome, dears."

Merrideth took off down the road at a brisk pace. "That does it! You've got to look at it now."

"What it?"

"That picture. I told you about it before. It's my house when it was the colonel's house in the olden days."

"I'm sorry. I don't have any idea what you're talking about."

"Never mind, I'll show you when we get home."

Merrideth refused to say anything more about it all the way home, which Abby found annoying, even though it was nice to see the way excitement lit up her eyes when she forgot to be bored. Her innate curiosity was coming out of dormancy at last.

When they got home, Merrideth tore open the door and raced up the stairs. "Come on. You've got to show me how to work the program."

When Abby got to the computer room, Merrideth had already launched *Beautiful Houses*. This time, an ancient castle, complete with moat and turrets, lit up the computer screen with the usual title, Beautiful House: Take a Virtual Tour superimposed over it.

"That's really cool," Abby said, sitting down next to Merrideth. "It's a famous castle—I can't remember its name. But it's the one Disneyland is copied from. It's French and dates from—"

"That's not the cool part," Merrideth said impatiently. She placed her hand on the mouse and clicked, and the Beautiful House slide show began.

"Yeah, I've seen that," Abby said dryly. "A lot. I thought you said you didn't play with this program."

"I don't. But it keeps showing up all the time, almost as if it wants me to, you know, play with it." Merrideth's voice trailed off. "I know that's impossible."

Abby had thought the same thing when the blue light

kept waking her, but at least she had sense enough to know the silly idea had sprung from her over-active imagination. "No, of course that's not possible."

Merrideth stabbed at the screen. "There it is! Look! Does that look familiar?"

"Oh, that is cool. It looks just like your house. Well, almost—" Then the image was gone, replaced by a quaint seaside cottage beside a lighthouse, and then after a few seconds, a converted barn. The houses continued to roll by.

"Do you know how to make it stop on that picture?"

"I can try." Merrideth got up from her chair, and Abby took her place before the computer.

"When it comes back, I'll be able to—"

"If it comes back," Merrideth said glumly. "The houses change every so often."

"There it is." Abby double clicked the mouse on the image, and it enlarged to fill the whole screen. "It does look like this house."

"I told you," Merrideth said with satisfaction.

"But it's not really this house," Abby said gently.

"I know it's not identical, but they could have taken down the rose thingies."

"The trellises on the front porch? Yes, and the carved wood trim at the eaves isn't there anymore either."

"Right, right. This picture must be from when the house was new. And see that smoke stack in the distance behind the house? That must be the grain mill Mrs. Arnold was talking about."

"But it can't be," Abby continued. "They didn't have photography back then—well, for sure not full color, high resolution photography like this picture."

"When did they first have color pictures?"

"I don't know for sure, but Mom and Dad's photo

albums are filled with black and white photos when they were growing up, until maybe the 1960s or 70s. And even though that may seem like the olden days to us, I'm sure no one had steam mills sitting around in their back yards then."

But when Abby scrolled down, she saw there was a caption under the picture that read: The Residence of Col. Jonathan Miles at Miles Station, Macoupin County, Illinois.

"There!" Merrideth said. "Read that!"

"Merrideth, I owe you an apology. But I don't understand. Why is this house—?"

"What do those do?" Pointing to the title bar at the top of the screen, Merrideth read, "Options, Setup, Location, Time Parameter, Extra Features."

"It looks a lot like my brother Aaron's architecture program. I wonder...," Abby said slowly, "...if it works...the same way."

When she clicked on the button marked with a little magnifying glass, the scene zoomed toward them.

"It does! See, you can use this tool to zoom in or back off."

They marveled over each tiny detail in the picture— the grain of the wooden shingles and wrought iron lightning rods on the roof, the lace curtains and shutters at the window.

And pink roses bloomed from the porch trellis, just as Mrs. Arnold had said.

They zoomed out again and spent time focusing on the steam mill and the tiny church in the background. Abby would have spent the rest of the day zooming in on each section of the picture, but finally Merrideth convinced her to try some of the other tools on the menu bar.

When she clicked the first few buttons, she got dialogue boxes asking for input that did not make sense to them. She ignored them because she was afraid to change any of the settings until she knew more about the program.

"We'll have to search for the program manual," Abby said distractedly, her eyes locked on the screen.

"Or maybe we can get instructions from the Help button."

"Right," Abby said dryly. "That could happen. Don't get your hopes up. I've never had much actual help with so-called Help."

One button had a little wheel-shaped icon, and Abby let out an excited yelp. "Awesome! It has video capability."

She saw the puzzled expression on Merrideth's face. "Watch." She clicked the icon and Colonel Miles' estate came alive. She laughed and pointed to smoke coming out of the smoke stack on the mill and cows walking down to the pond to drink.

"Isn't it cute? How did they ever make this program?" Merrideth asked.

"And why did they? Do you think it's a movie set?"

"Maybe. But it sure looks real." And then Merrideth shouted, "Look! There's someone at the window!"

"I think it was the curtain. That's cute. They're having a summer breeze, too."

"No, really. I'm sure I saw a person at the window. I want to have a turn."

Abby obligingly got up and Merrideth took the mouse and zoomed in closer on the window above the trellised front porch. A young woman in an old-fashioned white dress stood peeking out from behind the lace curtain.

"What in the world! You're right!"

"It must be Charlotte, you know, Colonel Miles'

daughter."

"If it is, you realize, don't you, that it's just an actress playing the part? And besides, no telling how many girls have lived in this house. It could be anyone."

Merrideth kept the view zoomed up as close as she could get to the window. "Well, I don't care. I know it's Charlotte."

"Maybe this is the newest reality show," Abby said. "Doesn't it creep you out to watch her walking around inside her room? I'm not saying she's real, but if she were?"

"She's real. And that's my room, too, you know."

"Maybe the manual explains it. You did get one, didn't you?"

"I don't know," Merrideth said absently. "Maybe."

"Well, where is it?"

"Probably still in the box," Merrideth said, pointing vaguely to the corner of the room where several boxes had been stacked.

Abby rummaged through the Styrofoam and bubble packing in the computer boxes until she found the instruction manuals for all the components of the system. But there was no documentation for the Beautiful House software. She did discover an 800-number for the computer manufacturer but knew they wouldn't help with the software.

"This is a lot more fun than Bubble Town," Merrideth said.

"There you are," Pat said from the door. "I called, but I guess you were so busy studying you didn't hear me."

"Mom, why are you home early?"

"I've got another migraine coming on." Pat rubbed her temples and turned to leave. "I'm going to lie down and try to head it off at the pass."

"Wait, Mom. Look," Merrideth said, pointing to the monitor. "I told you I found this house."

Pat looked over Merrideth's shoulder at the screen. "Too bad it doesn't look that good now. I wouldn't have to remodel."

"I think it must be part of a documentary, or something," Abby said.

"Isn't it cool, Mom?"

Pat pushed her hair off her forehead and exhaled. "It's great, Merrideth, but I think studying math and English would be a better use of your time."

"But, Mom—"

"Now that Abby's here, you shouldn't be wasting so much time playing computer games."

"Sorry," Abby said, stricken. "I just thought...well, she seemed to like—"

"That's okay," Pat said. "Only from now on, keep the fun and games for after school."

CHAPTER 8

"You can do this, Merrideth," Abby said, hoping none of her frustration was leaking out.

Merrideth sat at the kitchen table, staring blankly at the page of math problems before her. "Sure I can do it, if you let me have my calculator back." She put her head on the table.

"Don't you know your division yet?"

"I was absent that day." Her muffled voice came from beneath her crossed arms. "And you don't have to sound so shocked."

"It's just that you're so smart."

"I told you I'm stupid."

"So you think Mrs. Arnold's stupid?"

Merrideth's head popped up, and she scowled at her. "Mrs. Arnold's not stupid."

"Of course she's not. There's a difference between ignorance and stupidity."

"Oh, good. I'm not stupid. I'm just ignorant."

"Yes, actually you are. But there's a remedy for that. Come with me."

Abby pulled Merrideth's chair out from the table. "We're going back to the computer room, but no Beautiful House this time." She turned to look menacingly at Merrideth. "Or Bubble Town."

Merrideth followed her, shuffling along in protest until Abby said, "Shh! Don't forget. Your mom's sleeping." When she got to the computer, Abby opened up the math drills program she had noticed earlier. "Here, let's see how you do."

"But these are multiplication."

"I know."

"But the worksheet is division."

"I know."

It was painfully obvious after only a few problems that Merrideth was as behind in multiplication as she was in division.

"I thought so," Abby said. "No wonder you can't do long division. If you don't know that nine times seven is sixty-three, how are you ever going to know that sixty-three divided by nine is seven? And therefore, how will you ever be able to do the steps of long division?"

"By using a calculator?" Merrideth said hopefully.

"Wrong. You won't always have a calculator with you wherever you go. It's so much faster and easier to have it in your brain so you can travel light."

"So this is the miracle cure?"

"It's the second step of the miracle cure. The first one is for you to make the decision you can and will learn the multiplication tables."

"I didn't know you were a math expert, too."

"I, my dear, am practically perfect," Abby said.

"Way to brag," Merrideth said sourly.

"I'm kidding. That's a quote from Mary Poppins. I'm sure not perfect."

With a stern warning not to stop until she told her to, Abby left Merrideth practicing her multiplication tables, and went to see what she could rustle up for dinner.

It took a while to find anything promising. Most of Pat's food staples were still in boxes on the floor of the pantry in a confused conglomeration with various plastic containers and kitchen gadgets. Apparently, Pat had left Chicago in a hurry.

Abby began sorting everything onto the pantry shelves as she went through it. She found a box of macaroni and cheese in a stack of dishtowels and scrounged in the refrigerator until she had enough vegetables for a salad.

When she went to get Merrideth for dinner, she expected to find her playing games. Surprisingly, she was still hard at work with multiplication drills.

"Wait a minute. I'm almost done," Merrideth said. "I got a 93% on the last test, and so far I haven't missed any on this one."

Abby smiled but kept quiet until Merrideth finished the last problem and the digital version of fireworks burst across the screen along with the words, Congratulations. You scored 100%.

"That's amazing, although I'm not surprised. I knew you could do it if you put your mind to it."

"Actually, it is amazing," Merrideth said, blinking in surprise. Then she stood and stretched.

"I'm hungry. What's for dinner?"

Pat never came down, so Abby prepared a plate in

case she felt up to eating later. During dinner, she mentally prepared a speech about the responsibility of sharing the workload in a home, but Merrideth didn't need to be prompted after all. When she was finished eating, she took her dishes to the counter and said, "Wash or dry?"

"I'll wash," Abby said.

"Go ahead. Ask me a multiplication problem," Merrideth said, eager to demonstrate her new math prowess.

Abby gladly complied, and by the time the dishes were done they had made it to twelve times twelve. Merrideth missed only a few problems, and was sure she'd know them the next time. Abby smiled at her new self-confidence.

Maybe having to wash and dry dishes by hand wasn't really a hardship at all, but a blessing. Not that she wouldn't be happy to be back in the world of dishwashers when the time came. But how many mothers and daughters had spent time together talking around that sink? And time with her mother was something Merrideth was in short supply of.

She really was intelligent to learn that quickly. And yet it would be so easy for a teacher to miss that if they only went by appearances. Abby filed that thought away to be remembered when she had her own classroom of students.

"School's over, right?" Merrideth said, placing the last plate in the cabinet.

Abby smiled. "Yep. Let's go find out what Charlotte's doing."

Merrideth finally agreed her turn time-surfing was over and let Abby back at the monitor so that she could experiment with more of the program settings. Most of the icons on the menu bar still remained incomprehensible, and she wished more than ever for a manual.

But the volume control was familiar. She clicked on it to activate the sound feature, and the little world of Miles Station seemed even more real than before.

Once again, Abby marveled at the programmers' attention to detail. Now they could hear the steam engine grinding the farmers' grain, the cows stomping through the pasture on their way to the pond for a drink, the wind rustling through the trees, even the tiny sound of voices from inside the house.

Then came the eerie sound of a train approaching the village. It was like no train she had ever seen, certainly no speeding Amtrak. They heard the chugging of the steam engine and the screaming of its whistle for some time before it came into view. Finally, a black engine pulling its cars appeared, slowing as it approached the depot. A smoky haze hung in the air for a while before being dissipated by the wind.

The date indicated at the top of the screen was May 20, 1854, but Abby found that the Time Parameters drop-down menu allowed her infinite control of forward and backward movement on the time continuum, in actual real time or at any other speed. Laughing, they made the train back up across the screen at high speed then chug slowly forward out of sight again.

Merrideth was fascinated by how much detail they could see by zooming in on the train while it was in slow motion. Women in bright bonnets and men in hats peered through the windows of the passenger cars, and a man shoveled coal into the furnace in the engine. Abby found that by scrolling the screen with the two arrow buttons at the bottom of the monitor, she could move the depot into view and watch the passengers disembark at the Miles

Station depot.

Merrideth could wait no longer. "Let me have a turn." She sat down and began to fiddle with the controls, zooming in, increasing the volume, moving forward and backward in time.

Leaning over her shoulder, Abby said, "This is so cool, and I hate to be ungrateful, but doesn't this just make you wish for more?"

Merrideth sighed wistfully. "I wish we could shrink and jump into the computer."

"I know what you mean. I wish we could see the back of the buildings, especially the..." She blinked and said in a strangled voice, "No...there's no way that would work. I mean, no one could invent a software program that could do that. No way."

"What are you talking about?" Merrideth asked, staring at her.

Abby didn't answer, but taking the mouse from her, she placed the cursor on the View icon on the menu bar and clicked. "This is so similar to Aaron's architecture program," she began, "that maybe we'll be able to..."

A drop-down menu appeared, giving them the options of *Flip*, *Interior*, *Exterior*, *Virtual*, and *Lock*. She clicked on *Flip*. "Do this," Abby said.

The screen view had rotated on its vertical axis and now they were seeing the back of Colonel Miles' house. White sheets on a clothesline snapped in the wind. A woman in a long blue dress and bonnet was stooping to pull a wet sheet from the wicker basket at her feet. A gray cat came out of the barn and, stepping delicately through the wet grass, cautiously bypassed the flapping sheets to lie in the sun on the back step.

After a moment of stunned silence, Merrideth said, "It's Charlotte. Quick. Zoom in on her."

"Maybe it's supposed to be Mrs. Miles." Before she could manipulate the zoom function, the young woman picked up her wicker basket and, stepping over the cat, went through the back door into the house, saying, "Nice kitty."

"Make her come back out so we can get a closer look," Merrideth said.

"I've got a better idea." She moved the cursor back up to the *View* menu and clicked on *Interior* and *Lock*.

And then they were pulled out of their time and into Charlotte's.

Charlotte set the wicker basket on the floor, removed her bonnet, and hung it from a peg beside the back door. She walked dispiritedly to the chopping block in the middle of the kitchen and began to peel the potatoes and carrots that were heaped there. From time to time, she wiped perspiration from her forehead with her apron.

She glanced up at the clock that ticked on the wall and frowned. Nearly ten-thirty. Out the window she could see the depot down the street. The train to Alton would be arriving at noon, and on it would no doubt be many passengers on their way to the State Fair. But she would be stuck there sweating in the kitchen. She heard her father moving around in his study and felt anger well up again.

The day had started off so well. She hadn't even minded doing her usual morning chores—fire up the stove, put the coffee on, make the biscuits, etc., etc., etc.— because she was thinking about the deliciously exciting prospect of going to the State Fair with Billy Reynolds.

She had not been able to work up the courage at

breakfast to tell her father Billy had asked her, but as soon as she finished the dishes and got things started for the noon meal, she would march into her father's study and tell him it was about time he let her have a little fun like everyone else.

Then she heard a curious thumping sound coming from the front yard. She put down her tea towel and went out to investigate.

"Mama's beautiful roses!" Papa and her brother Frank were removing the trellises from the front porch. Their only explanation was a vague, "Never mind, Charlotte. Never mind."

Mama had planted the two pink Queen Victoria climbing roses two years before she died. They hadn't bloomed or even grown much the first year, but the second summer they had covered their trellises in a blanket of pink roses. Looking at the blooms and sniffing their sweet scent carried in on the wind had been Mama's one sure comfort when she lay on the settee in the sitting room all that final summer, too sick to get up.

Oh, Papa and Frank tried to avoid injuring the roses, but pulling them from the trellis, no matter how gently, left them broken and ragged and with nothing to hold onto.

As if that weren't bad enough, when she went in later to her father to ask about going to the State Fair, he immediately said a flat "no" without even considering it for one minute.

"The State Fair comes to Alton and I can't go?" she cried. "Samuel and Frank got to go to Alton when they were sixteen—all by themselves—on the train. What's the use of having a train run practically through your front yard if you can't get on it once in a while?"

"I'm sorry about the fair," Papa said. "I really wish I

could take you, but I just can't this year."

"But it's just to Alton. Billy Reynolds said—"

"I'll not let you go across the street with Billy Reynolds, much less to the State Fair!" he fairly shouted at her.

"I don't know why you don't like him, Papa."

"Never mind, Charlotte. I don't want to discuss it again."

She had stormed back to the kitchen to slave away the morning. Now, just the sound of her father coming down the hall from his study made her slam the knife down through the carrots she was chopping.

Jonathan Miles came through the kitchen door and paused. His hair was thinning on top, but still dark and silky like his full beard. His piercing brown eyes gentled when he saw the expression his sixteen-year-old daughter wore. She'd had to shoulder so much responsibility—too much responsibility—ever since her mother died. She was still furious with him. He only hoped she would find it in her heart to forgive him—and soon, before her temper caused her to hurt herself.

"I'm going to check on a few things at the mercantile before I meet the train, dear," he said mildly. "I'm hoping there'll be a letter from Mr. McGuire for me today."

"Yes, Papa."

"Do you need anything for that stew you're making?"

"No, Papa."

"Will it be ready for the noon train?"

"Yes, Papa. Isn't it always?"

"I'm going now," he said, realizing she wasn't ready to forgive him yet. "I'll be back shortly."

When he was gone and there was no one to see, she cried while she worked, stopping from time to time to scrub angrily at her eyes. With her tears and the steam from the cooking pot she could barely see what she was doing.

She brushed the chopped carrots and potatoes off the block into a blue crockery bowl and carried it to the cook stove. She lifted the heavy lid from the cast iron stew pot and dumped the vegetables into the rich simmering broth, stirring to make sure nothing was sticking to the bottom. Then she replaced the lid and wiped the steam from her face with her apron. Next, she gathered the peelings and carrot tops into the blue bowl and went outside, letting the screen door slam behind her.

Charlotte touched the flapping sheets as she passed the clothesline. They were dry and ready to come down, but she didn't have enough time before the passengers arrived. She looked to the sky and decided it was not likely to rain.

When she reached the chicken yard, she didn't bother to open the gate, just dumped the scraps over the fence. She usually loved the way the chickens, so calmly clucking and scratching about the yard one minute, became wildly squawking maniacs the next as they competed for the vegetable peelings. But today she did not take time to watch.

She started back for the kitchen, but decided there was time to check on the new litter of kittens first. They always cheered her up. She pulled the bolt on the half door and entered the dim barn, setting the blue bowl on the floor just inside the door. She reminded herself not to forget it this time.

Tiny mewing sounds were coming from the hay manger. "Momma Cat moved you again, didn't she?"

Miles Station was gone. Just the logo and the words, *Beautiful House: Take a Virtual Tour*, showed on the screen now. Abby gradually became aware of the computer room in which she sat. She glanced at her watch and saw that it was almost eleven-thirty. She turned to judge Merrideth's reaction.

She was staring back at her in a daze. "Abby?" Merrideth asked blankly. "Did we just travel back in time?"

"I don't think so. I mean no. Of course not. That's only in movies."

"Then what just happened?"

"I don't know, but my congratulations to whoever designed this software. That was the weirdest thing I've ever experienced. I'm calling customer support. I want to know what's going on."

Abby went to get the phone and dialed the number she had found earlier. The owner's manual boasted 24-hour service and the best-rated technicians of any computer company. The line was busy the first three times she dialed, but on the fourth try, the call went through. She felt a flutter of excitement until she realized that she was talking to a recorded voice.

"You have reached the customer service queue. Your call is important to us and will be answered by the next available service representative."

Merrideth kept whispering, "Hurry up, let's go back." And after ten minutes Abby couldn't stand it anymore and hung up.

"Well, I guess I'm not going to get any answers tonight." She pulled her own cell phone out of her pocket to check the time. "It's after midnight, Merrideth. We had both better get some sleep."

"Come on, I want to see Charlotte again."

Abby shut down the computer. "Tomorrow's Saturday. No school. We'll have all day to do whatever it was we just did."

CHAPTER 9

After Abby finished washing the breakfast dishes, she hurried up to the computer room. Beautiful House was on the screen, and Merrideth sat staring at the houses scrolling by.

"I thought you shut down the computer last night," she said absently. "Come on, come on! Where's my house?"

"I did. Maybe your mom used it before she went to work."

"She never uses this computer," Merrideth muttered. "There it is. Gotcha!" She clicked on it, and Colonel Miles' house popped up to fill the screen.

"Nothing's happening. No sound, no movement, no nothing."

"No anything." Abby sat down next to her. "I still can't believe this program. Some computer nerd—a really, really clever one—did a lot of research about the history of Miles Station to come up with such detail."

"I think a really, really smart scientist invented a time-travel program."

"If we had actually traveled back in time to 1854, Charlotte—or whoever that girl was—would have seen us, known we were there. Who knows how we would have changed history? No, *Beautiful House* invited us to take a virtual tour, and we did."

"Then how come we didn't have to be hooked up to wires and wear special goggles or something? Like in the movies."

"Like I said, it's really, really good. And in my opinion, what we did was way better than time traveling. I knew everything Charlotte was thinking and feeling. Like when I'm reading a good book."

"Okay, okay. Whatever. But how do I make Charlotte come out of the house?"

"You don't have to wait for that. We can go inside. Click on that drop-down menu," she said, pointing. "Then select *Interior*."

Merrideth followed her instructions, but nothing changed.

"Let me try." Merrideth got up and Abby moved into her chair. She clicked on *Interior* and the other controls she had used the night before. Nothing. She leaned in closer to the screen. The house looked so real, not like a photo at all. But it was so silent.

Duh. The volume was down. When she dialed it up, they heard birds singing and a breeze rustling through the trees.

"We're there," Abby said.

"Well, why isn't anything happening?"

"I don't know. I wish I knew how to work it better. Like last night. I had it set for Interior, but then we followed that girl—"

"Charlotte."

"Okay, we'll call her Charlotte. We followed Charlotte outside to the chicken yard and barn."

"But remember? You clicked on Lock."

"Oh, right. I guess it overrode the other setting. And the way it just shut down suddenly without me doing anything? I think there must be a default time limit. I'll check the Time Parameter and View options next time."

Merrideth sighed mournfully. "If there is a next time."

The front door of the house on the monitor opened and Abby jumped. "There. She's back."

The same young woman they had seen before came out onto the porch wearing a different, fancier dress and a lacy shawl. She paused to sniff the pink roses on the trellis and then walked down the path that would later become Merrideth's front sidewalk.

"I'm not hearing her thoughts, are you?" Abby said.

"Nope."

Abby clicked on Lock, which still didn't take them into complete virtual mode, but at least allowed them to follow the girl as she turned down the road and got farther and farther from the house.

"Don't get me wrong, it's still way cool," Abby said. "But it's not like last night."

"Do something."

"I'm afraid to mess with the settings or we'll lose her."

After a short walk, Charlotte—and Abby and Merrideth—arrived at the village. Charlotte stepped up onto the boardwalk and walked until she got to the building labeled Miles Mercantile. A man driving a buggy came down the street. She paused to wave at him and then went into the store.

She greeted the woman behind the counter by

name—Florence—and spent several minutes chatting happily with her. Then she told her she needed salt, beans, and sorghum. Florence dipped sorghum into a Mason jar and weighed out the beans and salt, wrapped them in brown paper, and tied the bundles with string. While she did all that, Charlotte admired several bolts of bright fabric at the other end of the store.

"I guess I should be happy for the little Podunk grocery store in town," Merrideth said.

"If this is a Hollywood movie set, it's way more detailed than I ever imagined them to be."

"This part's getting boring, Abby. Why don't we speed this thing up?"

"I guess we'd better, or we'll use up our own lives watching Charlotte live hers."

Abby turned the dial to fast-forward and experimented with speed. At first it was too fast to see what Charlotte was doing, and then when she eased back, it was too slow.

Eventually, she found a happy medium and they followed Charlotte as she left the store—apparently planning on coming back for the supplies later—and went on down the boardwalk. She stopped at a shoemaker's. She looked at several pairs of boots and shoes but didn't buy anything.

She left and went on down the street, passing various stores, a little school, and a huge structure that they determined must be Jonathan Miles' grain mill.

At the end of the street, she turned right and walked a short distance to a small white house. She knocked on the door, and it was opened by a smiling young woman. She laughed at something Charlotte said and they went inside together. They were drinking tea from pink cups when the program quit, reverting back to the *Beautiful Houses* title and the scrolling houses.

"Make it go back," Merrideth said.

"It's time we stopped stalking Charlotte—for a while anyway."

"It's not stalking. I think we should call it time-surfing."

"Okay. Let's stop time-surfing," Abby said with air quotes, "and go explore the Miles Station of today."

Michael showed up just as they went outside, and he decided to go along as their "Indian guide." When he went into the trees and came back with three sticks in case they came across any snakes, Abby named him "Boy-Who-Runs-In-Woods." She tried not to think about what adventures he got up to, wandering around on his own.

She used the plat map as a guide, but everything looked so different from when Charlotte had walked down the street in 1854. But they began to see evidence here and there of the stores and houses that had once made up the village called Miles Station.

They discovered remnants of a stone foundation overgrown by prairie grass where once, according to the map, a warehouse had stood. Where the school should be, they found a small stone building that someone was using for a storage shed. A fiberglass garage door had been installed, and the windows were boarded up. But the little cupola on top, where once a bell had hung, gave it away. Abby visualized barefoot children studying at wooden desks in a one-room schoolhouse.

There was only an empty lot where the little white house that Charlotte visited once stood. A pile of broken bricks was probably the remains of its chimney.

They noticed that Maple Street did not dead-end at Mrs. Arnold's house as they had thought. To be sure, the oiled and graveled surface ended at a barbed wire gate, but the road continued on as a grassy track through a pasture in which cattle placidly grazed.

After speculating on who owned the property and how likely they were to prosecute for trespassing, they opened the gate and followed the grassy path. The cattle paid no attention to them. The path led them to a good-sized pond glittering in the sun. A hundred frogs, croaking in warning, plopped into the water; a pair of red-winged blackbirds, clinging to cattails at the water's edge, scolded them for getting too close to their nest.

Cattle tracks meandered everywhere in the mud, some leading from the water's edge to an old hay shed that leaned precariously to one side. There was a strong cattle smell of manure and hay in the air.

Abby thought the scene pleasantly pastoral, but Merrideth wrinkled her nose, and Michael didn't say anything. In front of the shed, they found a round concrete platform, and she and Merrideth sat on it to rest. Michael still had energy to spare, so he amused himself by circling them, doing his version of an Indian war dance complete with chanting and occasional fierce whoops.

Just when Abby was thinking she couldn't take much more of his dizzying performance, he stopped and pointed to where they sat.

"Why is that there?"

"Maybe it's a well top," Merrideth said.

"No." Michael stepped onto the platform and squatted next to them. "This," he said, tracing the square hole in the center with his finger.

Abby started to say she didn't know, but then she realized she did. It was not concrete, but stone—Jonathan Miles' millstone—that had, as Mrs. Arnold told them, once ground the grain for every farmer for miles around.

CHAPTER 10

The whole house was quiet when Abby came downstairs at nine o'clock, showered and wearing a dress. Pat and Merrideth hadn't stirred from their bedrooms. The solitude was pleasant, something she always missed during the school year when she lived in such close quarters with her dorm mates.

After making coffee, she took a cup into the living room to enjoy the delicious peace of a quiet summer morning. Maybe she wouldn't go to church this one time. After all, she had worked so hard all week. And then she mentally slapped herself up the side of the head for following that train of thought. Being tired was all the more reason to go to church and be recharged for the coming week.

With a town the size of Brighton, Abby hadn't expected it to take so long to find the church she had seen listed in the yellow pages. She ended up seeing the whole town before finally pulling into the parking lot of

Westminster Presbyterian Church.

It was a small and rather plain brown building, and when she entered, five minutes after the service had begun, she saw it was equally plain inside. Certainly there were no stained glass windows or a towering ceiling. The only ornamentation was an oak cross and colorful, hand-stitched banners hanging from the white walls.

But a man, whose nametag said Jack, greeted her at the door with a warm smile and a bulletin, and led her to the entrance of the crowded sanctuary. He stood there frowning as he craned his neck every which way, scanning the room for an empty seat. The organist began an introduction to *A Mighty Fortress Is Our God*, and the congregation stood and sang enthusiastically.

At last, Jack grinned, put a friendly hand on her elbow, and whispered, "To your right—in the second row."

Abby smiled her thanks and eyed the long center aisle. Great. It would be like running the gauntlet. Only with luck, no one would hit her, and it would be accompanied by one of her all-time favorite hymns.

Taking a deep breath, she went quickly down the aisle to the second row. "Excuse me," she whispered and edged her way past a young mother and father, five stair-stepped young boys, decked out in matching white shirts and crooked red ties, and a sleeping baby dressed in pink in an infant seat on the floor.

Abby had a horrible moment of panic when her foot snagged on something and she thought she would fall and squash the baby.

But then a strong, tanned hand reached out to steady her, and she settled with an exhalation of relief in front of the last remaining seat in the sanctuary.

"Thanks," she whispered and looked up into a pair of

smiling blue eyes. He towered over her five foot, four inches. It had just been a glance before she averted her face. But that's all it took to see that the blue eyes were set in one of the most arresting masculine faces she had ever seen, all framed by silky, chocolate-brown hair.

Abby felt herself blushing and envisioned herself falling to the floor in a faint. Unfamiliar faces hovered over her saying, "What could be the matter with the new girl?" Mentally slapping herself for the second time that morning, she vowed not to look his way again.

But then he was offering her a hymnal, thoughtfully opened to the right page, so she glanced up to say thanks again. Her heart actually fluttered. Get a grip, she thought. She reached out to take the hymnal. When he didn't release it, she realized he intended to share it with her.

He must think her a complete idiot for trying to tug it out of his hand. She spared another quick glimpse and saw that he was grinning. Her face felt like a third-degree sunburn. She looked back down at the hymnal, but that meant she saw his hand, so masculine and different from her own slender one.

At last, she cast her eyes toward the song leader in front. But they were nearly finished with the fourth verse before her heart rate got back to normal and her traitorous brain began to concentrate on the beautiful words of the hymn instead of the handsome him and how well his baritone voice blended with her soprano.

When the hymn was finished, they sat and his shoulder scraped against hers. She supposed he couldn't help it that the chairs weren't large enough. Heat was radiating off him, and he shifted in his chair as if trying to take up less space. Then she saw in horror that the skirt of her white eyelet dress had landed on his khakis and she hurried to tug it back in place.

Another man came up to the pulpit and reminded the congregation to give generously, and not to forget the Building Expansion Fund, to which several people said heartfelt amens. He prayed and the plates were passed. The guy beside her put in a folded check and passed the plate to her, which meant she was forced to look at his hand again.

There were other hymns and choruses and then the pastor came to the pulpit, prayed, and began to speak. The sermon was titled "God's Grace in Time of Need." She knew that because the bulletin said so. But when it was finished she realized she had no earthly idea what the sermon had been about, because the guy next to her had taken up all the oxygen in the room, leaving her with nothing to breathe but the scent of his cologne.

Finally, everyone stood. Escape at last—but no. The family of eight in front of her was taking an inordinate amount of time to gather up Bibles, a diaper bag, coloring books and crayons, a baby bottle, five miniature boxes of raisins, a Tupperware container of Cheerios, and finally the baby in the infant seat. She marveled that the children had been so quiet and well-behaved. Of course, they could have been swinging from the chandeliers the whole time and she, in her own torturous little world, wouldn't have noticed.

Then, when the last boy had filed out, a smiling couple came up to block her escape. "Hi, I'm Mary and this is my husband George. We're so happy you could worship with us today."

Not as much of that had occurred as she would have liked, but she smiled and said, "Hello, Abby Thomas. It was a great service." She had never lied in church before. She wondered if it was worse than lying anywhere else.

"I see you've already met John," George said. Behind

her, he said, "No." His voice cracked a little as he added, "Not really."

Mercifully, George and Mary backed up enough to allow them to step into the aisle. She turned and saw that he was wearing a blue shirt that called attention to the blue of his eyes. He looked hot, his face as red as hers felt. He extended a hand and said, "Hi, I'm John Roberts."

As she had imagined, his hand dwarfed hers, but his handshake was gentle, like he was used to reining in his strength. Backing away, he said, "Nice to meet you, uh, Abby. But, I've, uh, got to go see someone before they leave."

Frowning, Mary turned to her husband. "Does he look feverish to you?" she asked with concern.

"I bet he is," George said, his eyes twinkling.

"I hope he's not coming down with a summer cold, bless his heart."

George and Mary introduced her to the pastor and lots of other people, who were all friendly and welcoming, and invited her to come back the next week.

"It's potluck Sunday," Mary said, smiling. "You won't want to miss that. We have the best cooks in town."

"Get here early," George said, knowingly, "and you can sit with us."

She had spent so much time meeting everyone, that by the time she got to the parking lot, her car was practically the only one left. She rolled down the windows to let the built-up heat escape and took out her phone. At last—four wonderful bars. She had several messages, one from her parents, the others from college friends, including Kate, which meant she was back from Europe. Abby was dying to hear about her trip but knew her parents would be worrying about her.

Her mom answered with a laugh. "Hi, Abby. Your

dad and I were just this minute saying we wished you'd call and put us out of our misery. We're dying to know how you've been managing."

"I'm fine, Mom. I have to admit I wanted to pull my hair out a few times. But she's coming along. Merrideth's behind in some areas, but she's no dummy, that's for sure."

"You'll have to bring her over for a visit."

"Mom?"

"Yes?"

"I just want to say thanks. I don't tell you nearly often enough."

"Why, what for?"

"I'm beginning to see more than ever how lucky I am to have parents like you."

Her mother didn't answer for a moment, and Abby thought she'd lost the connection. Then she heard her blowing her nose. Afterwards she said, "Oh, honey, that's so sweet."

Abby was a little teary-eyed herself by the time they finished talking and she disconnected. But Kate got her to laughing within mere seconds of hearing her voice.

"So how was your trip?" Abby said.

"It was fabulous. I got to see so many things. But I missed the tour of the Eiffel Tower. That...er...that was sort of my own fault."

Abby laughed. "Why am I not surprised? You're so terrible about time. So is it true about the French being snooty to Americans?"

Kate laughed. "Yes, but they treat everyone that way. So enough about me. How's it going for you, Jane Eyre?"

"Other than that my student doesn't want me here, pretty well."

"Tell her she should be glad she's not a fine young

Spanish girl. They have to have their duennas with them everywhere they go until they're eighteen or nineteen. Okay, so now for the good stuff. Have you met anyone down there?"

"Of course. Just this morning I met a lot of really nice people at the church. There's a couple named—"

"Abby?"

"What?"

"Don't make me have to come down there."

"Okay, so there was this guy I sat next to this morning."

"Yes, yes. Describe, please."

"His name is John. He has the most gorgeous blue eyes and brown hair, and when he smiles I can't breathe right. And he's got to be at least six feet two."

"I knew it! Tall, dark, and handsome! Did he ask you out, and if not, why not?"

"Don't be an idiot. I just met him. At church. And besides," she said primly, "it wouldn't be right to begin a relationship while I'm on the job."

Kate sighed loudly. "Must you always be such a straight arrow?"

Abby was still grinning when she walked into Pat's kitchen. She was just taking a casserole dish out of the oven.

"You're just in time. I thought we'd have Sunday brunch."

"It smells heavenly."

"It's sausage casserole. I didn't want you to think I never cook. How was church?"

"It was good. I think I'll go back next week."

"I wish I could get Merrideth to go to church. We used to go when she was little, but lately…. Maybe you can talk her into it."

"I'll try, but I don't know…"

"And as for me," Pat continued, "it's just that Sunday is my only day off, and I need the extra sleep, and since I still don't know anyone—"

"Hey, stop," Abby said, putting her hand up. "Don't confess to me. I have enough of my own sins to worry about."

Merrideth came in carrying Kit Kat.

"Put the cat down, Merrideth. You'll get cat fur all over the food." Pat began dishing out the casserole "So, Abby, did you meet anyone interesting at the church?"

"Yes, as a matter of fact, I met a very nice couple named George and Mary. Everyone was friendly. They're having a potluck next week. I'm going to ask my mom for one of her recipes. Do you want to go with me, Merrideth?"

"No."

"No, thank you," Pat added.

"Right." Merrideth rolled her eyes. "So, Mom, when are you going to take me to see Dad? You said we would go this summer. And guess what? It's summer."

"I'm afraid I can't take you right now." Pat smiled stiffly. "Isn't this sausage casserole scrumptious?"

"Yes," Abby said. "It sure is."

"But you promised."

"I know, I did, honey. But I'm just too busy right now to get away."

Merrideth looked imploringly at Abby. "Maybe, could you—?"

Abby looked at Pat who quickly said, "It's not fair to ask Abby to take you, Merrideth. I just wouldn't feel right about that."

Merrideth slammed her fork on the table, pushed her chair back, and ran from the room.

Pat closed her eyes, took a deep breath, and exhaled. She didn't make any effort to go to her daughter.

So Abby said, "Maybe I'd better go check on her."

When she got to Merrideth's room, she found her flung across her bed, face down.

Abby felt miserable. "I'd take you if I could, kiddo."

"I hate her."

"No, you don't."

"I hate him too."

"No, you don't."

"Yes, I do, because he hates me. He never calls me anymore. And he doesn't pick up when I call."

"Maybe he's having phone trouble."

"Do you think?" Merrideth turned over and Abby saw that her lashes were damp with tears.

"I bet he doesn't have a Rhapsody II, or even a Rhapsody I, does he?" Abby pulled playfully on Merrideth's sneakered foot. "I bet he still has an old Quasar or some other piece of junk phone. No wonder you can't get a hold of him."

Merrideth smiled crookedly and swiped at her eyes. "The one he has is not even as good as a Quasar."

"Just as I suspected. Hey, while you're waiting for him to get caught up with the latest phone technology, I know just the thing to take your mind off it."

"What?" Merrideth asked suspiciously. "Long division?"

"You wound me. No, let's go exploring again. I have an idea where we can get more clues."

Merrideth was smiling when Pat came to the door and stuck her head in. "Are you all right, sweetie?"

"Yeah," Merrideth said. "Mom, we're going for a walk. You want to—?"

"Oh, that's good, honey. I've got to go make some

phone calls."

"But it's Sunday."

"I know, I know. But it's important."

"Whatever."

The plat map showed a little square with a cross on top, which Abby figured indicated a church. It was no longer there. But they stumbled, literally, upon the cemetery, which, as she had hoped, was behind it. Now, only gravestones remained standing, and most of them, having sunken unevenly over time, bowed crookedly like grieving mourners who had drunk too much sherry at the wake. Some were completely flattened, broken by the weather or possibly by vandals. Butterflies kept vigil, silently fluttering over the tall grass and wildflowers that had taken over the cemetery. Ironically, Miles Station Cemetery, of all their discoveries, did the most to make the town really come alive for them.

One plot was enclosed by a black wrought iron fence. Flowing iron script spelled the name *Arnold* on the arch over the gate. Bouquets of gladiolas decorated several graves there, including one labeled, *George, Beloved Husband* of Susannah. Not a blade of grass dared touch any of the stones, and Abby smiled thinking of Mrs. Arnold ferociously whacking away at the weeds with her hoe.

Throughout the cemetery, the inscriptions on the granite gravestones were crisp and easy to read, no matter their age. But the sandstone markers were worn, some past all recognition. Merrideth bent to one and traced the eroded words with her finger.

Abby made her voice ghostly and dramatic:

Because I could not stop for Death,
He kindly stopped for me;
The carriage held but just ourselves,

And Immortality.

"Did you just make that up?"

Abby smiled. "I wish. No, it's a poem by Emily Dickinson. She wrote lots of poetry about graveyards. I'll show you when we get back."

A little smile played over Merrideth's face. "So you thought taking me to a graveyard would cheer me up?"

Abby grinned. "Is it working?"

"I thought it would be scary…walking through a cemetery." Putting her hand up to shade her eyes, she looked out over the gravestones around them. "But mostly it's just sad. Someday the names will be completely gone, and no one will know who is buried here."

"I feel the sadness too, but—" Abby said.

"See this one?" She knelt before a small tilted tombstone. "Clara-something—I can't make out the last part. Born April 9, 1802, and died May 20, 1805. Only three years old. Just a name and two dates. But she was a real person, you know? Probably no one remembers her or even knows who she was."

Abby was startled by the gloom in Merrideth's voice. She took it for granted that God would never forget. If he kept track of every hair on their heads, he surely knew who was buried in all the graves. Besides, the names were written down in his book. It was obvious Merrideth didn't have that assurance.

Merrideth gestured to indicate the whole cemetery. "And that's just one person, one story. Over and over. Time doesn't stop. People are born and die, born and die."

"Whoa! How old did you say you are? That sounds like something from my philosophy class, not an eleven-year-old. See, this is what I've been talking about. You're one of the smartest kids I know."

But what did you say to a girl so intelligent and so morbid? Was there a Bible verse somewhere? "A time to be born; a time to die." But reading Ecclesiastes probably wouldn't be such a good idea in her frame of mind. Touring cemeteries was definitely unhelpful.

"Let's go home and think happier thoughts," Abby said, patting Merrideth's arm.

"I want to find where Colonel Miles is buried."

Where the engravings were still legible, they began to recognize names from the plat map: *McPherson, Stubblefield, Logan,* and other families once a part of Miles Station that had lived and died there over a hundred years before.

Finally, working their way systematically through the cemetery, they found the Miles' family plot. The colonel lay next to Eliza Stratton Miles, his *Dearly Beloved Wife.* Nearby were other Miles graves—sons or brothers, perhaps, with their loved ones.

"But, why did it disappear?" Merrideth asked suddenly. "The town."

"I don't know, kiddo. But we could see if the library has any information. I saw one this morning when I was touring Brighton."

"Can we go tomorrow?"

"You know your mom wants us to focus on—"

"Please."

"Okay, but in the afternoon, after we work on long division."

"I'll do four million long division problems—without a calculator—only I want to find out more about Charlotte."

CHAPTER 11

The next morning, Merrideth had reverted to her cranky self, balking at everything Abby set for her to do. Forget four million math problems. She'd be lucky to get her to do four. Nor did Merrideth care to do anything else Abby suggested, but kept begging to be allowed to go play on her computer. How she could want to after spending half the night at it was more than she could understand.

Merrideth had settled herself in the computer room after dinner and stayed there for hours. She was still at it when Abby went to bed, promising her she'd shut it down "in a minute." First, it had been Bubble Town, and every sound effect and precious bubble-head comment had gone straight to Abby's brain as lay trying to get to sleep.

Then it got quiet and Abby assumed Merrideth had gone on to bed. But apparently she had only switched to watching Charlotte's window. She squealed in happiness every time she spotted her, which happened to be every time Abby managed to fall asleep. She had been about to go get Merrideth and chain her to her bed, when she finally heard her shut down the computer and shuffle off down the hall.

Sometime around 3:30 the blue light had come back on to torment her. She was too tired to go turn it off.

Now, she was starting the day without enough sleep. As if it weren't difficult enough to be perky and enthusiastic on a Monday morning.

Abby was looking over Merrideth's shoulder as she contemplated the sentence she was supposed to punctuate when Pat came into the kitchen carrying a large cardboard box.

Merrideth looked up in relief at the distraction.

"I won't feel settled until I get my treasures out," Pat said. "Can you girls help me figure out where to put these knickknacks?"

"That'll be a lot more fun than trying to figure out where to put commas," Merrideth said.

Abby helped Pat hang pictures, while Merrideth arranged various pottery pieces that she explained were souvenirs from past vacations in Colorado. She put a blue ceramic cat on top of the refrigerator.

"It's beginning to feel a little more like home, Mom," Merrideth admitted.

"Yes, it does, doesn't it? Unfortunately, I can't stay to enjoy the feeling. I've got to go meet a client in Alton."

"But, I thought since you were home we could—"

"You know someone's got to bring home the bacon, honey. Besides, you need to get back to your studies this afternoon."

"Mom!" She drew out the word like it had fourteen syllables. "I'm sick of studying math and English."

"I thought we'd study history this afternoon," Abby said. "Remember?"

"Oh, right, history," Merrideth agreed.

The library was small but well organized, and when they got to the history section, Abby spotted The History of Macoupin County, Illinois right off. Published in 1856, it gave a fascinating account of the various settlements and towns in the county at the time. The book also included a "biographical sketch" for each major landowner, along with a charming portrait of his farm.

"Aren't the drawings cute?" Abby asked.

"I guess."

"My brother Aaron said this style of art is called 'American Primitive.' See how the scale is not right."

Merrideth pointed to the name under the farm. "William Heal. You're in the H's. Keep turning."

Abby flipped a few more pages and found a three-page section on Miles Station. And there, on page 376, was Merrideth's house. The caption under the drawing was The residence of Col. Jonathan Miles at Miles Station, Macoupin County, Illinois.

"Wow," Merrideth said.

Abby leaned in closer. "It's just like the photograph on *Beautiful Houses*—down to the cows drinking from the pond." She pointed out a large building with a smokestack that stood beside the pond. "And there's the colonel's mill."

The accompanying biography of Colonel Miles made a big deal about the mill, explaining that Miles had bought, at great personal expense, the first steam mill in the area. He had built his house in 1843, and then other businesses, stores, and houses had grown up around him and his mill. He had convinced the Chicago & Alton Company to lay the railroad through the little settlement, donating his own land for the depot. By 1855, the little village had a population of five hundred citizens.

The biography was effusive in praising Colonel Miles, describing him as "one of the most substantial and estimable gentlemen that has claimed Macoupin county for his home; brave, patriotic, broad minded, God-fearing, zealous. He is known as thorough, competent, honest and able, a man held in the highest esteem by all."

And it listed his children as Samuel, Frank, and Charlotte.

"Whoever wrote the software must have had access to this book," Abby said. "But I still don't get how Mrs. Arnold knew all this. After all, she can't read."

"Well, duh. She's from the olden days."

Abby chuckled. "Yes, but not that olden. She's ninety-two, not one hundred and seventy."

All that was interesting, but it didn't shed any light on why the town had disappeared. They looked but could find no other helpful books. And when they questioned the librarian, she hadn't even known the town ever existed.

They might as well go home and time-surf back to Miles Station. Maybe the computer programmer knew what happened to the town.

Abby slammed on the brakes.

"What's wrong?" Merrideth squeaked.

Abby pointed out the side window. "There's a Tropical Frost." With its distinctive blue siding, white shutters, and gingerbread trim, the snow cone stand looked like a playhouse for children. "I think we need a treat after all our work at the library."

Abby and Merrideth got in line behind several teenage girls who were flirting outrageously with the guy behind the counter. Naturally, Abby tried to get a look at him, but he was so tall his face was shielded from view by the awning over the window. Finally, after confusion about who ordered what and nearly spilling a grape ice on one teen, the attendant gave them their change and the girls moved off, whispering and smiling back over their shoulders.

As she and Merrideth stepped up to the counter, the object of the girl's fascination leaned down. It was John Roberts.

She should have known. Probably every female he met got all fluttery and faint. She wanted to ask him what he was doing there. Didn't high school kids work summers at places like Tropical Frost? And he was definitely no high school kid.

"Abby," he said. "What are you doing here?"

"I saw the stand and just had to stop." She had a horrible thought. What if he thought she had stopped because of him, like the giggling high school girls? "I love snow cones," she said forcefully.

Merrideth looked with interest at Abby and then John. She swiped at her bangs and studied the list of flavors posted high on the wall behind him. "Don't you have Pineapple Passion? At home that's what I always order."

"Oh. Sorry," he said, turning to glance at the sign behind him. "I guess we just have plain pineapple."

"Oh, all right," Merrideth said grudgingly. "I'll take plain pineapple."

"Okay. Coming right up." He turned expectantly to Abby.

"Is your vanilla Coke good?" What a stupid question, she thought. How could it be anything but good?

"Oh, yes. We have the best. You know how some people make it too vanilla-y and some don't put enough in? Well, ours is just right." The expression on his face told Abby that he realized he sounded lame too.

"That's what I'll have then," she said.

Smiling, he straightened and turned away from the window. She saw that he had traded his dress clothes for jeans and a black T-shirt.

"I can't believe they don't have Pineapple Passion," Merrideth grumbled. "That's about right for a hick town. In Chicago—"

"What?" Abby said, pulling her attention back to Merrideth. "That's not a very nice thing to say."

"Well, it's true."

"Well, when in Rome…"

Merrideth looked like she was about to ask what that meant, but John was back. He handed them their orders. "Are you new in town?"

Abby handed him a five-dollar bill. "Yes. We are."

"So who's your friend there?"

"Oh. Sorry. This is Merrideth." Then she found herself saying, "I used to work at a Tropical Frost when I was in high school." As soon as the stupid words were out of her mouth she wished she could take them back. He was probably embarrassed working a minimum wage job.

"And where was that?" he asked.

"I'm from St. Louis, and Merrideth is from Chicago."

He handed Abby her change. "Oh," he said blankly. "I thought you were sisters."

"Actually, I'm just here for the summer for Merrideth."

"So you're the babysitter," he said, leaning on the counter.

Merrideth frowned and wiped her mouth with her hand. John kept his eyes trained on Abby, but pulled a wad of napkins from the chrome napkin holder and handed them to Merrideth.

"No, not exactly. Merrideth will be a sixth grader this

fall. She doesn't need a babysitter."

"I guess she's too old for that." He looked puzzled.

She smiled. "I guess you could say I'm sort of a Jane Eyre."

"Oh, I get it—like a governess."

"Yes, that's right." Abby grinned. "And the house is very old, the kind that might have an innocent governess and assorted ghosts and dangerous strangers."

"Let's go home, Abby. I'm hot." Merrideth's cone had dripped onto her T-shirt, and she wiped futilely at the spots with the wad of napkins.

"Merrideth," John said, "would you like extra pineapple syrup?"

"Okay," she said, handing him her paper cone.

"So, where is this old house?"

"Miles Station," Abby said.

"Oh, sure. That runs east of town, doesn't it?"

"Not the road. The town."

John looked puzzled.

"Come on, Abby. Let's go."

"Be sure to come back tomorrow," he said quickly. "We're having a sale…buy one, get one free." He seemed to be making it up as he spoke.

"Maybe," she said. Maybe it was a bad idea to get involved while she was on assignment.

"See you, Abby." John flashed her a smile. It was a friendly smile, not at all flirtatious, but with his brilliant white teeth against his tanned face, it was a killer smile all the same. And just as she'd told Kate, she had trouble breathing.

"We have to go so Abby can call her boyfriend," Merrideth said, grinning slyly.

John stopped smiling.

"I'm not leaving so I can call my boyfriend…I mean,

I don't have a boyfriend, and you know it, Merrideth." She felt her cheeks flaming. Now he probably thought she was one of those brazen, pushy females who chased guys, the kind he probably had to fend off constantly.

"I mean, the reason we have to go is because I have to get this brat—I mean girl—home so we can get back to our school work."

"You said you were going to call your friends," Merrideth said, grinning. "And I bet some of your friends are boys, right?"

"Goodbye, John," Abby said, tugging on Merrideth's arm. She steered her toward the car. "Come on, let's hurry. I know how much you love long division. Or maybe we should discuss participles."

She couldn't resist taking one little peek back. John was standing there, arms folded across his chest, watching them go. His smile had returned.

There was another postcard from Kate when they got home. A picture of Big Ben was on the front. Kate had mailed it right before her flight home from London. Abby read it aloud to Merrideth:

My Dear Poppet,
I say there, I'm having a smashing time, except, by Jove, everyone drives on the wrong side of the street, don't you know. And the tour guide—a bit barmy but still a jolly good chap—locked the luggage in the boot of the car. Then the lift wasn't working so we had to walk up three flights. The room was posh, but we had to share the loo down the hall. I'm sure the waiter (a cheeky bloke) thought I was a blooming idiot because I didn't know what bangers and mash are, but our tour guide explained everything so that even a Yank from across the pond could understand.

Love, Kate

Merrideth didn't get it, but Abby laughed, imagining Kate doing Brit-speak.

Merrideth went from very good to horrid in under thirty seconds when Pat announced at dinner that she would be away for a three-day real estate seminar in St. Louis. She was leaving in the morning and would be gone until Friday.

Pat tried to explain to Merrideth that this was a good opportunity to improve her skills, which would lead to more sales and thus, more commissions, and that really she had no choice if she wanted to keep her job. Through all her explanations, Merrideth sat sullenly unresponsive.

When Pat promised to take her to the State Fair in Springfield when she got back, Merrideth said sarcastically, "Wow, Mom. What a treat. You're really getting into this rustic scene. Only, I've got an idea. How about taking me to see Dad, like you promised."

"Merrideth, I don't have time to get into this with you," Pat said, rising from the table. "I've got to go pack."

"That's the problem. You don't ever have time."

"I'm sorry," Pat said tightly, her face growing red. "I'm doing the best I can—without any help from your father, I might add. I promised we'd go and we will, but not now."

"I'll call Dad and he'll come take me to live with them. Sylvia's nicer to me than you are."

Pat slapped her.

Abby couldn't tell who of the three of them was most surprised. Merrideth's eyes grew wide and she put her hand over the red handprint blooming on her cheek.

Pat's face seemed to crumple, and the angry red staining her cheeks blanched to white. "I'm sorry," she whispered.

Merrideth stood, her chair toppling backward. Pat tried to take her arm, but Merrideth wrenched out of her grasp and staggered from the room.

Abby started after her and then stopped. A voice inside her head was babbling warnings, "There's your temper again. Don't do it. Don't yell at your boss." But her résumé seemed really unimportant at the moment.

"You do know, don't you, that Merrideth calls him every night? I'd be happy to take her to see her dad. So why won't you let me?"

"There's more to it than you know, Abby. You don't understand."

"I understand that a girl needs her father."

"I know what you must think, but it's not because of Sylvia. She entered the picture after we left." Pat sighed and pushed her hair out of her face. "Two years ago, Brad's buddies got him involved with drugs. It started out with pot, just using it at first. But later he was selling it. I hated it, but he just laughed it off when I pleaded with him to stop.

"Don't worry. Don't worry," he told me.

"Oh." Abby blinked. "I didn't know…"

"Then I discovered they had gone from pot to meth. They were actually cooking meth in a shed in our backyard. He could have blown us all sky high. So there's no way on earth I'll allow her to go up there until I have the time to supervise a visit."

"I'm so sorry," Abby said. "I didn't realize. I shouldn't have said—"

"No, I'm sorry, Abby. Sorry you had to be sucked into our mess. And sorry I didn't say anything ahead of time about the seminar. I guess I'm a coward. I knew she'd get upset, and—"

"You're not a coward. In fact, you've been very brave.

And don't worry while you're gone. I'll keep her busy."

"Thank you. I know I can count on you."

When Abby went past Merrideth's room on her way to her own, she heard Pat murmuring something soothing. If Merrideth responded, she didn't hear it. At least no one was screaming or hitting.

Later that night, she heard Merrideth dialing the phone in the hall again. This time, apparently no one answered on the other end, and the phone was carefully replaced in its cradle. A sob escaped and hung in the darkness. Abby hoped for Merrideth's sake that her dad hadn't blown himself up.

"Merrideth?" Abby called softly from her bed. There was a soft flurrying sound. "Merrideth, come here." At first, she thought she had left, but she heard a creak and caught a glimmer of white and knew that Merrideth stood just inside the door. Abby sat up in bed and leaned against the headboard. "Come talk to me," she said, patting the sheets beside her.

Merrideth took two timid steps into the room. "I didn't mean to wake you."

"You didn't. I was just lying here thinking about that girl, Charlotte Miles, who used to live here. Did you ever wonder what sounds she heard at night a hundred and fifty years ago? Of course there wouldn't have been the sound of planes overhead or cars on the road."

Merrideth took another cautious step into the room and then sat at the foot of the bed. She laughed softly. "I guess she wouldn't have heard the sound of phones in the night, either."

"Listen!" Abby whispered. "There's one sound she would have heard." A train rumbled toward them from the north. Closer and closer it came, and then it was past, and the sound faded into the south.

"I guess you miss your dad a lot."

"Yeah, and ever since me and Mom moved down to this place—"

"Mom and I," Abby said automatically. "Yeah?"

"What?"

"Mom and I what?"

"You should have said—Oh, never mind."

"Well, of course I miss my dad 'cause he's so far away. But I shouldn't have to miss my mom too. At least Dad has the excuse that he lives in Chicago."

Abby remained silent.

"I know I should be grateful."

"That's true," Abby agreed.

"I know I was a brat tonight. I shouldn't have said that about Sylvia."

"That's also true. But, kiddo, I think it will get better when your mom gets her career off the ground."

"I guess." Merrideth sighed. "How about you? Do you miss your mom and dad?" She lay down on the comforter at the foot of the bed.

"Actually, I was surprised how much I missed them in college. I haven't been home since Easter break, but at least St. Louis is not that far away from here. They told me to bring you for a visit sometime. They want to meet you."

"I bet," Merrideth said.

"I mean it. They do."

"Do you look like your mom?"

"Mostly."

"Mom says I look just like Dad," Merrideth said mournfully. "And I know what she thinks of him."

"I'm sure she doesn't mean that in a bad way. After all, she married him, didn't she?"

"I could exercise a million years and never be skinny like Mom. And I could study a million years and never be a genius."

"Merrideth, you're very intelligent. But even if you weren't, you're you. You don't have to try to be your mom. And they don't expect you to be a genius, either."

"That's easy for you to say. You're beautiful and smart and you can have all the boyfriends in the world. I saw how the snow cone guy was drooling over you."

"He was not."

"Was so."

"Well, maybe slightly drooling. And I don't have a boyfriend."

"Why not? You're beautiful and really nice."

Abby blinked in surprise. "Thank you. I used to have a boyfriend, but not lately."

"What happened? Did he ditch you?"

"You're really nosy, you know that? If you must know, I ditched him."

"Really? Why?"

"He was only interested in one thing, and it wasn't my personality. Do you know what I'm saying?"

"I think I understand. After all, I may be ignorant, but I'm not stupid." Abby could hear the grin in her voice.

A companionable silence settled over the dark room and Abby had almost drifted off to sleep when Merrideth said, "Abby, can I ask you another question."

"Sure."

"Will you show me how to fix my hair like yours?"

"Of course, but—" Abby sat up straight. "I just had a brilliant idea. This weekend while your mom is gone to her seminar, we'll have a seminar, too. A self-improvement seminar."

"If you mean practicing my multiplication, no thanks."

"No, silly," Abby said, chuckling. "I mean a beauty

seminar. We'll do a complete makeover—hair and nails and clothes. When your mom comes home, we'll surprise her with the new you."

"Really?" Merrideth asked. Abby heard the doubt in her voice.

"Really," Abby said firmly.

"All right." While some doubt lingered, she seemed cautiously optimistic.

"But first we need to get our beauty sleep, kiddo, so get out of here."

CHAPTER 12

Pat had already left by the time they got up the next morning. But she left a note on the kitchen table telling them to have fun while she was gone, and that she'd see them on Friday.

"That means we can play on the computer, right?"

"I don't know..."

"And we don't have to do math while she's gone."

"Well, she did say to have fun," Abby said.

They convened their beauty seminar in Abby's room, and Merrideth sat facing the dresser mirror. "Okay. What's first?"

"The first thing is to trim your hair a little." Abby combed Merrideth's hair and then began to snip all around her face. After a while, she stepped back. "There. Look how much better we can see your beautiful brown eyes. And this suits the shape of your face better."

"Do you really think they're pretty? I wish I had blue eyes."

"I think brown eyes are gorgeous."

"The snow cone guy's eyes are blue."

"I know. They're a shade that's sort of a cross between—"Abby stopped herself. "Let's just forget John and focus on you."

"Okay, so how about my nails?"

"Slow down there, girl. The next thing is to wash your hair. Now that you're older, you need to shower and wash your hair every day."

"I hate to take a bath."

"That's obvious." Abby stole a cautious look at Merrideth. Her eyes were round.

"Oh."

"But you'll feel much better if you do." She paused. "And you'll be nicer to be around."

"Oh."

"And here. You need this now, too." She handed Merrideth her powder-scented deodorant.

"Oh."

"Why don't you try my vanilla shampoo? Lather up twice and don't put anything else on your hair."

"I always use mom's conditioner when—"

"Your type of hair doesn't need any conditioners. You'll see. And be sure to rinse well," Abby added. "When you get done I'll style your hair."

"Okay. I'll try it," Merrideth said, walking toward the bathroom.

"Oh, one more thing," Abby said off-handedly. "You can borrow my razor...if you want to shave your legs."

Merrideth's eyes went large. "I might."

Abby gave her a few tips so she wouldn't come away with too many wounds. Merrideth, part girl and part woman, skipped off to the bathroom.

Abby smiled after her, glad that she'd made the effort.

Merrideth was progressing nicely. She just needed a little help with a few things.

When Merrideth was finished showering, they went again to Abby's room, and she showed her how to style her hair so that it framed her face.

"I wish I had curly hair like yours," Merrideth said wistfully.

"Oh, you goose! Look how shiny and blond your hair is now that it's really clean. Why would you want mine? See, you're beautiful."

"Abby?"

"Yes?"

"Abby, would you mind if I used your makeup?"

"I think it would be all right. But just a little. We want the real you to show through. Then I'll do your nails."

Afterward, Merrideth demanded her turn. She painted Abby's toenails a bright pink and styled her hair in strange and exotic ways.

"I've been thinking," Abby said as Merrideth put the finishing touches on her hair. "I know the book I brought is not your favorite. So how about if we get you a library card? You can check out the kind of books you like best. And it will give us a chance to show off our fabulous hair styles around town."

"Like at the snow cone stand?" Merrideth asked with a sly smile. "After all, they are having that 'buy-one-get-one-free' sale."

"Right. Good idea."

Merrideth suggested that they take Michael with them, which was brilliant, Abby thought, not only because she wanted to give the boy a treat, but also because it gave them a perfectly good excuse to return to Tropical Frost. And it was all the better that Merrideth had come up with the plan. She didn't want John to get the wrong idea.

But first she had to find Michael. No one answered the door of his house when she knocked, and they didn't get even a glimpse of him all the way to the end of the road.

Mrs. Arnold stopped hoeing weeds long enough to say that she hadn't seen him all day. "If you ever find that rascally boy, tell him I got some cookies for him, too. Tell him not to worry, his have blue icing."

"I wanted to ask his mother if he could go get a snow cone with us. I knocked, but…"

"Oh, she's in there, but she din't hear you. Miz Richardson's stone deaf. That's why Michael can't talk proper, you know. Cause he ain't got nobody much to talk proper to him, 'cept me."

"But he's smart," Merrideth said a little defensively.

"Heavens to Betsy, yes!" Mrs. Arnold chuckled. "That boy's smart as a whip."

They had decided they would have to go on without Michael, but when they got back to the house, he was sitting patiently on their front porch. His eyes lit with excitement when they explained their plan.

"Let's ask your mom," Abby said.

"How are we going to do that if she can't hear?" Merrideth asked.

"How about an old-fashioned letter?"

They trooped back upstairs and Abby sat down at the computer. Merrideth and Michael watched with interest as she typed a short note introducing herself and asking Mrs. Richardson permission for the trip. Then she added, at Merrideth's suggestion, a request that Michael be allowed to stay on for dinner.

When they pulled up to his house, Michael jumped out of the car with the typed sheet and raced to the front door. After a short time, the curtain in the front window swished back and a woman's curious face appeared there momentarily. Then, face beaming, Michael ran back to the car and returned the letter to Abby. At the bottom of it, Mrs. Richardson had written:

Mrs. Arnold told me who you are, so it's all right with me. Thanks for being nice to Michael.

Betty Richardson

Michael was quivering with excitement about getting a snow cone, but he went with them into the library with no complaint. It didn't take long to get Merrideth's library card. When the librarian handed it to her, she smiled proudly and showed it to Michael.

Merrideth picked out several books for herself, and then, seeing the look on Michael's face, took him to the little kids' shelves and helped choose some books for him. Abby wasn't sure if he could read, but judging by his expression, he really wanted to.

When they got to the Tropical Frost stand, Michael raced ahead of them down the sidewalk. But before they could catch up with him, he came back, his smile replaced with a look of sad resignation. Abby saw a group of small boys in green and yellow baseball uniforms crowded around the window.

"I think the little creeps have come to town," Merrideth whispered.

Surely these weren't the bullies who'd taken Michael's cookies? They looked so cute and wholesome. Three of the boys were already busily slurping snow cones. A small red-haired boy was mining his pockets for the money he needed to pay for his.

When Abby and the others got into line behind them, the tallest boy nudged the redhead and said, "Hurry up, Jake."

Behind the counter, John patiently held a grape snow cone in one hand while accepting the nickels, dimes, and pennies the boy gave him with the other.

John looked up and smiled. "Abby, I like your hair."

She put her hand up to her hair and mentally groaned. The hair clips and elastic bands Merrideth had stuck all over her hair were still there. But when Abby saw that she was smiling proudly, she put her hand down.

She smiled weakly. "Thanks. Merrideth fixed it for me."

John grinned at Merrideth. "Maybe you'll have your own salon in the city one day."

She looked thoughtful. "Maybe I will."

The boy finally put the last penny in John's hand, and then he and the other boys turned away, whispering and pointing. At first, Abby thought they were pointing at her hair, and she really didn't blame them. But then they began to chant: "Tardo, tardo, Michael is a retard."

They must have thought they were far enough away to be safe from retribution, but John vaulted over the counter with the ease of a track star and, reaching the boys in three strides, grabbed the ringleader's shirt in one hand and the red-haired boy's in the other.

"You little punks!" he said.

The boys' eyes were huge and they didn't even bother to resist arrest, although their friends wasted no time mounting their bikes and racing away down the sidewalk.

"You come back over here and apologize right now." He hauled his two detainees back to the window, where she and Merrideth stood with their mouths gaping open, and Michael looked like he had just seen his favorite super-hero come to life.

The boys hung their heads and mumbled some- thing. Abby wasn't sure anyone knew what they said, including the boys themselves. But they seemed remorseful, so John let them go. They didn't stick around to chat.

"Since you apologized, you're welcome to come back," John called after them. "But tell your buddies if they want to come to Tropical Frost again, they'll have to come talk to me first."

Calmly he opened the side door and reappeared behind the window. "Now. What can I get for you ladies and gentleman today?"

"We came back," Abby said unnecessarily, "for the buy-one-get-one sale. That's the reason we came. And Michael—that's Michael—and Michael has never been to Tropical Frost before. So, anyway, that's why we're here." She closed her eyes in relief. At last her mouth had stopped.

"Hi, pleased to meet you." John extended his hand, and the boy smiled and shook it. "What flavor can I get you, Michael?"

"What kind do you got?" he asked.

"Have," Abby corrected automatically.

Merrideth began describing all the flavors on the chart to him.

"I wanted to come see your Miles Station," John said. "But I couldn't get off work."

"If you like historical houses like I do, you'd love it," Abby said.

"I meant I wanted to come see you."

"Oh." She panicked and began babbling again. "That's the trouble with summer jobs, isn't it? They don't pay much and you can't get time off when you want to."

Why was she talking about the blasted job again?

"Well, actually it does pay pretty well."

He had to have pretty low career expectations to think that. Before she could think of what to say that wouldn't sound patronizing, Michael announced the flavor he had chosen. John seemed embarrassed because he had to ask him twice to repeat it.

"He said Waikiki Lime," Merrideth said.

"And how about you, Abby? What do you want?" John asked.

"Hmm." She pondered the list on the wall. "I'll take Slurple Purple."

John's eyes were glued to Abby's face as he handed her the cone.

Merrideth watched John watch Abby sip her cone. "I would like…" She cleared her throat. "As for my order…" Merrideth began again, "I said…"

John shook his head and seemed to come out of a trance. Finally, he shifted his eyes from her to Merrideth.

She rolled her eyes. "I'll have pineapple, plain pineapple, please," she said patiently.

"Oh. Right," he said, clearing his throat. "Sorry, we don't have Pineapple Passion."

"That's okay," Merrideth said. "There's too much around here anyway."

They left in a hurry again. But, other than Merrideth's embarrassing remark, Abby was generally pleased with her behavior. This time she had managed to avoid staining her blouse and had acted as grown up as her makeup and new haircut. Best of all, she had been solicitous of Michael and seemed to enjoy her role as mentor and benefactor.

When they got home, she even offered to read one of the library books to Michael. Listening from the kitchen, Abby was impressed by the fluency of Merrideth's reading but even more with her kindness. When the story was finished, Merrideth suggested they go play computer games. He seemed reluctant to end the storytime until Merrideth told him they could read more after dinner, and he could come over and she'd read them to him again anytime he wanted.

"You can play games after dinner," Abby said. "But first, let's open the word processor, Merrideth. You need to practice, because you'll be typing more and more of your homework, especially in high school. Why don't you type a letter to your dad? You know, a good old-fashioned letter might be better than a phone call, anyway."

Merrideth stared at the blank screen. "I don't know what to say."

"Did you ever thank him for the computer?"

"No. He only got it for me because he felt guilty about the divorce."

Abby hoped he felt guilty for a whole lot more than that. "Well, you should still thank him."

After a moment, Merrideth began in a style that was somewhere between hunt and peck and touch typing. In an amazingly short time, she finished and shyly invited Abby to read her letter:

Dear Dad,

Thanks for the computer. There is a lot of neat stuff on it. I like Bubble Town the best. And there's a secret on my computer. I'll show you when you come visit. Dad, I miss you so much. Every night when I see the stars come out, I make a wish. Guess what I wish? I wish for you and Mom to get back together again. I also wish that I will wake up in the morning and find out that I am back in

Chicago. Do you think you will get un-busy before school starts so I can come visit you? Maybe you could call me and let me know. I'm here almost every day, except me and Abby might go back to the library later this week. So try to call right away, okay?

Love, Merrideth

Abby swallowed a lump in her throat. "That's very nice, kiddo."

"I guess a little practice doesn't hurt. Now I'll be warmed up for the usual what-I-did-on-my-summer-vacation essay."

"Don't forget the during-my-summer-vacation essay you're going to need to type for your heartless tutor."

Merrideth turned to Michael, who had been patiently watching. "I have a game on here called Space Invaders. You want to play?"

He grinned and nodded his head.

Abby made homemade pizza, which impressed Merrideth and Michael, but not so much that they hung around for very long afterward. They did willingly carry their dishes over to the sink, but then raced back upstairs to play Space Invaders. As she was cleaning up the kitchen and straightening the living room, she heard their whoops and groans and the bleep-bleep of the computer. The cats were also having a fun time, thumping up and down the hall and stairs in their usual evening hyper mode.

The bleeps and explosions stopped, and the house was uncannily quiet. When she got upstairs, she found Merrideth and Michael sitting on the computer boxes in the corner. He was listening intently as she read one of the library books to him.

When she came to the end of the story, he smiled and didn't stop, even when Abby told him it was time to go home. And since it was beginning to get dark, she and Merrideth walked him home, even though he assured them he wasn't afraid to go by himself.

The sun was low in the sky, but there was still no relief from the heat. The syrup-thick air pressed in on all sides as they walked down the dark road. Crickets chirped from the grassy ditches on either side of them. The pit bull rattled his chain and barked a few times when they passed. Blue-tinged lights flickered in one trailer's front windows and canned audience laughter came in bursts of artificial hilarity. Heat lightning to the north outlined cornfields against the sky.

"It's going to be hot trying to sleep tonight," Abby said after they left Michael at his house.

"I'm going to take another shower before I go to bed."

Abby's eyes widened in surprise. Two in one day. She kept the conversation impersonal. "It feels like it might rain. That would cool things down. As for now, it's so humid I think we could swim the rest of the way home."

"Can't." Abby heard the smile in Merrideth's voice. "I didn't bring my floaties."

CHAPTER 13

Michael showed up right after breakfast the next morning and looked adoringly up at Merrideth. "You want to play in my clubhouse?"

"Sure, Michael. Lead the way."

Since Merrideth had just been urging her to hurry so that they could get back to time-surfing upstairs, Abby knew it was a huge sacrifice on her part.

Abby assumed he would be taking them to the woods or at least somewhere near his home, but instead, he led them to their own barn.

Michael tugged at the iron latch until it gave way and pushed the door open for them. Abby hadn't gotten around to checking out the barn, and she stepped forward, eager to appease her curiosity. Something black and furry came at her, and she yelped and jerked back, stumbling into Merrideth. Finally, her brain processed what she had seen: a black cat had jumped down from the top rail of a stall and then fairly flown away into the gloom. There was no way to judge who had been more frightened—she or the cat.

Michael laughed. "Wild cats."

"Not panthers or cougars," Merrideth hurried to reassure her. "He means untamed cats."

Abby let out her breath and laughed. "I certainly hope so."

"There's some pretty ones, but they won't let you near them," Merrideth said.

Abby paused before entering, hoping there were no other surprises. The barn was dim, and the stalls that had once held livestock were empty. A splintered and worn manger on the right held hay so shrouded in dust that surely no self-respecting cow would ever eat it. The barn's rough-hewn walls and rafters were festooned with dusty cobwebs. A lonely feeling seemed to float in the air and permeate the very timbers.

Merrideth came in behind her and promptly tripped over something that went skittering across the barn's stone floor.

It was a dirty blue crockery bowl. Michael picked it up and held it out to Abby. "Miss Ruth used to feed the cats in it."

She had no inclination to take it but made a mental note to see about getting more cat food. "It's an antique, I think. Could be valuable."

Merrideth looked at it closely. "Abby, it's Charlotte's bowl. Remember? I bet she took scraps out in it and forgot it. Just think. It's been out here all this time."

"It sure looks like the one on the computer," Abby said guardedly. "But that's an incredibly long time for it to survive. You nearly broke it just now."

"We could go back to that first day we met Charlotte and look at it again."

"Wait a minute. What am I thinking? There's no way on earth that a computer programmer could know about this blue bowl."

"But it looks just like it."

"Well, even if it's not Charlotte's, it might be pretty under all the filth. Let's take it up to the house."

"Yeah, Mom loves pottery."

"Okay, then, Michael. Set the bowl down and show us where this clubhouse of yours is."

He led them farther into the barn to a primitive ladder of rough boards nailed to one of the barn's massive supporting posts. The ladder led to a square opening into the loft. He clambered up the ladder like a monkey and disappeared from view.

Then he grinned down at them through a flurry of straw drifting down on their heads. "Come see."

"Oh, Michael, be careful up there," Abby said.

"Miss Ruth always let me play in the loft." The tone of his voice said he was fearful this privilege might be denied him by the new ownership.

"I'm sure Pat will let you, too, but you really should ask first."

"Come on up." He waved encouragingly.

Abby put her foot on the first rung, searched until she found a handhold, and began to pull herself up. When she was high enough to look in, she saw sunbeams arrowing through a thousand cracks and knotholes in the board walls, gilding the dust particles that floated in the air. Bales of straw—or perhaps hay, she had never figured out the distinction—were stacked at the perimeter of the loft.

When she had conquered the ladder, Abby lay on the loft floor next to Michael and reached a hand down to Merrideth. "Come on. It's not so bad."

"Oh, all right." Merrideth struggled to pull herself up

each rung. "No telling how many people have fallen off this so-called ladder and killed themselves," she griped between breaths.

Abby grabbed her arm and pulled her up. "You know, Merrideth," she said, "I think you've lost weight."

A smile lit up Merrideth's face. "Do you really think so?"

"Ha. That's what you get for giving up your couch potato ways, kiddo."

Michael scampered across the straw-strewn board floor, waving for them to come see his "clubhouse." But she and Merrideth clung for a moment to the security of the post, staring in trepidation at the floor of the loft. Through cracks between the boards, they could see the barn below. Firmly reminding herself that her foot couldn't possibly fit between the cracks, she started toward Michael, the floorboards creaking with each step.

Michael's "clubhouse" was just an old green tarp draped over a wooden frame of some sort. But they spent considerable time admiring its features.

"This is nice, Michael," Abby said.

"It's pretty cool," Merrideth added generously. "Did you build this all by yourself?"

"Yep," he said and smiled proudly.

They crawled through the entrance, which he had positioned to take advantage of what light there was. The tarp above them, like the barn walls, had so many holes that the clubhouse was not all that dark. They sat on bales of straw. A plastic milk crate in one corner served as a table. Abby smiled to see a peanut butter sandwich in a plastic bag.

Abby studied the walls of his clubhouse in the dim light. "You didn't nail all this together, did you?" she said, running her hands curiously over it.

"Naw," he said.

Abby squinted in the dim light and then smiled. "I know what it is. Merrideth, does this look familiar?"

"No. What is it?"

"Think pink roses."

"The missing porch trellises! What in the world are they doing up here?"

"They're in excellent condition. Just need a coat of paint."

"Mom will love it."

Abby saw that Michael's eyes had gone wide and alarmed. "Don't worry. There's no way we could get them out of the loft anyway."

Michael offered to share his peanut butter sandwich. They thanked him but declined.

"I want to do more research," Abby said.

"You just want to go back to Brighton and see—"

"Ha. That's where you're wrong. We'll surf the web for what I want to know."

"And what do you want to know?"

"I think the computer programmer got careless with his history."

"What do you mean?"

"Well, I've been thinking. You know how Charlotte was mad because her father wouldn't let her go to the State Fair when it was so close to home? Since when was the State Fair ever in Alton instead of Springfield?"

"I'm beginning to think this must be a documentary," Abby said. "And man, did they ever sweat the details. 1854, the one and only year the State Fair was in Alton. I'd like to have seen that. But since Alton was founded only thirty years before, doesn't it seem like it would have been too small to host the fair? Of course, all of Illinois was growing so fast."

It suddenly occurred to Abby that she was the only one talking, babbling really, and she turned to look at Merrideth.

Her arms were crossed over her chest and she was rolling her eyes. "That part about the fair just proves it's not a documentary, Abby. Who would put a little thing like that in there? When we time-surf, it's real. And that girl really is Charlotte."

"Kiddo, I don't think—"

"And if you want to go see Alton back in the day, then lets time-surf there. You'll see it's real too."

"How would we?"

"Charlotte's going to get on the train sooner or later and when she does—"

"We lock onto her and go with. You're brilliant, kiddo. You know that?"

"I know," Merrideth agreed with a grin. "Now let's get surfing."

"Guess what?" Jonathan Miles asked, coming in the kitchen door, "Mr. McGuire didn't send a letter. He came in person from Springfield to talk over the case."

Charlotte's only comment was "Oh?" She wiped the perspiration from her face with a corner of her apron and then, taking the heavy cast iron pot of stew, started for the dining room.

When Charlotte saw the visitor, she got mad at her father all over again. Why hadn't he told her how handsome and young Mr. McGuire was? Her first impulse was to smooth her hair, but since she was holding a heavy pot of stew, that was out of the question. Her calico dress was stained, but there was no time to do anything about her bedraggled appearance now. Passengers expected their food on the table hot, and plenty of it, so they could get back to the station on time.

Mr. McGuire's clothes were ordinary, those of a country lawyer, but without the somberness she might have expected. Her eyes were drawn to his brown hair glinting in the afternoon sun. Then he looked up as she approached, and she nearly stumbled. His strong face was clean-shaven. His eyes were a leafy green, fringed with the longest dark lashes she had ever seen. And they were peering into her blue ones with interest. She set the pot down in front of him and turned quickly away, intending to go back to the kitchen to wash her face.

But he stood politely and held out his hand. "Thank you, Miss. My name is McGuire—James McGuire. I do appreciate a hot meal when I'm traveling."

"You're most welcome," she said, taking his hand after wiping hers on her skirt. At last, she drew her eyes away and noticed the other guests sitting across the table, a pale and nervous man with his pale and nervous wife and their active—very active—little boy.

"I'll just go get the cornbread then," Charlotte said, smiling weakly.

"My Charlotte has been cooking for years," Jonathan Miles said as he took his seat at the head of the table. "She took over after her mother passed on."

"Oh, Papa," Charlotte said and hurried to the kitchen to take the skillet from the oven.

When she returned with a basket of cornbread, the men had risen and Mr. McGuire was politely seating a dazzlingly beautiful woman next to himself. He looked up as Charlotte approached.

"Miss Charlotte, may I introduce Clarissa?" Charlotte nearly dropped her basket. His wife must have been in the parlor. The smile Charlotte had been wearing felt wobbly, but she fixed it as best she could. She hoped it didn't fall off.

"Pleased to meet you," she said and went to her seat at the end of the table. Clarissa's silk skirt rustled as she settled it around herself. Mr. McGuire said something Charlotte couldn't hear and Clarissa laughed softly, her shining blonde curls bouncing.

From his seat at the head of the table, her father turned to the pale young husband. "Where are you folks headed, if you don't mind my asking?"

"We're going to take Joshua to the fair," he replied.

Charlotte shot her father a pointed look.

"That is, if he finishes his dinner in time," the pale mother said. The little boy bounced in his seat and hurriedly stuffed a bite of cornbread into his mouth.

"Time to go, time to go, time to go!" he said as soon as he had swallowed the cornbread.

"Now, Joshua," his mother warned, wiping crumbs from his face. "You're going to choke."

"It's fortunate that Clarissa could go with us," the pale husband said.

"It will be fun for me, too," she said, smiling at Joshua.

Charlotte frowned in confusion. "Did you meet Mrs. McGuire on the train?" she asked the pale husband.

James choked and smothered a laugh with his napkin.

Clarissa gasped. "I'm not Mrs. McGuire," she said, darting a look at the man next to her.

"But I thought—" Charlotte broke off, horrified.

"Clarissa is my sister," the pale young husband said.

"Oh, of course," Charlotte said. She felt her face burning and knew it was flaming red. She had an overwhelming urge to be somewhere far away. Maybe she'd walk to Alton.

"I'll go get the dessert," she said at last and escaped to the kitchen.

When she had washed her face in cool water and stalled for as long as she dared, she went back, carrying the warm blackberry cobbler. She was grateful that everyone had resumed conversation.

"I'll wager Joshua's enjoying his ride on the train as much as he will the fair itself," James McGuire said with a laugh. "Trains are the ride to the future, but I'm sure I don't have to tell you that, sir," he said with a nod at Charlotte's father.

"No, indeed, Mr. McGuire. I had to do some talking, but I convinced Mr. Godfrey to put the railroad through this land on its way to Alton. It's the first rail line to the Mississippi, you know."

James smiled and said, "And with immigrants from Kentucky and Tennessee pouring into Illinois, I predict your little village will take off like a house afire."

"Papa came from Kentucky, too, and when he first got here there were no roads, no fences, and no houses—just unbroken prairie. Now there are twenty-seven houses and we have a school, a church, a blacksmith's shop, and Papa's mercantile. Of course, there's also Mr. Puckett's tavern—if you want to count that progress. And it's been just four years since the railroad was finished. It all started when Papa built the mill—it's steam powered, you know. Farmers used to have to travel for a week to get to the nearest mill. Now they come from miles around to have their corn and wheat ground. Papa says—"

"Charlotte, you're making me blush," Jonathan said.

"What a charmingly loyal daughter you are," Clarissa said.

"You have every right to be proud of your father,"

James added.

Charlotte's face flamed again as she realized she had been chattering on like a child.

"I just wish your mother could be here to see it all." He coughed into his napkin and changed the subject.

The talk turned to the fair and the weather until the depot whistle sounded. The young family rose abruptly and, saying quick goodbyes, gathered their belongings and left. When Charlotte began to gather the dirty plates and cups, James hurried to get the stew pot. "Let me help you with these heavy things, Miss Charlotte."

"Let's speed it up, okay?" Merrideth said. "She's obviously not going to get to go Alton yet. And besides, this is getting boring."

"I don't think it's boring," Abby said. "The plot is thickening. Don't you think James is cute?"

"Not that cute. Let's fast-forward and see if Charlotte ever gets on the train."

Abby clicked the Time Parameters menu and increased the speed. They laughed when Charlotte and the others began scurrying around, doing the washing up in double time. Even that speed was too slow.

Abby moved the dial again and the screen became a blur of colors all blending together, then shades of gray speeding past. Every few minutes, she slowed the rate to real time so that they could follow Charlotte as she lived out her life. They watched her weeding her garden and picking flowers for the church. They watched a lot of work being done around the house: ironing, cleaning, sewing. Once in a while, a woman came to help with heavier housework.

They saw Charlotte and her father, dressed in their best clothes, drive off in a horse-drawn buggy to the little church down the street where they joined her brothers Samuel and Frank and their families for the Sunday service.

Only a dozen or so headstones jutted from the neatly mown churchyard, a fraction of the number Abby and Merrideth had counted in the cemetery.

They went with Charlotte as she walked down the boardwalk of the village and got a chance to see the blacksmith shop, the school, and even the grain mill when Charlotte went with her father there one day.

Abby took her hand from the mouse and rubbed her eyes. They were tired and burning, strained from staring at the monitor all day. "We'd better stop for a while. I'm starting to feel like a stalker again. We can't spend our whole life up in this room reliving someone else's life."

But then Abby saw Charlotte walk to the depot and sit on the bench in front. She grabbed the mouse and nudged the speed up a little. The train pulled into the station.

"Hey, Merrideth. Maybe she's finally getting on the train."

James stepped down from the train and stood on the platform smiling at Charlotte.

"Or not." Merrideth said.

"I should have realized she wouldn't be going anywhere without luggage."

Abby started to shut down the program, but Merrideth's squeal to "wait" stopped her. Abby squealed, too, when she recognized the traveler who had stepped down from the train and stood chatting with James and Charlotte.

CHAPTER 14

"Charlotte, may I introduce my boss, Mr. Abraham Lincoln," James said.

Mr. Lincoln was very tall. His hands looked too large for the rest of him, perhaps because the sleeves of his suit did not cover his wrists. He tipped his hat, briefly revealing bushy black hair, and gave a polite bow.

"Miss Miles, James has not ceased enumerating your charms ever since he was last here. I see he has not exaggerated one whit."

Charlotte's face went hot. She couldn't make her eyes turn toward James, although she was curious to see his reaction to this outrageous statement.

"And, Mr. Lincoln, may I present Miss Charlotte Miles."

"We're glad to have you, sir. My father would have been here to meet the train, but he had business at the mercantile. He should be here soon. I know he is anxious to talk over the case with you."

"Yes, indeed. Now, Mr. McGuire, if you wouldn't mind—no, I'm sure you wouldn't—escorting Miss Charlotte back to the house, I will meet you there presently. I need...er...something from the mercantile. I'll walk back with Mr. Miles."

"Is there something I can get for you, sir?"

"No, James. That's quite all right. I'll be back before you miss me."

When Charlotte and James got back to the house, she excused herself to finish the meal preparations. James, refusing to stay put in the parlor, followed her to the kitchen. She put her apron back on and tried to concentrate on making gravy, a process tricky enough even without knowing James' green eyes were following her every move. She was just putting the last of the food on the table when her father and Mr. Lincoln came through the front door.

James took the heavy platter of roast beef from her hands. She smiled in gratitude and called out, "Dinner is ready, Papa."

"We'll be right there, dear." After hanging Mr. Lincoln's hat on the hall hat tree, he escorted him into the dining room.

"These are surely the best jellybeans in the state," Mr. Lincoln said, stuffing the bag into his coat pocket. "I always like to visit your mercantile when I pass through."

"I'm glad you like them, sir. I send all the way to Boston for them. But I have another treat for you," Jonathan Miles said. "Wait until you taste Charlotte's cooking."

"Yes, I seem to recall Mr. McGuire telling me something about that."

The computer whirred as the allotted time expired and the screen blinked and reverted to the *Beautiful Houses* page.

"Can you believe it?" Merrideth said. "Abraham Lincoln in this very house!"

"This is so cool! I am a little disappointed in their portrayal of Lincoln, though," Abby said. "I mean, didn't they go a little overboard on the homespun routine? And that voice. It was so twangy. You would have thought they would have made Lincoln a little more presidential."

"But he's not the president yet," Merrideth said.

"No, you're right. Just a simple Springfield lawyer."

"You can't still think this is just a computer game? This has to be real!"

Abby yawned and stood, stretching her arms over her head. "Well, whatever it is, it's amazing. I'm going to call Kate. She won't believe this."

She was right: Kate didn't believe it—she literally didn't believe it. She insisted that Abby was trying to get back at her for all the practical jokes she had pulled on her. She laughed the whole time. "Good one, Abby," Kate said. "Of course, Lincoln slept in your house. He slept in every old house in Illinois."

Abby kept trying to describe Lincoln, but Kate said not to bother—everyone in Springfield was an expert on the subject of Lincoln.

"But you're good," Kate said. "You should apply for a job on the Springfield Tourism Board. They shamelessly use Lincoln to sell everything. My personal favorite is the 'Gettysburger' served at the Anne Rutledge Restaurant. I have an idea myself that I might submit to them for the cover of the Springfield telephone book: Let Your

Lincolns Do the Hawking. Ha, ha, ha. Get it? Instead of let your fingers do—"

"Yeah, I get it, but that's not the point," Abby said. When Kate was in one of her hyper moods, there was no use trying to talk to her. So when a beep signaled a call coming through, she told her rather tersely that she had to go.

The call was Pat letting them know she would be delayed getting home. She would be staying on for a panel discussion and some "essential" networking opportunities. She would be back by Sunday at the latest. Merrideth grabbed the phone from Abby. But Pat told her she couldn't talk for long, because she was getting ready to go back and, besides, she didn't want to run up the phone bill.

Then Abby tried again to call the computer customer service number. This time the call went right through the first time she dialed, but regular customer service was closed for the day. However, after only a momentary delay, the mechanical operator switched her to their "award-winning after-hours technical service group."

At last! A real person she could talk to. But when Abby tried to explain that she wanted to get information about the *Beautiful Houses* software included with the computer, the technician, who sounded about fifteen, couldn't seem to grasp the idea. He put her on hold for ten minutes while he consulted his "resources," then was back to tell her that she would need to call during regular office hours and talk to someone in customer service.

"I'm in a loop," she said, slamming the phone down in exasperation.

Merrideth was gone. She finally found her sitting in the dark on the front porch steps, gazing up into the night sky.

Abby sat down next to her. "I still can't get over the difference from the city. It seems like there are a zillion more stars here than we ever have there."

She glanced at Merrideth, who sat resting her head on her knees. Faint strains of Elvis came from somewhere down the road.

"It's about time for the train."

"Yeah. I know."

"You seem sad tonight, Merrideth. Is it because your mom's not coming home tomorrow?"

"Oh well," Merrideth answered. "I guess that just gives us more time before we have to get back to long division."

She squeezed Merrideth's arm.

"I wish Dad would come. But it's not just that."

"What, then?"

"Charlotte, I guess. I feel sort of strange now after being with her all day."

"Yes, me too. It's kind of a letdown." She chuckled. "It's like we're just home from a foreign country, only no postcards to show for it."

"But it's so sad," Merrideth blurted out. "I feel sorry for her being stuck in that town...er...this town— whatever—and having to work all the time. After all, she's only sixteen. 'Too busy. Too busy.' They're always too busy— even in the olden days."

Abby was pretty sure her psych professor would say Merrideth was projecting. "Charlotte doesn't seem sad to me."

They watched the lights of the Amtrak approaching fast from the south. When it neared the old depot, its whistle wailed, even though no passengers would be disembarking at Miles Station, and hadn't in over sixty years. Was it from some longstanding tradition of respect for the old train stop?

When the train was even with the porch, they could see, where window shades were up, the unsuspecting faces of passengers lit up like actors under stage lights. Then the train was past, on its route north and east through all the small towns of the prairie, then the larger ones, and finally Grand Central Station in Chicago.

Merrideth followed its progress until it had disappeared from view behind the shadowy trees. "If I were her, I would have just hopped the train to the fair. Get out of this place."

Abby put an arm around Merrideth. She didn't even shake it off. "Charlotte's life seems pretty happy to me. Just because she didn't get to go to the fair doesn't mean she's not basically happy. I wonder how far forward in time the program goes? It would be cool if it came all the way to our time."

"But maybe we don't want to go forward too far."

"Don't you want to see what happens next?" Abby said.

"Sure, but…well, I just don't want to go too far."

Abby thought about Charlotte and the passing of time. Maybe Merrideth was right. She didn't know if she could stand to watch her grow old. "How about tomorrow we try going back farther in time? Maybe we'll see when Miles Station was first settled, depending on how extensive the software researcher got."

"That would be interesting, I guess. But I still want to see Charlotte go to Alton," Merrideth said.

"Okay, the future it is—just not too far. You know, maybe I'll use this for a term paper this fall."

Merrideth stood and started back to the house. "And I'll tell all the kids at school that Lincoln slept in my house."

CHAPTER 15

The next morning, Abby told herself that she would show some self-control by taking the time to call Customer Support before she let herself go back to stalking Charlotte. Merrideth set no such restrictions on herself.

"That was the biggest waste of fifty-five minutes I've had in a long time," Abby said when she finally got to the computer room.

"What'd they say?"

"That I should try calling the Montel Williams Show," Abby said in disgust. "The guy said they would probably have a spot for me when they do their show on reincarnation. That little gem of wisdom came after I had waited in the queue for twenty minutes, then got transferred to various baby techs as I made my way up the hierarchy to the Technician in Chief."

"You could have saved yourself a lot of time, because this is not a software program," Merrideth insisted. "Well, not a regular one."

"I'm telling you, Charlotte's not real," Abby said, pretending to pull her hair in frustration.

"Of course she's real. We read all about the Miles' family in the history books."

"Haven't you ever read historical fiction? The characters may be real people, but the author makes up a fictional story about them. Nobody could know all these details about Charlotte's life."

"I don't care what you say. She's real." Merrideth turned back to the monitor to watch Charlotte.

"I want to go to the library again to look up some stuff about Lincoln," Abby said as they finished eating lunch.

"You mean you want to go see John," Merrideth said.

"Don't be silly. I need to do some research on—"

"Hello. If you wanted to do 'research,' you'd be surfing the web right now," Merrideth said with a smug smile.

"And even if he is cute, I'm not interested at the present time."

"Sure."

"Besides, I want a man with ambition. I could never get interested in a guy who thinks working at a Tropical Frost is a high-paying job."

"Whatever."

They browsed the library's Lincoln collection, such as it was, and settled down in old but comfortable chairs in one quiet corner to read the books they had selected from the shelves. Abby and Merrideth found they did not do well studying together. Every few minutes, one would interrupt the other's concentration by blurting out nuggets of interesting information.

Abby looked up from a book about Lincoln's life married to Mary Todd. "Hey, guess what? Lincoln was ambitious. I never thought of him that way, but the author says part of the reason he married Mary was because she came from a wealthy, socially prominent family, which was sure to help his political career."

"Hey, you said you admired ambition in a man," Merrideth said without turning from her book on Lincoln's early life.

"I don't mean Lincoln was ambitious in a cut-throat way. And that's sure not what I'm looking for either."

"Did you know he didn't go to school? He did all his reading and studying on his own, even Shakespeare and stuff like that. He read for hours at night, laying on a pile of leaves, twigs, and animal skins. That was his only bed up until he was a grown man," Merrideth said in wonder.

"Lying," Abby said.

"He never lied; he was 'Honest Abe,' remember?"

"No, I mean you should say he was lying on a pile of leaves."

"Give me a break, Abby. We're not in English class. Anyway," she said, giving Abby a pointed look. "He did all his studying without a teacher standing over him with math and grammar books."

"That's because he knew how important education was." Abby grinned. "If he had an amazing tutor such as *moi* to help him, who knows how brilliant he would have been."

"Right. Anyway, I'm getting tired of this. Let's go get a snow cone."

"But isn't research fun?"

"Actually, it is when it's someone you know."

A long line of people was waiting to be served when she and Merrideth got there. When they discovered John wasn't there, Merrideth nudged her arm, and she tried not to show her disappointment. There was an elderly woman at the counter. She seemed rattled by the crowd and was slow and inefficient at taking money and handing out cones. Fortunately, everyone seemed to be cutting her some slack. Eventually, the line shortened and it was their turn.

"Sorry about the delay," she gasped, wiping her face with a paper napkin. "First day on the job. My name's Elsie. What flavor do you want?"

"Pineapple—just plain pineapple—for my friend, and I'll have the Cheery Cherry." Sooner than they had expected, they had their cones in hand and Abby asked, "Doesn't John work here anymore, Elsie?"

"Why, mercy. Yes, girl. Where else would he work?"

"I suppose there aren't many places to work around here."

"There's some. And as smart as he is—got a full scholarship to the University of Illinois, you know—anyway, he could work any place he wanted. Like maybe at Rural King or the Farmer's Co-op or—"

"So why here?" Abby said.

"Hey, don't knock it. It's better than being a greeter at Walmart. That was my last job. But he works here because he owns the place. Has ever since he was a junior in high school, and now that boy's a junior at the college, believe it or not."

"No wonder he said the pay was good," Abby said.

Elsie snorted. "Course the pay's not good. He knew that when he saved his money to buy this place. He opened it for the kids to have a little fun in this town. Not to get rich, though with his ambition I'm sure he will be someday. He's studying to be a lawyer."

"Don't you think ambition is so important in a young man?" Merrideth said sincerely.

"Oh, be quiet, Merrideth," Abby said under her

breath. "Speaking of ambition, we've got to go home and get to work." She smiled at Elsie. "Thanks for the snow cones."

When they opened *Beautiful Houses*, Abby set the controls and they occupied themselves watching the mundane details of Charlotte's life. Merrideth agreed not to speed up too fast for fear they would miss something interesting.

Abby was more interested than Merrideth in the developing romance between Charlotte and James McGuire. And she liked to hear James' accounts of his work with Lincoln in the Springfield law office. They never did get all the details of the case Lincoln was working on for Jonathan Miles—some complaint against the railroad company for failing to compensate for timber he sold them.

But James seemed to make many trips to Miles Station to confer with Jonathan—not that he actually spent much time in the office. More often, he strolled with Charlotte in the garden or around the village. And he always stayed behind to help with the heavy pots and pans after one of Charlotte's meals.

Merrideth was beginning to be bored by the adult conversation, and Abby was just about to speed up when they caught the announcement James was making at the table. Mr. Lincoln would be seeking a seat in the Senate.

James' face was a comical mixture of conflicting emotions. On one hand, he was proud and excited that he would continue to be the assistant of the new senator, when he was elected—and he was sure he would be. And he had nothing but praise for the character, honesty, and kindness of the man for whom he worked. He was confident Mr. Lincoln would be the best senator the state had ever had, far greater than that windbag Stephen

Douglas who was running against him.

But on the other hand, James knew that his free time would be limited for the next several months, and he probably would not get to see Charlotte for a while.

James' announcement that Lincoln would run against Douglas for the Senate was no surprise to Abby. She knew that the campaign would focus on whether or not slavery should be allowed into the Western territories of the United State. And she knew that the two candidates would square off against each other across the state in a series of seven debates that would capture the attention of the whole country.

What she had not realized until she heard the announcement at the Miles' dining room table was that the last of the famous Lincoln-Douglas debates took place only twenty miles away in Alton on October 15, 1858.

They did not have to time-surf past very many months—boring, lonely ones for Charlotte—before they began to see flyers posted around the village listing the dates and times of all the debates. Everywhere in Miles Station, the conversation turned to the progress of the political campaigns of the "elegant" Democratic candidate Stephen Douglas and the "homely" Republican candidate Abraham Lincoln.

Travelers passing through were kind enough to leave copies of the Daily Courier from Alton or the Illinois State Register from Springfield. The newspapers were eagerly read and re-read by the villagers, and Abby and Merrideth began to realize the huge importance such events were in the lives of an earlier generation. Entertainment of any sort was a rarity that no one took for granted.

Reporters boasted their skill with the new shorthand method and promised to capture the "full phonographic verbatim reports" of the "Last Great Discussion." Some villagers made plans to hear the debate in person, and many more made that decision when the newspapers informed them that the Chicago and Alton Railroad Company would carry passengers at half-fare.

Abby and Merrideth were happy that at last Charlotte would get her chance to ride the train to Alton. And although it was not the State Fair, the entertainment would be every bit as exciting for her. An added attraction for Charlotte was that she and her father would meet James there.

And now, if Abby could keep the lock on Charlotte when she left the vicinity of Miles Station, she and Merrideth would get to go along too.

Abby checked all the settings and told Merrideth to keep her fingers crossed. But when the porter handed Charlotte up the steps into the train, they were right there with her. And they stayed with her the whole trip to Alton.

The day was cool and overcast and rain threatened, but nothing could dampen Charlotte's excitement, or that of the nearly five thousand people crowding the streets of Alton. People had come for many miles for the chance to hear the two politicians debate. When they stepped from the train, the bustle and noise of the crowd was at first overwhelming, but Charlotte felt safe at her father's side and observed everything with interest. Then James appeared out of the crowd and Charlotte's felt joy well up and threaten to spill over.

"There you are, James," Jonathan said above the noise of the crowd.

"Mr. Lincoln," James said, "calls all this 'fizzlegig and fireworks.'"

"It is for sure. I'll leave Charlotte in your capable care—as we discussed earlier." She saw that a silent message passed between the two men. At her questioning look, her father added, "I'll be right back—railroad business."

"But, Father, how will we find you in this crowd?" Charlotte asked.

"Don't worry, sir," James said to Jonathan. "The hotel is just two blocks down. It's quiet and Charlotte can rest there until the speech begins."

"Surely you're jesting, James," she said in alarm. "I want to see every bit of this...this fizzlegig and fireworks."

Jonathan took out his pocket watch and pondered it for a bit. "We've got about two hours before the speeches are set to begin. Where can I meet you, James?"

"I have reserved seats in the tenth row right in front of City Hall. We'll meet you there."

Charlotte smiled in relief and took James' arm. "Let's do see it all."

Red, white, and blue bunting hung from every imaginable surface, and a marching band was coming up State Street behind them. A souvenir seller hawking his wares caught Charlotte's attention, but she had so little spending money that the thought of stopping never occurred to her. Watching her face, James was quick to interpret the wistful look and insisted that Charlotte have a memento of the occasion. She picked out a miniature log cabin with the words Honest Abe inscribed on its roof.

After James paid the vendor, they decided to walk the two blocks to the landing on Front Street to watch the passengers disembarking from the steamboat White Cloud, up from St. Louis. Charlotte knew that her dress and accessories would never compare to those of the belles and matrons in crinolines with tiny parasols being escorted by gentlemen in frock coats and silk high hats. But she didn't care. She was wearing her best and knew, with a passing recognition of her vanity, that she at least out-dressed the farm women in their gingham.

They dodged their way through the crowd until they found the seats James had saved for them not ten feet from the platform that had been built just outside City Hall. Soon, Jonathan rejoined them, and they settled into their seats to wait.

"You know we're in enemy territory now." James' expression was determined.

"I know this is a staunchly Democratic county," Jonathan Miles answered calmly. "But I have every confidence Mr. Lincoln will bring the crowd around."

The crowd was loud and eager for the debate to begin, but James carefully turned so that the people near him wouldn't hear what he was about to say. "I'm sure you're right, sir, but I can't help wondering if the citizens of Alton have had much of a change of attitude since Elijah Lovejoy."

"Who's Elijah Lovejoy?" Charlotte asked in a whisper.

"He was before your time, dear, nearly twenty years ago," her father answered. "He was an editor, here in Alton, who was opposed to slavery and was not shy about printing his views in his newspaper. The citizens of Alton took exception to that."

"What happened?" Charlotte said.

"First they tried destroying his printing press," James said. "They dumped it in the Mississippi, but he just bought another one and continued to call for the abolition of slavery. They destroyed his press three different times, but when that wouldn't make him stop, a drunken mob torched his printing shop and shot and killed Mr.

Lovejoy."

"That's horrible!" Charlotte said. She thought for a bit and then blurted, "But, Father, Illinois is a free state!"

"Even so, many citizens, especially here in southern Illinois, are sympathetic to the South. There are plenty of slave catchers turning in runaways for the bounty. They feel no remorse at all about sending them back to their angry masters."

"And weren't they just thrilled when Douglas and his friends managed to get Congress to repeal the Missouri Compromise," James said. "It would have kept slavery from spreading into the Territories. That's why it's crucial that Mr. Lincoln be elected our new senator."

"We can take comfort," her father added, "that Mr. Lovejoy's martyrdom was not in vain. Many good men have taken up the cause of abolition because of what happened."

"And they aren't afraid to put their lives on the line for the cause, either," James added quietly.

"As a matter of fact," her father said, casting his eyes over the crowd, "I just met some gentlemen from Brighton—Dr. Thomas Brown, for one—to discuss how Miles Station might become a stop for a very special train coming up from the South."

"Ah, Sir, I think I get your meaning," James said, smiling with satisfaction. "I've heard about the good use Brown and Herman Griggs and the others have been making of their attics and cellars."

"What? What are you two talking about?" Charlotte asked, indignant that she was left out of the secret.

James whispered in her ear, "Your father means the Underground Railroad."

"You're going to build another railroad—?" she said, darting a glance to her father. "Underground?"

"Shhh. No." James couldn't help laughing, but he stopped when he saw the hurt expression on her face. "Not a literal train at all, but a way to help slaves get to freedom in the North." When she would have continued to question him, James said softly, "Your father will explain more when you get safely home."

Her father nodded to her and got his pocket watch out again. "It's about time."

"Time to start praying," Charlotte said.

"Indeed! Mr. Lincoln will have his work cut out for him. By the time we get to the election next month, I figure Mr. Douglas will have out-spent us fifty to one. And this is the last debate," James said gloomily.

"Then Mr. Lincoln will just have to out-talk Mr. Douglas fifty to one," Charlotte said.

"Just wait," James said with a smile. "He will."

"We'll be in for it now," Jonathan said. "Here they come."

The music blared and spectators furiously waved their banners as the debaters mounted the platform steps and faced the crowd. Charlotte had no doubt about where the sympathies of her nearest neighbors lay when the man on her left shouted, "Hurrah for the 'Little Giant.'"

Douglas strutted across the stage and pulled himself to his full five feet, two inches. Although Lincoln's posture was a little stooped, he still was at least a head taller than his opponent.

When Mr. Lincoln had visited in her home, Charlotte had not thought much about his attire, but now she was acutely embarrassed for him because of the contrast between the two orators.

Stephen Douglas' shirt was ruffled and dazzlingly white. His dark blue frock coat was ornamented with shiny buttons, and his boots were glossy and fine. On his head was a soft-brimmed hat much like those worn by wealthy southern planters.

What could she say about Mr. Lincoln? His coat was a worn rusty black color and his trousers were baggy and short enough to reveal his rough boots. Charlotte realized that the stovepipe hat that he politely removed was sadly out of date.

Mr. Douglas was allotted the first hour, and his oratory style, Charlotte soon discovered, was as flashy as his clothing. However, it was difficult to hear much of what he was saying, for his voice was hoarse, and at times only emphatic words like democracy, equality, and abolition could be clearly heard above the boisterous crowd's encouragement and assent.

One man in the crowd kept crying, "Popular sovereignty!"

Finally, Douglas addressed his fan directly. "You, sir, are right on the money." He slammed his clenched right fist into his open left hand. "I, for one, care more for the great principle of self-government—the right of the people to rule themselves—than I do for all the niggers in Christendom! Whereas Mr. Lincoln, here…"

His words trailed off and only when he reached his grand finale did she hear clearly his emphatic statement that "America was established on the white basis for the benefit of white men and their posterity forever."

The crowd's cheering was deafening. Charlotte looked first at her father, then at James. Both were frowning in disgust. She wondered how Mr. Lincoln would hold up with this crowd.

When he rose to take his turn, someone in the back cried out: "No black Republicans!"

But Mr. Lincoln ignored him and began his speech. His shyness was abundantly obvious. He began in a low tone of voice—as if he were used to debating outdoors, and was afraid of speaking too loudly. His oratorical gestures were no match for Douglas' practiced style. Lincoln moved his lanky body in absurd side-to-side and up-and- down movements, trying to emphasize his statements, and every time he did, he emphasized the inadequate length of his sleeves and pant legs.

He had a few supporters in the crowd—some called out "Old Abe," and some in the back were holding a banner that read "Free Territories and Free Men."

Fewer were cheering for Lincoln, but at least Charlotte could hear better, and after a while she forgot his personal appearance and his individual peculiarities as the fervency of his beliefs began to shine through. Soon his shyness was replaced with what she recognized as righteous indignation.

Lincoln's position that slavery was morally wrong contrasted with Douglas' purely pragmatic position of political practicality. Douglas had spent most of his speaking time appealing to his audience's feelings of racial superiority. Any real arguments had been based on the economic problems that abolition would incur or the fact that so many prominent southern plantation owners were opposed to it.

Lincoln, however, called his audience back to the foundational laws of the Constitution, explaining that when the Founding Fathers said "all men," they meant the Negro, too, and intended for slavery's ultimate extinction. But, contrary to Mr. Douglas' assertion, Lincoln emphasized that he did not expect to eradicate slavery overnight. It would be foolish to destroy the whole economy. But they had to begin somewhere. America could begin by preventing slavery's expansion into Kansas and the remaining western territories.

Toward the end of Mr. Lincoln's speech, the rain that had threatened all day started to fall in a depressing drizzle, and the audience began to drift away to find shelter. Nevertheless, he received a respectable applause from the crowd in general, with pockets of more enthusiastic clapping, including that of Charlotte, Jonathan, and James.

Charlotte clapped long after everyone else had stopped. "That was wonderful," she said, clutching James's coat sleeve in her excitement. "He has such a way with words. At times it was almost poetic."

"Mr. Lincoln is a poet," James said with pride, "although not many people know that. I'll ask him to send you a copy of some of his poems."

Then turning quickly to Jonathon he said, "I'm sorry, sir. I've got to go. I'm not much of an entourage, but I want to escort the Lincolns back to the hotel. Goodbye, Charlotte. I'll come see you as soon as I can get away from Springfield."

"Goodbye, James. God bless and keep you."

He took her hand, and pulling her close, looked lovingly and long into her eyes. "I count the days to our wedding, my love," he whispered. At last, he turned to go.

"Wait!" She opened her reticule and drew out the bag of jellybeans she had brought. "Give him this and tell Mr. Lincoln—tell him it was the best speech I ever heard."

James smiled and took the bag from Charlotte's outstretched hand. "I'll tell him," he said hurrying away.

The rain came in earnest now. The red, white, and blue bunting along the street hung in sodden ruin, and a man was taking down the post office flag.

"He's not going to win the election, is he, Papa?"

Her father took her arm. "We'd better start back for the train station, honey, before you catch your death."

CHAPTER 16

Abby heaved a deep sigh and looked at Merrideth, who was wiping her eyes with the sleeve of her T-shirt. Kit Kat jumped up on her lap in sympathy, and she smiled a watery smile.

"So did he?" Merrideth asked.

"Lose the election? Yes."

"That's so wrong. Didn't they listen to what he said? He was so good."

"I know," Abby said. "Wasn't it a great speech?"

"Only the beautiful people win in America."

Abby looked at her in surprise. "Wow. That's an incredibly cynical thing to say." But then a picture popped into her head of Lincoln in a modern televised speech. "You may be right."

Merrideth took the seat at the monitor and began time-surfing on high speed. "Let's get out of all this sadness." The screen was a flash of white when they approached and passed June 1859.

"Slow down for a minute, would you?" Abby said. "It's June and Charlotte's wearing white."

"The wedding!" Merrideth said.

When they reversed, they saw Charlotte enduring numerous fittings for a gorgeous white wedding gown. By zooming in very close, they could admire the delicate lace and tiny stitches on her dress.

The excitement of the wedding plans took Abby and Merrideth's minds off the tremendous letdown they felt about Lincoln's defeat, just as it seemed to for Charlotte and her friends and family. Abby was amused to find she was as excited by Charlotte's wedding preparations as if they were for Kate or one of her other college girlfriends.

Then they watched in teary happiness as on a bright Saturday morning in June, Jonathan Miles escorted his daughter to the church in his buggy. Nearly everyone from the village came. Some of the area farmers who patronized Jonathan Miles' mill stood respectfully outside the church so that there would be room inside for their wives and the relatives from Tennessee.

The ceremony and vows were simple and sweet. Charlotte thought often of her mother, praying that she would know how happy she was.

Cake and punch were served in the shade of the oak trees in the churchyard. Then under a shower of rice and calls for happiness, the newlyweds climbed into Jonathan's buggy, and he drove them to the train station.

"Wasn't it a beautiful wedding?" Abby said dreamily. "There's something so romantic about that buggy ride. Maybe I'll have one when I get married."

"Hey, Abby, snap out of it. Charlotte's getting on the train."

Then it dawned on her that Charlotte wouldn't be at Miles Station anymore. The train was getting up steam to pull out of the station on its run to Chicago with stops along the way. The newlyweds planned to reach Springfield by 4:00 p.m.

"Quick!" Merrideth said. "You have to lock onto Charlotte. I don't want to lose her."

Abby reached for the computer mouse just as Kit Kat, for reasons known only to her tiny feline brain, decided to claw her. Abby cried out and grabbed her leg. When she looked up again, she saw that she had bumped the dial too far forward. Charlotte and James were gone. Only Jonathan remained, looking wistful as the train steamed away.

"I'm sorry," Abby said. "I'll run the time back so I can get a fix on her." She replayed the wedding reception and the train station send-off. But even though she tried three times, she couldn't get a lock on Charlotte.

"Something's wrong," she said. "I've lost her."

"Maybe you should try to call customer service again."

"That's useless. You know it is."

"But Charlotte. What about Charlotte? How will we know how she is?"

"I don't know what to tell you, kiddo. We could try again later. But for now, we might as well try moving forward in time again from Miles Station. I'm kind of curious about what happens during the war. We won't have to go forward very much. The war begins in only a few months. Right after Lincoln is elected."

"You go ahead," Merri said. "I'm going to my room."

"Don't you want to watch?"

"It'll be boring without Charlotte."

"Merrideth, come quick!" Abby called.

The reply from down the hall was a muffled, "I'm busy."

"Hurry, kiddo, I've found Charlotte."

Merrideth made it from her bedroom to the computer room in record time. "Really?"

"Yeah, look. I went forward several months. You were right. It was boring without her. But then, she came back to Miles Station to live."

"Why would she do that?" Before Abby could answer the question, the expression on Merrideth's face went from curious to anguished. "They got a divorce?"

"No, no, kiddo. Nothing like that. She came back to help. To keep the mill running while her father and the other men went off to war. You'll see. She and James are still happily married, even though they're separated from each other. I'll show you a few of the scenes I found."

Charlotte sat on the sack of cornmeal to rest while she waited for Joshua to bring the horse around. She was tired, but in a satisfied sort of way. They had worked all afternoon at her father's mill, and now they would have enough cornmeal for every household in Miles Station for at least a week. It was after five and the village was nearly empty. Her sister-in-law Florence had already closed the mercantile and gone home.

Charlotte needed to go home too to check on her upstairs guests and on the two pots of stew simmering on the stove. When the Chicago & Alton train came in at six, she would serve any passengers who wanted a hot meal, including probably a half a score of soldiers making their way to the front lines. She prayed that James, her brothers, and Papa—Colonel Jonathan Miles now— would have a hot meal, too, wherever they were camped for the night.

She hated the war that was tearing the nation apart, and she hated that her men folk were so far away from home—near her birthplace, actually. Tennessee was only two states away from Illinois, but it might as well be a million miles. Her father's letters were full of the agony of knowing he was fighting against cousins and uncles— some of the same guests who had thrown rice at the wedding and wished them God's blessing.

But James' letters were filled with sweet words of comfort and dreams of the day he would return and everything would be just as it was before the war. They would live in their little house in Springfield, and on special occasions, they would ride the train to Miles Station to visit her Papa and her brothers and their families.

Even though she missed them ferociously, Charlotte took pride in knowing that she and other women in Miles Station were helping to "hold the fort," as James called it.

Her fifteen-year-old cousin Joshua came around the corner of the mill leading her gray mare, still wearing the scowl he'd first put on when he learned he would be staying to run the mill instead of going along with the men to fight the rebels in a blue coat with shiny buttons.

Rested, Charlotte rose from her impromptu seat and helped Joshua hoist the grain sack onto the mare's back. That is, she wanted to help him, tried to help him, but he only frowned harder at her efforts until she relinquished the job to him.

His masculine pride soothed, Joshua mumbled what might have been an apology, and they began the short walk to her father's house.

Unfortunately, the train arrived before Charlotte could tend to matters upstairs, and she fretted even as she dished up stew for the seven passengers off the six o'clock train. Six of them were soldiers, stragglers from the 33rd Illinois Infantry Company out of Bloomington, bound for Cairo, Illinois for training under General Grant.

"Thank you, ma'am," Lieutenant Hollis said with a tired smile when Charlotte handed him a bowl.

"You're very welcome." When she realized the men were waiting politely for her to sit before they did, she blushed. "Oh, you all just go on and eat your stew before the train takes off without you."

The soldiers, not waiting for a second invitation, took their seats and picked up their spoons.

The seventh passenger, Reverend Robbins, remained standing and cleared his throat loudly. "Mrs. McGuire, it behooves me to insist that we offer our gratitude to the Supplier of all blessings before we eat."

Charlotte blushed again. "Of course, Reverend Robbins."

When he finished—it was a lofty prayer mostly spent reassuring God that his army in blue was up to the task of annihilating the South and protecting the Union—the men began eating.

"Thank you, Reverend," Charlotte said. "I'll get that fresh bread I promised."

In the kitchen, Joshua was bolting his stew like a young dog, but he paused long enough to say, "He sure is a jackass."

"Joshua! I'm sure your mother wouldn't like you using such language." Charlotte wiped the perspiration from her face and hurried to pile the fresh rolls she had baked that morning into two baskets.

"You want me to take some of those upstairs?"

"Not just yet. But thank you."

The men had wasted no time eating their stew and

were happy for the rolls, some of which they ate and some of which they tucked into pockets for their journey.

Unfortunately, they were in no hurry to leave. Their hunger having been assuaged, they seemed starved for conversation and peppered her with questions about her family. When had her father founded Miles Station? Where were her husband and father fighting? What was it like running a train stop kitchen all alone? Charlotte knew their questions were friendly. Perhaps they saw in her the sister or cousin they had left behind. But she wished them gone, the sooner the better.

"You should have more than a boy here with you, dear," Reverend Robbins said.

Charlotte heard a snort from the kitchen. "We're fine," she answered. "And I have my sisters-in-law and neighbors."

"Well, you be on the lookout for runaway Negroes," he said. "They will rob you as soon as look at you. And a pretty white woman like you…"

Charlotte opened her eyes wide. "Surely, they're not stupid enough to run, what with a bounty on their heads?"

"And there's the prison sentence and a thousand dollar fine for those aiding and abetting them," Lieutenant Hollis said, smiling grimly at her.

"I apologize. I'm sure the citizens of Miles Station are law-abiding Christians," Reverend Robbins said.

"I'm sure they are," Lieutenant Hollis said. He seemed eager to change the subject. "Do you and Mr. McGuire have children?"

"No, we haven't been so blessed," Charlotte answered. No sooner were the words out of her mouth than a child's faint cry, abruptly shut off, drifted down from above.

"What was that?" Reverend Robbins asked.

Lieutenant Hollis stood and gave her a small bow. "Thank you for the meal, ma'am." He took out his wallet, as did the other men, and paid Charlotte. "My men and I will stretch our legs in the garden before we leave, if that's acceptable."

Charlotte sent up a prayer of thanks. "Of course, Lieutenant."

Joshua stumbled into the dining room carrying the cat Charlotte had just seen in the kitchen sleeping by the stove. "I got her, Charlotte. Pesky thing was upstairs crying to be fed."

"The cat," she said. "That's good you brought her down then."

Charlotte followed as the men filed out. Lieutenant Hollis paused on the porch. He glanced at the gourd dipper hanging beside the front door and then back at her. "You better hurry to feed her." After putting on his hat, he followed the others out.

Hand at her throat, Charlotte went back inside and locked the door behind them.

Joshua, white-faced, stared at her. "What do we do?"

"We feed the cat."

"Did you see how much Charlotte's cat looked like Kit-Kat?" Merrideth said. "Wouldn't it be cool if she was the great, great, great, great granddaughter of Charlotte's cat?"

"But I thought Kit-Kat came with you from—"

"Chicago. She did, but wouldn't it be cool?"

Abby grinned. "We can still pretend."

"What was up with the gourd?"

"It sure wasn't pretty," Abby said. "I was wondering why they had that hanging by the front door."

"That soldier was looking at it funny, and I could tell Charlotte was a little scared."

"I imagine she was always a little nervous about having strangers there in the house with her father gone. I don't know if I'd be brave enough to do it. Even though that preacher was a bigot, I think he was right to be worried about her."

"At least she had her cousin Joshua there."

"But I still don't know how she ever managed to keep up with the cooking for all the train people."

"Speaking of cooking," Merrideth said, "I'm hungry. What's for dinner?"

They worked together to heat tomato soup and make grilled cheese sandwiches. And then after eating lunch in record time they hurried back to the computer, agreeing they'd wash the dishes later.

CHAPTER 17

Charlotte put the bread and cheese she had prepared for her lunch in her pocket and went to take down the rifle her father had left for her. Papa had taught her well. As much help as Joshua was, she was glad she wasn't totally dependent upon him. The gun was still awkward and heavy for her, but she had a good eye. She put it over her shoulder and headed for the stand of oaks east of the barn.

The afternoon sun was playing tag with the leaves and she thought about how nice it would be to just sit and enjoy the peace and quiet with no thought of her responsibilities.

. Taking a deep breath, she lifted the gun and began to systematically train her eyes over each branch above her.

After twenty minutes of patient observation, she knew the only thing moving were the leaves. Maybe she should get back to her kitchen and start supper.

She put her right foot forward and then her left. When her right foot touched the ground the second time, it seemed to ignite with a fiery pain that began at her ankle and then radiated up her leg—a pain so shocking it drove her, screaming, to the ground. The gun discharged when she hit the ground, but she hardly heard it. She writhed helplessly on the ground, blindly clawing at her foot.

When her hands found the metal jaws and teeth that were gnawing at her ankle, the pain that had been monopolizing her brain was pushed back by a healthy dose of anger: poachers were back with their filthy traps on her father's land.

The second thought, after the anger, was fear, because now she understood firsthand how a trapped animal could bring itself to chew off its own leg.

Joshua wouldn't be home from the mill until suppertime. She wondered how long it would be before he came looking for her.

She forced herself to sit up and assess the damage. The trap had captured her leg just above the top of her shoe. She reached down and tried to pull the jaws apart, but blood covered everything and made her fingers slippery. She tried to rip a piece of her skirt to help her grip, but her fingers felt boneless and were much too weak to tear the sturdy cloth.

Then she remembered her bonnet hanging down her back. She untied it and wrapped it around the steel jaws. They moved a little but she lacked the strength to open them sufficiently to pull her foot out. The jaws slipped out of her hands and snapped together. She cried out and nearly fainted. On her second try, the jaws moved a little more, but she couldn't hold them long and had to let them go back, more carefully this time, to their death grip on her foot. There was more blood now. So much blood. The bonnet was saturated with it. The leaves under her leg were a glossy scarlet, brighter than the most colorful autumn foliage. She stopped for a minute to concentrate on breathing.

By the fifth attempt, her fingers wouldn't obey the command to grip. She fell back and lay there, gulping the cool air. The light coming through the leaves was so pretty. After a while, the only sound was the leaves rustling ...

"She's dead. Oh, Abby, Charlotte's dead." Merrideth bolted from her chair.

"Wait, Merrideth." Abby reached out to stop her, but she slipped away and rushed from the room. Down the hall, her door slammed shut.

Abby glanced back at the computer screen, but quickly turned her face away at the sight of Charlotte bleeding to death under the trees. In a small part of her brain, she had worried about this very thing. Merrideth, in her fragile emotional state, was bound to take it hard when it came time for Charlotte to die. But she had assumed they had plenty of time. Who could have known she would die so young in such a freak accident?

She went to her door and tapped softly. "Merrideth? May I come in?"

She didn't answer. Abby tried to turn the knob, but the door wouldn't budge. "Open up, kiddo. Let's talk." Putting her ear to the door, Abby heard a soft sob and a muffled, "Go away."

"Come on, Merrideth."

"You don't even care that Charlotte just died."

"Of course I care," she said. Even if she was only a fictional character it would be sad. But if she was real…

"Just go away."

"You had to know that Charlotte was going to die," Abby said. "She's been dead for over a hundred years, Merrideth."

She sobbed louder. "Is that supposed to make me feel better? Go away."

Abby felt a stab of irritation. If she was going to indulge in a childish pity-party—well, obviously, there was no sense talking to her until she calmed down.

The door opened and Abby jerked in surprise.

"Wait! Abby, I know," Merrideth said, sliding past her.

"What?" Abby followed her back to the computer room.

"We'll go back. Back before the accident." Merrideth took the mouse and began a fast reverse until Charlotte was back in the kitchen.

"Now what?"

Merrideth began clicking on the icons at the top of the screen. "We'll warn her not to go into the woods. There's got to be some setting on here that we can change."

"Merrideth, you know we can't—."

"We've got to talk to her! Warn her." She continued to click frantically on each menu icon.

"Listen to me!" Abby said, grasping her arm. Her touch seemed to break through Merrideth's panic, and finally she looked up at her and blinked.

"If this is real," Abby said, "and not some computer game, then we can't just go back and change a setting. There's nothing we can do about it. It happened to Charlotte before we were even born. We've just been ignoring the fact that it was going to happen eventually. It's done."

"You finally believe it's real?"

"It's either real or the computer nerd who invented it really needs to get a life—and I do mean one of his own."

Awkwardly, Merrideth stood and stumbled over to stare, unseeing, out the window. "It's not fair," she said.

"Did you think we control our lives? God is in charge—you do believe in God, don't you?" What was that verse about things working together for good? Somewhere in Romans. Abby fervently wished she had overcome her timidity about talking to Merrideth about her faith much earlier.

"Yeah, I believe there's a God, and he does whatever he wants. We're the little puppets he plays with. We live for a little while and then we die. There's no sense in even trying." Merrideth leaned her head against the window frame and began to cry.

Abby was at a complete loss for words. If one of her college friends had said something so wildly blasphemous, she would have been shocked. But for a kid this age? What on earth should she say to something like that? Finally, stepping to the window, Abby put her arms around Merrideth and rubbed her back, hoping she could give some comfort, even if she was woefully unprepared to give sound biblical explanations.

Merrideth stopped crying, and Abby felt a wave of relief. Maybe she wouldn't have to come up with answers to such cosmic questions. Maybe the worst was over. After all, Merrideth had been making such progress, at least academically and socially—even in the area of hygiene. Abby looked hopefully at her. "It'll be all right."

"No," Merrideth said wrenching herself away from Abby. "It won't." There was a thick film of scorn coating her words. "What's the use of all the work Colonel Miles did to build this town?" Merrideth furiously wiped at her tears.

The cessation of her tears turned out not to be an accurate indicator of a lessening of Merrideth's pain. Beyond the well of despair that Abby had sensed from the very beginning and had been confident she could heal, something burst and Merrideth's words came out in a raging torrent.

"If Colonel Miles could see this pitiful so-called town, I bet he'd puke. And you saw Abraham Lincoln—such a good man—pouring out his heart in that speech, standing up for what's right. But no one listened. No one voted for him."

"Yeah, but…"

"It's the same for me. It's my fate to be a failure, isn't it? Fat and stupid, right? No wonder Dad left! Who would want to be around such a loser?"

"Merrideth, you're not a loser! Maybe you have a few areas you're weak in—we all do—but you're making such improvement."

"And Mom stays away as much as she can," Merrideth said as if she hadn't heard. "I used to try so hard to be good, but I never could make them happy. So I stopped wasting time. Why did you ever come here and start making me want to try again? I was doing just fine before you got here."

With that bombshell, Merrideth ran from the room.

"Oh, Merrideth…"

She'd known all along that she had a good brain, but clearly, Merrideth had been thinking more deeply than she had. And she was supposed to be the teacher? Abby felt ashamed that she had been so glib, so sure she—a silly college girl—could cure Merrideth. It had taken the death of Charlotte—be she real or only virtual, Abby still wasn't sure—to reveal to her that Merrideth's depression and spiritual pain were far worse than she had imagined.

"And I was so worried about her bathing habits. I haven't helped her at all." She sank into the chair and lay her head down next to the keyboard.

"Dear God," she whispered, "I can't do it. I realize that now. Please help me to help Merrideth."

CHAPTER 18

"Merrideth," Abby whispered. "Wake up, kiddo." She gently laid her hand on the sleeping girl's shoulder. The room was dark except for the light from the hall. Wind blew in through the windows, bringing the sound of rustling leaves, and at long last, the sweet smell of approaching rain. Abby's hair blew softly around her face.

"Wha—?" Merrideth sat up in bed and rubbed her red and tear-swollen eyes like a toddler.

"Hurry. I want to show you something before the storm gets here."

"What time is it?"

"Three-thirty. I couldn't sleep so I did some more time-surfing."

"You're crazy if you think I'm going to watch any more of that." Merrideth fell back onto her pillow and turned away.

"It's Charlotte. She didn't die. Come see."

Abby was afraid she would have to coax her, but

Merrideth stumbled from her bed and followed Abby down the hall.

"She didn't?" Merrideth asked, confused.

"Nope. Look. There she is."

Abby clicked the mouse and the action on the screen that she had paused resumed. Charlotte sat in the parlor with her bandaged foot on a pillow. She looked pale and in pain, but smiled when Lucinda came in from the kitchen carrying a tea tray.

Abby paused it again. "If only I had remembered the dates from the library book, I would have known that Charlotte lived for many years after the war."

Merrideth started to take the mouse, but Abby stopped her. "Charlotte did some pretty amazing things after this. I want to show you, but some of it's hard to watch."

Merrideth put her hands over her eyes. "I can't stand to see any more of—"

"I don't mean that. Remember the gourd hanging on Charlotte's front door?"

"Yeah?"

"It kept bugging me, so I looked it up. Gourd dippers were often used during that time as a symbol of the Big Dipper and thus the North Star."

"I think I'm still asleep. You're not making any sense."

"As runaway slaves went north following the North Star, they knew that a gourd dipper hanging on a front door meant it was a safe house. The reason Charlotte seemed so nervous when the soldiers were there was because she was harboring slaves in her attic."

"You're saying this house was part of the Underground Railroad?"

"That's exactly what I'm saying. Remember that part

about the cat?"

"Yes, that was weird. That sound wasn't a cat, was it?"

"Nope. It was a little boy crying because he was hungry. He and his older brother and mother were up in the attic the whole time Charlotte was serving train customers as cool as a cucumber in her dining room. Later, she sent them on their way to another safe house."

"I want to see."

"Good. But I'm going to skip over some of it, just because there's so much I want to show you."

"And Lord protect those under this roof from those who would do us harm. In Jesus' name—Oh, and please, dear Lord, give me the strength—and time enough—to get everything done that needs doing. Amen."

Charlotte rose from her knees and dressed quickly. It was too cold to dawdle. In the kitchen she stoked her cook stove and made a trip out to the smoke house for a slab of salt pork. She sliced it and then made cornbread batter in her blue bowl. She put the cornbread on to bake in one iron skillet and the salt pork on to fry in another.

Someone knocked on the back door and then opened it before Charlotte could finish wiping her hands on her apron.

"Lucinda Brown, what are you doing here so early in the morning?" At twenty-five, she was six years older than Charlotte and considered herself well on the shelf.

"Early, late, and middle of the day. I'm here, Lottie, to lend my assistance if you're going to be foolish enough to continue conducting passengers on the Underground Railroad while also tending to the passengers of the

Chicago & Alton."

"Well, I expect I've got railroading in my blood. You're one to talk, Lucinda. As if you and your father don't do the same thing in Brighton. And how is Doctor Brown?"

"He's well, thank you. And besides him, I've got a sister and two brothers to help with the cause. You've got no one."

"Don't let Joshua hear you say that."

"Well, yes, of course, dear Joshua." Lucinda took her bonnet off and hung it on a peg by the back door. "Where is the boy? He can bring my case in."

"You're serious about staying?"

"You know me. I'm always serious."

Charlotte hugged her friend in relief. "That's wonderful, Lucinda. So would you keep watch down here while I take breakfast up?"

"Certainly. I aim to please."

"If anyone should happen to stop by—"

"Don't worry, Lottie, I know what to do."

Charlotte stood on the porch between Joshua and Lucinda, praying Sally and the boys on their way down the dark road.

"It's always difficult to see them go," Lucinda said.

"Every time," Charlotte said, brushing a tear from her cheek. "There's never time for proper goodbyes."

The sound of the cart's wheels was barely out of hearing when Joshua whispered, "Listen!"

Someone was singing softly in the woods behind the house. Charlotte listened carefully for a moment and then smiled. The song was *Amazing Grace*, one of the signals area conductors had agreed upon.

"Indeed, how sweet the sound," she said.

"It's Jemmy," Lucinda said. "I'd know his off-key singing anywhere."

They hurried through the front door and on to the kitchen. Joshua went out onto the back porch while Charlotte lowered the wick on her worktable lantern until the room was as dim as she could make it. Jemmy and Joshua came in leading three men. They varied in age and physical condition, but all wore the same expression she had come to recognize as a combination of hunger, exhaustion, and wariness.

"That makes two times in one week, Jemmy," Charlotte said. "Your poor legs must be tired."

Jemmy tipped his cap. "Only nine miles to Shake Rag Corner, Miss Charlotte."

"You and Joshua take the men up, Charlotte," Lucinda said. "I'll bring up the leftover cornbread and bacon directly."

Lucinda was smiling at Jemmy in a way Charlotte had never noticed before. He stood awkwardly near the back door, his hat in his hand. Even in the dim light it was obvious that he was blushing. So that's the way the wind blew. Charlotte smiled broadly at Lucinda, who was suddenly fidgeting and frowning. And not looking at Jemmy.

Joshua must have picked up on it too because he grinned. "I'll go finish the chores in the barn," he said on his way out the back door.

"All right," Charlotte said. "Bring up the food when you're ready."

She led the men to the pantry and opened the door to the stairway. "It's steep. Mind your step."

They climbed the stairs after her, weariness obvious

in their shuffling steps. She opened the door at the top, and they went into her dark bedroom. She turned with her lantern and saw that the men's eyes had gone wild. They had been trained from birth, she knew, to keep their eyes averted from a white woman's face. Forgetting that rule could mean fifty lashes. How much worse would the punishment be for entering her bedroom? She hated to frighten them so, but she also knew that if anyone came snooping around looking for runaways, they'd never imagine in a thousand years that she'd allow Negro men into her room.

"It's all right. Don't be afraid." She went across the room to the door that led to the attic. "Up this way."

The stairs were even steeper, and she kept one hand on the rail. When she got to the top, she covered her lantern to keep the light as low as possible. It wouldn't do for anyone outside to begin wondering what she was doing in the attic in the middle of the night.

Even so, there was enough light to see the big man in the corner turn away on his pallet as he did every time she came to the attic. There hadn't been room for him on the cart with Sally and the boys, and besides, his feet were still too ravaged from his barefoot trip half-way across the state to Miles Station.

She showed them the cornhusk pallets in the corner that Sally and the boys had used. The three men eyed the man in the corner cautiously and then settled onto the pallets.

When Lucinda brought the food, Charlotte distributed it the newcomers, and they began wolfing it down. As always, she was distressed to see that degree of hunger.

While the men ate, she went to her wooden trunk to retrieve her journal and pen. She sat down on the trunk and studied her guests.

"I have stories in this book," she said. "Stories about the people who come through here. Would anyone like to tell me his story?"

The three men stole nervous but curious glances at her.

"It's all right," she said. "You don't have to worry about me being here."

That only seemed to remind them of the peril of looking at her, and they turned away again.

"Someday, I'll have all the stories published, and people—white people—will know what you went through. Why you went North. Who wants to tell me first?"

The men rustled on their pallets but said nothing.

"Won't you help me?"

The smallest of them, a wiry man of about thirty years of age, braved a glance at her.

"That's right," she said. "It's quite all right to look at me. What's your name?"

"Lucky, ma'am. Just Lucky."

"Good." She dipped her pen and wrote the name in her journal. "Where are you from, Lucky?"

"I belonged to Master Rawlings at Cedar Grove."

"Is that in Missouri?"

He looked confused and averted his eyes again.

"That's all right. Tell me your story. And, Lucky? You don't ever have to call that man Master again."

"He a mean man, Master Rawlings—that man. I got my share of beatings just like everyone, but when he start in on my Ceely…well, I couldn't let him do that. I hear her screaming from clear out in the cornfield where I was chopping weeds. When I got up to the yard that man was whipping her—whipping her hard. He say she lazy and useless. Say she ruin his good shirts. I saw she must a forgot to stir the wash kettle. That man, he done flung the shirts on the ground. They be ruined sure—with black scorch marks and dirt. And Ceely's blood splattered all over 'em."

"What did you do, Lucky?"

He ran his hands over his eyes as if to erase the memory in his head.

"She was on the ground screaming so. The whip had done cut through her dress. And I saw I still had the hoe in my hand...and I hit Mas—that man."

"Did you kill him?"

"No, but I hurt him bad. Then Ceely, she laid there looking all wide-eyed at me. She say I have to run or he kill me." Lucky hung his head. "I didn't want to leave her. She say she can't run but I can. So I did."

Charlotte watched a teardrop fall from his chin onto his knee. Hearing their stories never seemed to get any easier, but she steeled herself not to begin crying too. She could help best by keeping her emotions in check—at least until she recorded the story.

"Lucky, I'll say a prayer for your wife Ceely. I'll ask God to help her. Maybe she'll join you one day."

"Ma'am, Ceely ain't my wife. She my child. She be six."

Charlotte closed her journal and sat hugging it to her chest while she cried and cried.

Merrideth held her hand to her mouth. "I feel sick. Why are you showing me this?"

"Just one more story. This one's not as bad."

CHAPTER 19

Charlotte blew her nose and went back to the trunk to sit. Taking up her journal and pen again, she looked at the men.

The youngest of them, the one named Wilson, returned her gaze. When she saw the pity in his eyes—pity for her—she nearly started crying again. "Would you like to go next?"

"Yes, ma'am. Only please don't cry any more, ma'am. I haven't been whipped in all my life. Thank you, ma'am for writing the book. Can you write in it about the cold and hunger? The children are only given coarse shirts to wear, even in winter, and there's never enough food.

"I was seven when I got my first trousers, and that was only so I could go up to the big house and work the pulley on the fans to keep the flies away while the family ate. I couldn't stop looking at all the food on the table, especially the ginger cakes they ate for dessert."

He closed his eyes and took in a huge breath as if he

could still see and smell the cakes.

For a while the only sound was the scratching of Charlotte's pen as she wrote Wilson's account in the journal. At last she finished and looked up. "Forgive me, Wilson, but you sound different."

"My mistress was kind, ma'am. She taught me to read and write. Master Reeves got so angry when he found out. I heard him tell her that once a man knew how to read he was forever unfit to be a slave." Wilson chuckled softly. "I knew then that he had just given away the secret of how white men keep black men enslaved. Mistress was forbidden to teach me anymore. But she made sure I had books, whenever she could sneak them to me. And she kept badgering her husband until, at last, he set me free."

He dug into his tattered coat and pulled out a folded paper, which he opened carefully and held out for her to see. At the top of the document in large letters was the title Certificate of Freedom.

Wilson didn't offer to let her hold it. She wouldn't have let it out of her hands either. He refolded the document and tucked it safely back in his pocket.

"But, Wilson, why did you leave? With your certificate, you could live free anywhere. And you certainly don't have to hide in my attic."

He smiled sadly at her, almost as if he pitied her again. "I stayed there for a while. But it's not safe, ma'am, even with the freedom papers. Not until I get farther north. I want to go to Chicago. I hear the abolitionists there are doing good work. Perhaps I can lend them assistance."

"There's a man there named Dwight Moody. You should try to find him if you can."

She turned to Andrew. "Are you ready to tell your story?"

"We'll stop here," Abby said. "I watched and listened for another hour as the last man told his story. It was even worse than the others, and I don't want you to hear it."

Merrideth put her head down on the table. "What does any of this prove, Abby? That life is horrible and then you die? I already figured that out. And if you're trying to show me that Charlotte's life wasn't so bad compared to theirs, well, okay. I admit it wasn't. But still…"

Merrideth's voice was muffled, and Abby couldn't tell if she was crying or not. "I know, kiddo. People do horrible things. Bad things happen. I don't want to upset you by showing you this, but…."

"Maybe I should force myself to watch all the stories," Merrideth mumbled. "They all wanted Charlotte to write them down so people would know. But it makes me sick."

"I know. Think how discouraging it must have been for the abolitionists living back then. Progress must have seemed so slow. Like no one was listening. And when Lovejoy was assassinated—in Illinois, a free state— it must have seemed hopeless. Charlotte and the others had to get discouraged during those dark days. But it was all part of God's plan."

Merrideth's head popped up from the table and she glared at her. "What kind of a plan was that? How could he let people be so mean?"

"I don't know."

Merrideth snorted. "What do you mean, you don't know? You've got to know. You're a Christian, aren't you?"

Abby smiled at her indignation. "No, kiddo, I don't know. Anyone who tells you they have it figured out is lying—or maybe delusional. "But I do know this: 'All things work together for good for them that love God.'"

"But—"

"Sometimes, we have to hang onto that verse by our fingernails when times are hard."

"Some people say God is in charge of the good things that happen, and the Devil is in charge of the bad things," Merrideth said. "If that's true...well, God's losing. So I guess he's not very powerful after all."

"If that were true," Abby said, "he wouldn't really be God, would he? But on the other hand, God isn't some power-hungry sadist who gets a thrill out of pulling our puppet strings, as you called them. That's saying God is evil, and that's just wrong. The Bible says God is love."

Thunder rumbled, low and menacing, and the curtain flapped even more wildly. Abby got up and went to tug the window shut.

"We'll have to hurry, before it storms, but I want to take you back to something we saw before." She sat back down and quickly set the dial for fast reverse with an automatic stop on June 13, 1856. The images on the screen flew past in a blur. She stopped the action when she got to the right place.

"I found out why the trellis was removed."

"What does that have to do with anything?" Merrideth rolled her eyes and put her face back on the table.

"Everything, actually."

Though it was nearly the middle of June, the night was

cool and the air clear. With no moon present and the last light in the house extinguished, the sky was black velvet, and the stars were showing off their brilliance for any who cared to look. A man came stealthily around the corner of the house and stood in the deep shadow of the front porch.

Though he looked up, it wasn't to admire the night sky. After checking again to see that no one was around, he stuck his hand among the roses clinging to the trellis, found a foothold, and began to climb. The thorns tore at his clothes, but it would be worth it.

When he reached the top rung, he eased his body onto the porch roof and lay there for a while, letting his heart calm. Finally, when he was sure the unavoidable sounds of his movement had not alerted anyone to his presence, he shimmied his way toward Charlotte's window.

When a light appeared in her room, he smiled in anticipation and prepared to inch forward for a better view. Unfortunately for him, Charlotte did appreciate the night sky and appeared at her bedroom window to gaze at the stars. This gave him a moment's fear, and he thought about making a quick retreat off the porch roof. He knew that if she looked hard enough, she would see him there, though he always wore black for these little expeditions. But she stared only at the sky while she slowly and carefully brushed her long hair.

At last, Charlotte put her brush down and began to pray in a soft voice. "Dear God, bless us. Help me to be more patient and kind. Please keep us safe. I know Mother is in heaven with you, so please tell her I'm doing fine. Amen."

Charlotte yawned. It had been a long day, and she could barely keep her eyes open as she unfastened the buttons that ran down the front of her dress. When she had drawn it over her head and laid it aside, she began to untie the ribbons that fastened her shift.

The view was better than Billy had even imagined. The trouble was, his breathing was getting so loud he was afraid she would hear it. All too soon, Charlotte blew her lantern out, and the show was over.

He remained still as a statue for a minute more. Finally, he began to slither back across the roof and down the trellis. Just as he stretched one leg to the ground, two hands reached out and rather roughly helped him the rest of the way down.

"What the devil are you doing, you slimy little creep?" Jonathan Miles said in a low but furious voice.

"Nothin', Mr. Miles, nothin'"

He held the younger man's shirtfront in his fists. "You listen to me, Reynolds. If I ever find out you've been hanging around my property again, I'll personally lock you up and lose the key. Do you understand?"

"Yes, Mr. Miles. I was just funnin'. I wasn't doin' nothin' wrong."

Jonathan Miles pulled him to the edge of the front yard. "Don't bother to lie to me, Reynolds." He gave him a shove that nearly sent him to the ground. "You keep your eyeballs in your head and don't ever come around here again."

"Yes, Mr. Miles, sir." Billy slunk away into the night.

Abby and Merrideth sat staring at the screen. A gust of damp evening air slapped at the curtains and brushed against them.

"The next day is when we first met Charlotte, all mad

at her father because she couldn't go to the fair with Billy Reynolds."

"Okay. He's a creep. But why are you showing me this now?"

"Let me take you back to Charlotte's accident."

The afternoon sun was playing tag with the leaves, and Charlotte thought about how nice it would be to just sit and enjoy the peace and quiet with no thought of her responsibilities. Taking a deep breath, she lifted the gun and began to systematically train her eyes over each branch. After a while, she knew the only thing moving were the leaves, so she decided to walk a little farther down the gully.

Stealthily she put her right foot forward and then her left. When her right foot touched the ground the second time...

"Stop that!" Merrideth covered the screen with her hands as if that alone would prevent Charlotte from being injured. "I don't want to see that again."

Abby stopped the action. "You won't."

"You promise?"

"I promise. I just want to show you what I found when I changed the perspective."

Abby adjusted the view settings and turned to look at Merrideth. "This is the same place. Same moment in time. But, watch. This time I'm focusing on the house instead of Charlotte."

Three men rode cautiously out of the timber and reined their dusty horses behind Jonathan Miles' barn. Billy Reynolds reached into his jacket pocket and pulled out a flask. "This is the place." He took a long swig and then laughed. "Now we'll have us some fun, boys."

"You sure no one's around, Reynolds?" the man on the roan said, staring nervously at the house.

"I happen to know Colonel Miles is way off in Kentucky chasin' Rebs," Reynolds said. "Though in a way, I wish he was here." His lips turned up in a sneer. "We'd do to 'im like my grandpappy and his friends did to that nigger-lovin' Lovejoy." He took another swig and laughed. "Nigger-lovin' Lovejoy. That's kinda poetic, ain't it?"

"Well, hurry up, will you?" said the man on the bay horse. "We ought to try to be in Missouri by sundown."

"All right. You boys stay behind the barn out of sight and I'll go in first." Reynolds spat on his palms and ran his fingers through his greasy hair. "When I give the signal, you can sneak in the back door there."

"What makes you think you can handle her by yourself?"

"And why do we have to wait out here?"

"Because she don't know you." Reynolds laughed. "She trusts me."

"Just don't you forget to give the signal, Reynolds."

He peeked in the kitchen window and then, seeing no one, eased through the back door.

After five minutes had passed, the two men behind the barn began to fidget.

"He's keeping the girlie for himself."

"I should've knowed it! Let's go."

After looking carefully around, the two men stepped

from behind the barn. When they had gone only a couple of steps, a gunshot rang out behind them. Not stopping to ask questions, they turned and ran to their horses. At the same time, Reynolds bolted out of the back door and ran for the barn, stuffing a handful of jewelry into his pocket.

"Do you get it now?" Abby searched Merrideth's red, puffy eyes, hoping to see understanding. Instead, all she saw was an angry glint.

"Sure. Billy Reynolds and his friends were going to hurt Charlotte."

"But, why didn't they?"

"Because they heard the gun and ran."

"Take it a step further. Why did the gun go off?"

The anger left Merrideth's eyes and she slumped again in her chair. "I'm tired, Abby. Do we have to play Twenty Questions? I just want to go back to bed."

"In a minute, kiddo. I don't know why God let Charlotte get hurt. All I know is that our world is totally messed up by sin. But when you think about all we saw, time after time, God brought good out of the bad and blessed his people."

"Yeah, well he must not have blessed Colonel Miles very good, because—

"Blessed them well."

"Well. Because everything he built rotted away, and now here we are in this dump."

"God's thoughts are so far above ours we'll never understand—at least in this life. But he has a plan. Because Colonel Miles worked so hard to get the railroad, a lot of soldiers and supplies were transported and helped win the war. Sure, maybe he didn't have enough time for his daughter sometimes. But because Charlotte worked so hard and was forced to take on so much responsibility when she was young, she continued to thrive while he was away. She helped keep the mill going, and the flour and cornmeal from it went to feed the Union Army. And she was courageous enough to help who knows how many slaves make it safely through Miles Station.

"And even Jonathan Miles' legal mess with the railroad company was part of the plan. It brought Lincoln into their lives, and he might very well have been the influence that made Charlotte so determined to help the slaves in the first place.

"And, speaking of Lincoln. We were sad that he lost the Senate election, but what he said during that failed campaign won him an even better job—the one he was born to do—lead America through the Civil War and end slavery."

Abby decided it was time for her to shut up. She stroked Merrideth's hair and let the silence draw out. Thunder rumbled again, closer, and a sprinkling of raindrops hit the window.

"The fair." Merrideth sat up and looked at her. "Charlotte was so mad her father wouldn't let her go to the fair. But that guy was a creep."

"That's right. If Charlotte's father had let her go off with Billy Reynolds, she might never have met James McGuire, who just happened to stop in that very day."

Merrideth thought again. "I guess if she could sit with us at the monitor and see her whole life the way we did, she wouldn't be angry with her father."

"And not her heavenly Father either, kiddo. And do you understand what happened to Charlotte in the woods?"

"If she hadn't been out hunting for squirrels, those

men would have hurt her. And if she hadn't dropped the gun...if the gun hadn't gone off..."

"Exactly. Time and again, God was working and—"

"And caring," Merrideth added.

They didn't say anything else, just sat staring at the dust settling on a bright sunny afternoon in 1862 in Miles Station. A loud clap of thunder brought them back to their own time and place.

"Okay, now I've really got to shut this thing down," Abby said.

"I get it," Merrideth said quietly.

"No, I'll shut it down. Why don't you start closing the windows?"

"No, I mean, I get it." She hurried to the door and was gone.

Abby breathed a prayer of thanks.

CHAPTER 20

In spite of the late night, Abby woke early the next morning when she heard noises coming from overhead. A glance at her clock through puffy eyes confirmed that it was six-thirty—A.M. The noises came again. Someone was in the attic? If it had been midnight instead of morning, the thump would have sounded like a dead body falling to the floor and the scraping sound as if someone were dragging it away. At least there were no rattling chains or ghostly wails.

She dragged her carcass out of bed and into the hall. The door to the spare room stood open and so did the door to the attic. Yellow light fell weakly on the stairs.

When she got to the top of the stairs, Merrideth looked up from where she knelt by an old wooden trunk riffling through its contents.

"What on earth are you doing, Merrideth?"

"Oh, sorry. But, look, Abby. I found Charlotte's trunk. It was under a stack of newspapers."

Abby lowered the lid and ran her hand over its scarred surface. "Well, what do you know? Can't you just picture Charlotte sitting on it writing away? Anything interesting in it?"

Merrideth sighed. "No, just old clothes."

"Cool,"

"Not that kind of old. Just dorky jeans and T-shirts. I was hoping Charlotte's book would still be up here." She stuffed the clothes back inside and closed the lid.

Abby grinned. "And if this were a true Nancy Drew summer, we would have found Charlotte's journal in the attic. But I've got the next best thing. I was so tired last night I completely forgot to show you."

As soon as they got to the computer room, Abby clicked on the PDF document she had downloaded the night before. An image of an old book popped up on the screen. The title embossed on the leather cover was Following the North Star: True Stories, as Told by Former Slaves.

"So she got it published?"

"Yep. It's out of print, but I did a web search and found it on the State Archive website. That's got to mean it's important. Click on it and the pages will turn."

Merrideth clicked and the book opened to the title page. The author's name jumped out at them: Charlotte Miles McGuire.

"Do you want to read it?" Abby asked.

"Maybe later. But shouldn't we go get ready for church?"

Abby enjoyed the church service much more than she had the previous week when she had been so distracted by

John. Although they sat next to him, this time it was Merrideth who occupied her thoughts. Abby spent the whole time seeing the service through her eyes, wondering what Merrideth thought of the pastor's words, praying for God's blessing on her young friend.

Merrideth seemed thoughtful, although she didn't say anything afterwards.

John walked with them out to the parking lot. "I thought I might come see you this afternoon, if that's all right."

Before Abby could get her tongue untangled, Merrideth piped up, "Sure. Come on by. You can help us with our surprise."

"I love surprises," John said.

Abby frowned. "What surprise?"

"You know. The rose thingies. You said we should put them back on the porch. We need to hurry before Mom gets home tonight. She's going to love it."

"Sweetie, I don't know how we'd ever get those trellises down from the loft. They're so heavy."

"That's where he comes in," Merrideth said, pointing to John.

John grinned. "I'm glad to know I'm good for something."

Abby felt her face heat. "Merrideth, we can't just expect—"

"I'll be right over as soon as I change clothes."

"I'll make sandwiches," Merrideth said. "Which do you like better, peanut butter or tuna?"

"Definitely peanut butter," John said.

They were making the sandwiches when the doorbell

rang.

"Oh, no! I hope she's not home early," Merrideth wailed.

Fortunately, it was just Michael, who wanted to know if anyone wanted to play in his clubhouse in the loft.

"We would like that," Merrideth said, pulling him into the kitchen. "But Michael would you—I mean, if we think of a way—would you let us take the trellises? It would look so pretty if we put them back on the porch."

"We'll help you build another clubhouse," Abby said.

He looked up at Merrideth, his brown eyes worried. "But will you still play with me? After, I mean."

"After what?"

"After you get the trellises."

"Of course I will, Michael," she answered softly. "I'm your friend."

They took their sandwiches up to Michael's clubhouse and sat companionably on straw bales to wait for John. Michael seemed happy that membership in his club had increased by 200 percent. Having his permission to recover the trellises was the first step, but Abby wondered how on earth they would get them through the small opening of the loft and down the rickety stairs.

But Michael showed them the fifteen-foot loft doors farmers had used to bring in their bales of hay and straw. He stepped onto an upturned bucket to wrestle with the latch. He gave a heroic shove, and the doors swung open and clattered against the side of the barn. Abby didn't even want to think about what exploits he must have had in the loft before they arrived.

She and Merrideth gasped in horror when he leaned out to call to a cat in the yard far below.

"Don't worry," Michael said. "Come see."

They cautiously stepped closer to the open door and

found a whole new perspective of Miles Station.

"Wow!" Abby said. "You get the big picture up here."

It was frightening to stand that close to a drop-off of twenty feet, but it was easy from their vantage point to see the remaining traces of what had been Miles Station. There was the old schoolhouse and the foundations of what had been thriving businesses. Where graceful homes had once lined the streets of Miles Station, humble mobile homes now stood.

Mrs. Richardson, appearing Lilliputian, stepped outside the little brown house that had once been the Miles Station depot, and Merrideth cried out, "See, Michael, there's your mom!" The shining tracks of the Chicago & Alton line ran parallel to their lane, disappearing from view beyond the stand of oaks at the edge of the village.

And straight ahead, rich Illinois farmland stretched to the horizon—a patchwork quilt of corn, beans, and wheat. Behind the last field and the farthest line of trees, a steeple from one of Brighton's churches reached for the sky.

They saw a blue car winding its way from the west on Miles Station Road and watched as it came closer and then turned into their lane.

"It's John," Abby said, brushing some dust off her jeans. She smoothed her hair back from her face and turned to Merrideth. "Quick, how do I look?"

"Not as good as when we finished our beauty seminar," she began. "But pretty good...considering you've been playing in the barn."

This time Abby rolled her eyes. "Thanks, I'm underwhelmed with your praise." She stuck her head out the loft door and called, "You're just in time."

John smiled up at them, and Abby felt the power of it smack her in the head from all the way up in the loft.

"Come on up and see Michael's clubhouse," Merrideth called.

"We got sandwiches," Michael said.

"Soon as I get a few things." Laughing, John went to the trunk of his car and gathered the supplies he had brought.

When he got to the top of the ladder, he handed up a coiled rope to Michael. "Here you go, buddy. Take this. We've got man work to do."

Smiling proudly, Michael took the rope and "helped" John tie it to the trellis so they could lower it to the ground. Then he supervised as John used his power drill to reattach the trellises to the front porch.

"Thanks, John and Michael. That looks great," Abby said.

"You're welcome."

"Just the way it's supposed to look," Merrideth said. "Except for the roses."

"Maybe Mrs. Arnold will have something," Abby said. "Come on, John, you've got to meet the first lady of Miles Station."

CHAPTER 21

They found her busily picking green beans, but she seemed glad to stop for a rest. "It's gettin' hot as a firecracker around here," she said, fanning her face with her apron.

"Mrs. Arnold," Abby said, "this is John Roberts. He helped us put the trellises back up on the Colonel's house."

"I'm right pleased to meet you, John Roberts. And pleased as punch you put them back where they belong. Come along, and I'll show you what you need to finish the job. Michael, run to the shed and bring me my shovel. Mind you get the good, sharp one."

Michael was there with the shovel when Mrs. Arnold stopped and pointed at a flowering vine twining up the side of her garden shed.

"You can dig up some of my honeysuckle," she said.

"It smells wonderful," Abby said.

"Roses would be prettier, but it's the wrong time of

the year to transplant them. Nothin' can kill honeysuckle."

John took the shovel and went to work digging. Michael stood nearby lending his moral support.

"No sense in all of us standing out in the heat. Let's go sit in the shade." Mrs. Arnold led Abby and Merrideth to her back porch and they sat on an assortment of chairs and watched John work.

"Maybe we can find some roses like the ones Charlotte used to have," Merrideth said to Abby.

"Yes, you should still be able to get Queen Victoria roses," Mrs. Arnold said. "They'll look pretty with the honeysuckle."

"How did you know what kind of roses?" Merrideth asked.

Mrs. Arnold put her hand to her mouth. "Probably Ruth told me."

"You said that before, but you know that's not right," Abby said softly, but firmly. "Please tell us. How did you know about the roses and the trellises?"

"And the jellybeans?" Merrideth added.

Mrs. Arnold turned to look at Merrideth. "Toward the end, your Aunt Ruth took to dreaming—dreaming 'bout the old days." She reached up to pat Merrideth's hair. "And she wasn't shy about telling anybody that came to see her all about it either. The hospice nurse said she was crazy on pain medicine. Shoot, I thought she was too—at first. But she could tell it so clear, just like she was seeing it all happen. And I'd sit there by her bed and hold her hand when the pain got bad and listen to all the stories. And then one day I saw it too. I know it sounds crazy, and I wouldn't blame you for not believing a word—"

"Oh, I believe you," Abby said. "I don't know how it happened, but I believe you."

Merrideth nodded her head in agreement.

"Well, don't say nothin' to my grandson. He's always hintin' it's about time I went to live in a an old folks home. That'd be bad enough, but a crazy hospital would be a lot worse."

"We won't," Abby said.

"Anyway, she was a brave woman, your Aunt Ruth. I expect you are too, child," she said, patting Merrideth's hand. "After all, you come from good stock, yes indeed you do. Just think how brave she was to sit upstairs in that attic listening to story after story of meanness and inhumanity while her stomach roiled and her heart broke."

"Charlotte? You saw Charlotte?" Merrideth asked.

"Why she was as heroic as any soldier in the war."

Abby and Merrideth looked at each other and then back at Mrs. Arnold.

"Are you saying Great Aunt Ruth was related to Charlotte Miles?" Merrideth asked.

"Why, yes. Didn't you know?"

"No…I didn't."

Abby gave Merrideth a hug. "How about that. You and Charlotte."

"I don't feel very brave," Merrideth said.

"You'll see. And God's got a purpose for your life too, child. Don't ever forget that."

Michael came skipping up. "Me and John got it digged up."

Mrs. Arnold chuckled and pulled the boy in for a hug. "Even this little scalawag. Who knows? God might decide to make him president someday."

Mrs. Arnold told John where to get burlap sacks to "tote" the plants home in. She agreed with Abby that a red geranium would be just right for the blue bowl and insisted on digging one for them herself. She gave them another plate of sugar cookies, this time in the shape of flags, even though the Fourth of July was still two weeks off.

When they had praised the cookies, paid sufficient tribute to her horticultural expertise, apologized for not visiting sooner, and promised to come again, they left.

They planted the honeysuckle as soon as they returned and then painted the trellis with paint they found in the barn. Afterward, they decided that was not the best order of events, for the leaves got speckled with paint. But they still looked pretty good against the white trellis.

After they had all removed their muddy shoes and washed their hands, Abby set the geranium in its blue bowl on the kitchen windowsill, and everyone thought that it was perfect.

They invited Michael and John to the computer room to see the *Beautiful Houses* program, but when Merrideth tried to load it, an error message came up on the screen.

"Maybe the storm last night messed up something," John said. "So what's so special about *Beautiful Houses*?"

"Well, you see… the program lets us—"

"Abby didn't think it was real. At first. But I knew it was Charlotte."

"Who's Charlotte?"

"That's the girl who used to live here," Merrideth said.

"I don't know how it works," Abby said. "Or even exactly what happens."

"Abby calls it stalking Charlotte, but I call it—"

Abby squeezed Merrideth's arm and telegraphed a warning before time-surfing came out of her mouth. Once that word was out, John would go from friendly to concerned. He'd probably start looking for the nearest mental health facility.

Why wouldn't he? How could John possibly understand from mere words what they had experienced— what they had lived— in Charlotte's world?

After all, Pat had brushed them off, and Kate had laughed when they had tried to tell her. And Customer Support had clearly thought they were insane.

No, it would be much better for him to see for himself.

"We'll invite you back when we get it working again," Abby said.

They thanked him again, and when he had driven off, Abby sat on the porch step next to Merrideth.

"Maybe it's a good thing the program is down. We'd never want to get back to your schoolwork if we knew we could visit Charlotte." Abby thought about some of the things that the minister had said that morning.

"And there's so much more that I want to teach you."

"By the way, I'm changing my name."

"Oh?"

Merrideth grinned. "Yeah, I'm beginning to think Dad's nickname for me isn't so lame."

"Good! 'Merri' will suit you perfectly!"

The End

A Note from the Author

The History Behind Time and Again

According to *The History of Macoupin County*, Jonathan Miles, born in Kentucky 1820, pioneered with his parents in Brighton Township in 1832. He married Eliza Stratton, also a native of Kentucky and they had three children, one of them a girl named Charlotte. The town that bore his name grew up and thrived at the nexus of Miles Station Road and the Chicago & Alton Railroad, which he was instrumental in getting to run through the town.

On more than one occasion, Abraham Lincoln took the train from his law office in Springfield, stopping in Miles Station to discuss a suit Miles had filed about nonpayment for lumber he had delivered to the railroad.

At the beginning of the Civil War Jonathan Miles formed a company of soldiers of the Twenty- Seventh Illinois Cavalry and had a brilliant career in the Union Army, being promoted to the rank of colonel in 1862. Jonathan Miles may or may not have actually helped fleeing slaves, but he was a staunch supporter of the cause. And there were several important stops on the Underground Railroad in nearby Brighton, including one at Dr. Thomas Brown's house.

The stories told by Charlotte's attic guests are inspired by the experiences of real people such as Booker T. Washington, Frederick Douglass, Andrew Jackson (not the U.S. president), Maria Adams, and many others. Their stories deserve to be heard, no matter how distressing. We must never forget.

For Further Study

Abolitionism and the Civil War in Southwestern Illinois. John J. Dunphy. Charleston: The History Press. 2011. Growing up Black. Jay David. New York: William Morrow. 1968.

History of Macoupin County, Illinois: Biographical and Pictorial. Vol. 1. Hon. Charles A. Walker, ed. Chicago: S.J. Clarke Publishing Co. 1911

Slaves, Salt, Sex & Mr. Crenshaw: The Real Story of the Old Slave House and America's Reverse Underground R.R. Jon Musgrave. Marion, IL: IllinoisHistory.com. 2004.

About the Author

I loved researching the "Olden Days" for the trilogy. It would have been so much easier to do if I could go back in time to see what it was really like. I let the characters in my books get to do just that. I stuck to virtual time travel because I didn't want them to accidentally mess up the whole space-time continuum thingy.

Some Christians have told me they're a bit uncomfortable about this fantasy concept of time-surfing. But as Brother Greenfield says in *Every Hill and Mountain*, (book 3) "Our God is omniscient, omnipotent, and omnipresent. Hallelujah! If he wants to give us a gift like that, he can."

It's an amazing gift, all right. Except sometimes Abby and her friends learn more than they ever wanted to know about people from the past. Still, studying their lives teaches them about God's love and goodness in a new way. From the distance that only time gives, they clearly see that God has a plan for his people, that He's in the business of redemption, that He makes all things new. I hope my readers get that. Writing about it reminded me, too.

I was born not far from the setting of *Every Hill and Mountain* and grew up "just down the road" from the settings of *Time and Again* and *Unclaimed Legacy*. Today I live with my husband in Monroe County, Illinois, the setting of *Once Again* (book 4). I enjoy reading, gardening, and learning about regional history. We have three grown children, three grandchildren, (and another on the way) and two canine buddies Digger and Scout (a.k.a. Dr. Bob in *Unclaimed Legacy*).

Let's Keep in Touch

I'd love to hear what you think of *Time and Again*. If you enjoyed it, please write a review for it and post it wherever you can, especially on Amazon and Goodreads. Or if you're not a customer, please post your review on my website.

And sign up to get V.I.P. Perks (in the right sidebar of my website). You'll get updates on my latest books and insider information about contests, giveaways, and when my books are scheduled to be free or reduced.

I'd really appreciate it if you'd "like," "follow," or otherwise connect with me. Thanks for supporting independent authors.

www.deborahheal.com

www.facebook.com/DeborahHeal

www.twitter.com/DeborahHeal

www.goodreads.com/deborahheal

If you liked *Time and Again*,
you'll love *Unclaimed Legacy*.
This series gets better by the book!

Unclaimed Legacy

book 2

**An old house + A new computer program =
The travel opportunity of a lifetime...
...to another century.**

The People

Abby Thomas' 11-year-old student Merri is finally
warming up to her. Her friendship with John Roberts is
also heating up. He's definitely marriage material. Except
for the fact that when she tells him about *Beautiful Houses*
he thinks she's crazy.

Because a computer program that allows you to rewind
and fast forward the lives of people from long ago is
surely pure fantasy. Except it's not.

Abby and John use *Beautiful Houses* to help the "Old
Dears" next door with their family tree. Rummaging
around in their history, they discover that the 85-year-old
twins have been keeping a secret from each other since
1941. And the ladies' ancestors have a few secrets of their

own.

Convicted in 1871 of murder and arson, Reuben Buchanan is a blight on the family name. But was he really guilty? Abby and John must get inside the mind of a murderer to find out.

But there are also heroes in the family tree—like Reuben's ancestor Nathan Buchanan. That doesn't mean he didn't have a few secrets, too. And Abby and John find one that's lain undiscovered for over 200 years.

The House

It began life as Nathan's log cabin built outside the walls of Lewis and Clark's 1803 Camp River Dubois. It was added onto through the years, and at one time it was a stage coach inn called Shake Rag Corner. Today it is a condemned derelict. While watching its history unfold, Abby and John discover a legacy waiting to be reclaimed and that God's promise to bless a thousand generations is really true.

WHAT READERS ARE SAYING ABOUT

Unclaimed Legacy

Wow! Unclaimed Legacy is in a class of its own! There's no sophomore slump for Heal--Unclaimed Legacy is an absolutely fantastic book. It picks up right where Time and Again leaves off…and the action doesn't quit until the end of the book. I loved digging into the past with Merri, John, and Abby, and I'm anxious to finish the story with book three!…Unclaimed Legacy does deal with some weighty issues, like spousal abuse, infidelity, and drug use, so I wouldn't recommend it for kids younger than 13 or 14. But for older teens and adults I highly recommend Unclaimed Legacy. **5.0 out of 5 stars**

—R.Ritta

Sometimes in a series, the author pours their heart and soul into book one and then fizzles out when it comes to book two. This is not the case with the Time and Again trilogy. Debbie actually puts more into this book. Not only more quirks, mishaps, and excitement are packed into this book, but also hard hitting subjects such as murder, domestic violence, and drug trafficking too. It's only getting better, folks!…I can't wait to see what explorations Abby will have with her best friend Kate. I have a good feeling lots more adventure, mystery, and troubles await them. **4.0 out of 5 stars**

—C. Estrella

A fantastic story geared to keep the reader entertained and on the edge of their seat through the whole book….I adored every single bit of this. It has just the perfect blend of history and action packed suspense to keep young adults glued to the pages as they work with the characters to uncover a crime from history ….She has mastered a home run here. **This one easily rates a 5 out of 5 stars**… *and I hope it will work its way to the top of the best seller lists.*

—Pirate Kat

An excerpt from

ᴜNCLAIMED ᴌEGACY

Chapter 1

Abby managed to get her mascara on without smudging it.
It was not an easy task, knowing that if she glanced at the
other reflection in the mirror she'd see Merri's sorrowful
eyes staring back at her. At least she wouldn't have to
spend any time on her hair. Whatever she did, it dried in a
mass of brown curls.

She smoothed on a bit of lip gloss and then, trying
not to feel guilty, smiled encouragingly at the pudgy
eleven-year-old beside her. "Come on, Merri, it's just a
lunch date. I'll be home before you know it. And while
I'm gone you'll get to spend some time with your mom."

Merri sat on the edge of the tub and morosely petted
Kit Kat, her chocolate-colored cat. "But this is just the
beginning. I'll never see you again now that you're going
out with John."

Abby was glad Merri wanted her around. It was a big
improvement from her first two weeks at the old house in
Miles Station. Thankfully, the troubled girl had finally
begun to accept her help and her friendship.

"I don't know if I'll keep 'going out' with John. It
depends. Besides, I'm your tutor; I can't go away. You'll
be seeing me all summer."

"What do you mean, 'it depends'?"

"Depends on if he turns out like the last guy I dated."

"The one who wasn't interested in your personality?"

"Yeah, that one. But as for John... well, so far so good. He's already earned a star in that department."

"A star?"

Abby blushed. "Well...see, whenever I meet a guy I'm interested in going out with, I imagine a chart for him labeled *Possible Marriage Material*. Then I give him imaginary stars for things I like about him."

"Like being tall and handsome?"

"He is that. But, I'm looking for character qualities." Abby gathered the last of her things and zipped her toiletry case. "Like I always say, beauty is more than skin deep."

Merri continued to pet Kit Kat thoughtfully and Abby wondered if she should stay and expand on the topic. She had already determined that her service project for Ambassador College included much more than tutoring Merri in academic subjects.

But John would be there any minute. She put her arm around Merri's shoulder and said, "We'll talk more when I get back."

Merri's mother Pat Randall poked her head past the door and said, "He's here. You didn't tell me he had a vintage Mustang."

When Abby got downstairs she saw that John was dressed in khakis and a shirt that made his eyes look even bluer than usual. And then, even before she got close, she picked up the scent of the killer cologne he always wore.

"You clean up nice," he said with a grin.

"Hi." She mentally grimaced, just thinking about the last time he had seen her— wearing cobwebs in her hair and old paint-stained jeans. This time she was dressed better, in tan capris and a white camp shirt, but the circumstances were just as awkward. Merri, still sulking, was watching every move she and John made, and Pat was hovering like she was her mother instead of her employer, which was ironic, of course, since she spent so little time with Merri, her actual daughter.

"So, John Roberts," Pat said, "what are you majoring in?"

"I'm in the pre-law program at the University of Illinois in Chicago."

"Do you have a summer job?"

"I work at the Tropical Frost in Brighton," he answered.

"That's...nice."

"He forgot to mention that he owns it." Abby glanced at her watch and adjusted the purse straps that were already digging into her shoulder.

Pat seemed to be assessing John's height. "I bet you played basketball in high school."

"No, I'm not much into contact sports. But I did run track for a couple of years."

Abby moved a little closer to the front door. John didn't seem to get the hint. Her stomach growled and she wondered where they were going to eat.

Pat's expression was serious, like it was her responsibility to screen for terrorists, serial killers, or other generally un-American guys. Maybe Pat was practicing for Merri's dating debut. But at age twenty, Abby was out of practice with parental inquisitions. Her own parents hadn't been so intense when she went on her first date in eighth grade with Jimmy Gale. Of course his mom had driven them to the junior high and stayed to chaperone at the annual St. Patrick's Day dance. But still.

"What are your hobbies?" Pat continued relentlessly.

Abby glanced over to see if John was getting annoyed.

But he was still smiling as if he enjoyed getting the third degree.

"I love reading—"

"What kind of books?"

"Mostly sci-fi. And I love music." Pat opened her mouth and John quickly added "Classic rock."

"Who's your favorite Beatle?"

"Paul." John blinked and darted a glance at Abby.

She smiled and nodded her head encouragingly. Pat folded her arms over her chest and frowned.

"I also restore vintage cars with my dad," John continued. "Oh, and I like theatre. I'll be in my college's production of *My Fair Lady* this fall."

Pat let her arms fall to her side and Abby wondered if that was a sign John had passed her test. She smiled and mentally assigned a star for *patience* to John's imaginary chart.

"So, where are you taking Abby?"

"We're going to see a few things in Alton and then have lunch at Genevieve's."

"Alton?" Merri looked imploringly at Abby. "I'd sure like to see what Alton looks like in modern times."

Abby put an arm around Merri's shoulder and said, "I'll tell you all about it when I get back."

"And when will that be?" Pat said.

"We should be back by 3:00." John checked his watch. "Make that 3:30 or 4:00." At last, he opened the door and said, "Well, we'll be going now."

Pat's cell phone rang and she flipped it open, holding up a hand to signal for them to wait. "That's great," she said into the phone. "I'll meet you in about twenty minutes."

Merri's face went from sullen to outraged in .002 seconds. "Mom, you promised we'd do something fun."

"It won't take me long to show my clients the house," Pat said, closing her phone. "You can wait in the office for me, Merrideth."

Abby understood Pat's need to get her fledgling real estate business off the ground, but she also knew Merri needed her mother's attention, especially since her father was so distant—both geographically and emotionally. She wondered again, if she should stay home with her. Maybe it wasn't even ethical to begin a relationship while she was on a tutoring job.

"But, Mom . . ." Merri wailed.

"Why don't you come with us?" John said, darting a look at Abby.

Abby's mouth dropped open and she scrutinized his face. No guy she knew willingly hung around kids, especially not bratty pre-teens, and never on a date. She checked closely for signs of martyrdom, but John was actually looking excited at the prospect.

"Could I?" Merri said.

"If you're sure it's all right," Pat said, looking relieved.

"Sure," John said.

Merri turned to see Abby's reaction. "Another star?" she asked, grinning knowingly.

Abby's eyes grew wide in alarm and she put her arm around Merri and leaned in close. "We won't mention the stars, Brat," she whispered. "Will we?"

But it was true. In her imagination, she added a big star for *kindness to children.*

John was a knowledgeable guide. He had grown up in nearby Brighton, but explained that everyone went to Alton for shopping and entertainment. "I guess it doesn't

5

seem like much to you two since you're used to Chicago."

"Well, it's a lot more interesting than Miles Station," Merri said.

"But you'd have to admit Miles Station *was* pretty interesting in the 1850s," Abby said.

John looked puzzled for a moment, but then they reached College Avenue and he pulled the car over and stopped. "Come on. I want you to meet one of our famous sons." He led them to a bronze statue of a tall, thin man leaning on a cane. "Abby and Merri, meet Mr. Wadlow."

"What's he famous for?" Merri asked.

John stood next to the statue. "Take a guess," he said, stretching as tall as he could.

After reading the plaque beside it, Abby looked up in amazement. "Merri, this statue is life-size. Robert Wadlow was 8 feet 11 inches tall, the tallest man ever recorded."

"They have a lot of stuff about him in the little museum across the street, but I think they're closed right now."

After saying goodbye to the so-called "Gentle Giant," John offered to take them to the mall, but Abby wasn't interested and Merri apparently had enough discretion not to offer suggestions for someone else's date.

"I'd like to see the older parts of town," Abby said. She turned to look at Merri in the back seat, who nodded her head in confirmation that it was time to tell John. "We want to see if it looks familiar," she said carefully.

"That's where we're going," he said. "Genevieve's is downtown and—wait a minute. I thought you were both new to the area."

Abby looked again at Merri. "I know you're going to have a hard time believing this," she began.

"And the computer hasn't been working right so we

6

couldn't show you," Merri explained.

"We were going to wait until it's fixed, but we've been having trouble with customer service."

"And since we're in Alton we can't resist seeing if we recognize . . ."

"You're familiar with Alton?" John inserted into the volley of comments.

"At least, Alton in 1858," Merri said.

John's eyes were darting from Abby beside him to Merri in the backseat. He looked so confused Abby had to swallow a laugh. "There's a stop light, John," Abby said, pointing to the intersection they were about to slide through. "You see, when Merri's dad sent her the new computer—"

"He was just trying to buy me off since he never spends time with me after the divorce."

"And there was this program on it called *Beautiful House*." Abby paused to gauge John's expression. "Maybe you'd better pull off and stop somewhere. You seem to be having trouble concentrating."

John ignored the suggestion, so she continued. "And one night when we were fooling around with it, something really weird happened."

"Abby tried to talk to customer support, but they thought she was just kidding with them."

"We could see Merri's house in Miles Station," Abby continued.

"Only instead of being run down and crummy, it was brand new," Merri added.

"And then we met Colonel Miles, well not actually met of course— "

"He's the man who built the house."

"In 1846."

"Wait a minute, wait a minute," John said. He flipped

his right turn signal on, moved across two lanes of traffic, and then pulled into the Quick Trip and parked. "This is a joke, right?"

Merri frowned at Abby. "I told you we should have waited to show him."

"You're saying you went back in time to 1846?" John said.

"No, silly," Merri said. "We weren't there the year the house was built. We found that date from the library."

"Oh," he said. "I thought you were trying to tell me—"

"We were there in 1858," Abby interrupted. "But I'd have to say it was a virtual trip only. I mean, Charlotte never saw us or knew we were there."

"Who's Charlotte?" John asked desperately.

"Colonel Miles' daughter. We got to know her quite well," Merri said.

"As I was saying—try to concentrate, John—no one knew we were there, and as far as I know we never changed the course of history."

John closed his eyes, put his head on the steering wheel, and began mumbling.

"*Beautiful Houses* is sort of like my brother's architecture software," Abby continued. "We could zoom in and control the view of the Miles' house. We could follow Charlotte, inside or out, and feel and experience what she did, go where she went. Like, for instance, when she got on the train and went to Alton for the Lincoln-Douglas debate."

Abby's voice trailed off when she saw John shaking. "What's wrong?" She put a comforting hand on his arm.

But then he lifted his head from the steering wheel and she saw he was laughing.

Abby quickly withdrew her hand. "We can prove it,"

she said indignantly. "Take us down to the old part of town."

John continued to laugh and Abby thought how satisfying it would be to hit him with her purse. Really hard. Her roommate Kate had laughed her head off too when she had tried to explain the program to her. She had continued to believe Abby was trying to play an elaborate practical joke on her. Abby snorted her displeasure and crossed her arms tightly across her chest. She'd have to make a new column on the chart for check marks instead of stars. She'd be adding a big black check mark for *mocking* or *disbelieving* or. . . something.

Still grinning, John restarted the car. "Let's go eat lunch."

As they got closer to the old part of town, the streets began to get narrow and steep. And then Abby saw the river and a tugboat pushing a barge upstream.

"Is that the Mississippi?" Merri said.

"That's right, squirt." When they reached the bottom of the hill, John pointed to a huge grain silo that stood near the river. "Do you see that red line painted up there? That's how high the river rose in the great flood of 1993. Whole houses were washed away."

"You're kidding."

"No. They don't call it the Mighty Mississippi for nothing. Alton has always been an important port on the Mississippi River. St. Louis is just across from us."

John turned left onto Broadway. "Many of the buildings here date from the early 1800s. Most of the businesses have moved out onto the new parkway. Now, downtown is mostly for antique hunters and tourists."

Abby wished she could explore some of the old buildings—better yet, do a little time-surfing in them. Who knew what stories they had to tell? Interspersed with them, other buildings, some plain and some outright ugly and obviously lacking the same character and soul, had been built where previous old buildings had given up the ghost in years past.

John parked the car in front of River Bend Pottery and they got out of the car. "Come on," he said. "Genevieve's is just up ahead."

A man carrying a little walnut table came out of an antique store as they walked past. John and Merri paused to admire the paintings in the window of an art gallery, but Abby's eye was drawn to the restaurant next door called My Just Desserts.

"Oh, look, you guys," she said. "Peanut butter pie. I'm trying not to stare, but I think that man in there's eating peanut butter pie." Abby's stomach rumbled and she felt her face turn red.

John laughed. "Don't worry. You'll eat soon."

Genevieve's was a combination gift shop and tea room swarming with visitors. The hostess took their names and suggested they might enjoy browsing in the gift shop while they waited for a table. Abby looked longingly at a tray of salads and sandwiches that a waitress carried past but obediently followed John and Merri to the gift shop.

It was crowded there too. They eased past three over-dressed women who were oohing and ahhing over a display of peach-scented potpourri.

Merri sneezed three times in quick succession. "Wow," she said, rubbing her eyes. "That's strong stuff."

"Wow is right," Abby said. She wondered if customers ever freaked out from the sensory overload. Vases of silk flowers in every hue sat among calico tea cozies, beaded handbags, miniature Beatrix Potter books, along with innumerable other girly treasures. Overhead, garlands of yellow forsythia, each bud with its own tiny white light, cast a warm glow.

John held up a turquoise T-shirt emblazoned with sequins spelling the words *Grandma's Are Just Antique Little Girls*. "My mom's birthday is in a couple of weeks. Do you think she'd like this?"

Not if she's sane, Abby thought. Or understands the rudiments of punctuation. But she was saved from having to come up with a kind reply when the "Robertson party of three" was summoned over the loudspeaker. Following the hostess, they made their way to the dining room, which unsurprisingly was another estrogen-powered extravaganza. The walls were papered with pink roses and each of the round tables was covered in a different floral print skirt, dripping with cream lace.

Abby had trouble seeing John over the centerpiece— an oversized tea pot filled with pink silk hydrangeas. She studied the menu of salads and sandwiches, all of which seemed to feature raspberries. But it was hard to think in the unrelenting pink of the room. The conversational buzz didn't help. The majority of their fellow diners were women over forty, and the majority of *them* wore dresses in floral prints much like that of the table cloths. They all seemed to be enjoying their fruity salads and sandwiches. Obviously, something was wrong with her, Abby thought, because she had the urge to run into the street screaming for a hamburger.

But then John peeked over the hydrangeas and smiled proudly at her. "I hope you like it. Mom said this would be a good place."

Abby's heart melted and she forgot she was annoyed with John. Would this star fall under *romantic* or *considerate*?

Of course it couldn't get too romantic with Merri there, even though she was good as gold and didn't say

11

much while they ate and tried to carry on a conversation over the centerpiece. But then Merri's phone warbled and she squealed. "It's a text from Mom. She says Dad is coming down to see me tomorrow!"

The women at the table next to them looked annoyed and Abby mentally cringed. But then she thought, tough luck, ladies. She was just relieved that Merri was so much happier.

"Merri's been wanting to go to Chicago to visit her dad, but her mom hasn't been able to take her," Abby explained. She couldn't tell him with Merri there that Pat had been stalling because she didn't want Merri to be around her father's criminal activities, or that it was the reason she had taken Merri and begun a new life in Miles Station in the first place.

"He wants me to pick out a place to go for lunch and I get to choose something fun to do afterwards. What should I say?"

"Well," John said. "There's the Brown Cow. They have really good burgers and steaks."

Abby nodded her head in wholehearted agreement. "That sounds good. I bet he'd like that."

Merri's thumbs were a blur as she texted her mom. "Okay, but what should we do after lunch?"

"Let's go." John tucked cash into the leather check folder the waitress had laid on the table. Then he stood and pulled Abby's chair out. "We'll think of something."

When they stepped outside, Abby pointed to an old brick three-story building across the street. "Isn't that City Hall?"

"I think that's it." Merri started to cross the street, but

John held her arm just before she would have stepped in front of a motorcycle.

"It used to be. Now it's the Alton History Museum," John said. "You'd probably like it since you're so keen on the past."

"Keen? Does anyone use that word anymore?" Abby said, laughing.

"Hey, I like retro words."

A *Closed* sign hung on the door, but Abby and Merri shaded their eyes and blatantly stared through the window. "There's a big picture on the wall," Merri said. "Look, Abby, do you see it?"

"That's it. See, John, there's Abraham Lincoln and Stephen Douglas shaking hands."

"Remember how goofy Lincoln looked, Abby?"

"Yes, but he was passionate about preventing the expansion of slavery, even if his voice was all twangy and weird," Abby said. "We need to come back when the museum is open."

"Do you mean the re-enactment?" John said. "They hold it every October."

"That's right. It was October 16th, 1858. There were chairs set up in front, but most people stood. Hundreds of people were here. They came from miles around."

"It was a really big deal to them," Merri said.

"The band marched along Front Street and then up Henry Street past the hotel where the speakers were staying. Lincoln's son Todd was marching along with the other cadets from the Alton Military Academy."

"Listen," John said. "Enough, already. I'm impressed that you two have studied a lot of history this summer."

Abby sighed when she saw the expression on John's face. "Oh, never mind. Just take us home, John. When we get the computer fixed, I'll show you."

John walked Abby to the front door, which although it was polite, was not very romantic since Merri was also there and didn't seem to be in any hurry to leave.

"Don't the trellises look nice?" Merri said. John had helped install them on the sides of the porch, and the honeysuckle their neighbor Mrs. Arnold had contributed was already starting to bloom. Indeed, the porch was looking good, the perfect place to say goodbye.

"Merri, your mom will be wondering why we're late," Abby hinted.

"Maybe John can help us fix the computer."

"Not this time," he said.

Then Merri suddenly seemed to realize that it was time for her to go. "Oh, right. See you," she said and tripped over the threshold in her haste to get inside the door.

And then finally, Abby was alone with John and it started to seem like a real date.

"Thanks, I had a good time."

John smiled and her stomach fluttered. "Me too, Abby."

She felt herself blushing and knew there was not one thing she could do but wait it out. What? Was she fifteen again? She was startled to find she couldn't maintain eye contact with him either. But when she glanced away she saw his hands, and that was almost as nerve-wracking as looking into his blue eyes. She remembered how strong and capable his hands had been when he helped her with the trellis last week—and how gentle with Merri's little friend Michael when the bullies teased him.

Then he leaned in closer, and his cologne, an intoxicating blend of something citrus and spicy, went right to her brain and she actually felt faint. He was going to kiss her, and she was going to faint right there on Pat and Merri's front porch. She took a breath and closed her eyes.

Nothing.

Abby opened her eyes and saw that he was looking at his watch. And frowning. "Well," he said, "it's 4:00. I've got to go."

"Oh. Of course." Abby felt stupid. How could she have gotten it so wrong?

"Well, you know when you own your own business you've got to keep early hours."

"Oh."

"See you tomorrow at church?"

"Okay."

She watched as he hurried back to his blue Mustang and continued watching as he drove away down Miles Station Road toward Brighton. She waved, but he didn't look back.

Abby sat down on the porch step and wondered where it had started to go wrong. After a while, she took her phone out of her purse and smiled when she saw there were five missed calls from her roommate Kate. Had it been anyone else, she would have been concerned that there was some dire emergency, but since it was Kate, she knew it was just impatience to hear all the nitty-gritty details of her date.

"Okay, give," Kate said right off.

"Hi, to you too, Kate."

"Oh well, hi, then. You know I'm dying to know how it went, so don't think you're going to torture me with this."

"It was nice. He took me to a fancy-schmancy tea room for lunch."

"That's so romantic."

15

"Yeah, well, I'm still hungry. Merri, too. She almost asked him to pull through McDonald's on the way home, but I wouldn't—."

"Wait a minute, wait a minute. Back up there, girlfriend. Are you telling me the chubster—I mean youngster—went with you? On your date with tall, dark, and handsome?"

"Hey, don't call her that. Her name's Merri."

"Well, excuse me. You called her that. Chubster, brat, slug, couch potato."

"Yeah…well…I shouldn't have. She's got issues, but she's working through them."

"Okay, *Merri*, then. I guess it wasn't much of a date with her along. No wonder you sound all frowny."

"I'm not frowny! Well, all right, I am now, but that's because you're being so annoying."

"Tell Auntie Kate all about it. What's wrong?"

"It's just that I thought John had such potential. He already has ten stars, and counting. But it got all weird and he rushed off. Right when I actually thought he was going to kiss me."

"Did you ever think it might be because Merri was there?" Kate's laughter made her even more annoyed.

"Don't be an idiot, Kate. Merri went in the house and there was plenty of opportunity, but he left like I had a contagious disease or something."

"But isn't that a nice change from the last guy who couldn't keep his paws off you long enough to carry on a simple conversation? And maybe next time, when Merri isn't tagging along…"

"Yes, but…well…if you must know, I think the real reason is…John thinks I'm crazy."

"Don't be ridiculous. You're the sanest person I— wait a minute. You didn't tell him about all that time travel hocus pocus, did you? You did, didn't you?"

"It's not hocus pocus. I tried to tell you, we really—"

"Okay, a joke, then. But, Abby, some people just aren't going to think it's funny when you keep on like that."

"Oh, never mind," Abby sighed. "When I get the computer fixed, I'll show you. You and John both. You are still coming down for a visit, aren't you?"

"I will as soon as I can get untangled from some things here. I can't wait to meet John—and the new improved Merri."

"Good. Maybe you can help me get a read on him," Abby said, and then muttered after she hung up, "And I'll introduce you to Charlotte and Abraham Lincoln too."

Merri was waiting for her when she opened the front door and Abby wondered if she had been spying out the window.

"Did he kiss you?" Merri demanded.

"Merri!" Pat said.

"Let's just say you won't have to worry about not seeing much of me this summer, Merri," Abby said and then described John's odd departure.

"What's the matter with that boy?" Pat said. "Why, any red-blooded guy would want to kiss you . . ." Pat's eyes widened. "He did say he likes theatre. I bet that's it. He's . . ." She nodded toward Merri and lowered her voice. "You know… of another persuasion."

"Mom, you don't have to talk in code," Merri said. "I'm not stupid."

"Why would he take me on a date if he's gay?"

"Some gay guys like to use a girlfriend as cover," Pat said. "I saw it on TV. And he's too nice. I mean, what guy wants to take a kid along on a date?"

"I'm sure that's not true, Pat." But then picture of

John sitting so at ease among the crowd of women in the flowery tea room popped unbidden into her head.

So, either she was crazy or he was gay—or, hey, maybe both.

ℰVERY ℋILL AND ℳOUNTAIN

book 3

An old house + A new computer program = The travel opportunity of a lifetime… …to another century.

The People

Since *Beautiful Houses* worked so well for the Old Dears' family tree project, Abby's college roommate Kate hopes the computer program will help her find out more about her ancestor Ned Greenfield.

Abby and John reluctantly agree to help Kate, but only on the condition that she and her fiancé Ryan promise to keep the program a secret, because if the government ever discovered they possessed a computer program that allows you to rewind and fast forward the lives of people it would surely want to get its hands on it.

The two couples take a trip to the tiny town of Equality, set in the hills of southern Illinois and the breath-taking Shawnee National Forest. According to Kate's research, Ned Greenfield was born there at a place called Hickory Hill.

The mayor, police chief, and townspeople are hospitable and helpful—until the topic of Hickory Hill comes up. Then they are determined to keep them away. Eventually they find Hickory Hill on their own—both the mansion and the lonely hill it sits upon.

The House

Built in 1834, Hickory Hill stands sentinel over Half Moon Salt Mine where the original owner John Granger accumulated his blood-tainted fortune with the use of slave labor. In the free state of Illinois—the Land of Lincoln.

Abby and her friends meet Miss Granger, Hickory Hill's current eccentric owner, and they eventually get the chance to run *Beautiful Houses* there. Their shocking discovery on the third floor concerning Kate's ancestor Ned Greenfield is almost too much to bear. What they learn sends them racing to the opposite end of the state to find the missing link in Kate's family tree. And there they are reminded that God is in the business of redemption— that one day he'll make all things new.

What Readers Are Saying About

ℰVERY 𝓗ILL AND 𝓜OUNTAIN

"This is one of those series that I reluctantly agreed to read when the author contacted me but then begged for the next book to be released. It's been quite a while since I've gotten this wrapped up in a YA series. . .Don't fool yourself — this series isn't just for teens!"

—Regina Hott
www.HottBooks.com

"Deborah writes the kind of historical fiction that I love to read. BELIEVABLE! I am drawn into her books so much that I really think I'm there with the characters. . . I admire Deborah's attention to detail and the voice she gives to her characters... The ending was more satisfying than a delectable bar of chocolate. I believe that high school kids and adults will love the ride the author takes us on as we discover the secrets of Hickory Hill."

—Robyn Campbell
www.robyn-campbell.blogspot.com

An Excerpt from

$\mathcal{E}$VERY $\mathcal{H}$ILL AND $\mathcal{M}$OUNTAIN

Chapter 1

"Did Doug say how long this is going to take?" Abby said, blowing her bangs out of her eyes. "And remind me. Why exactly are we using this antique instead of an electric one?"

"He said using an electric ice cream maker meant it didn't count as homemade," John said, wiping his forehead with first his left T-shirt sleeve and then his right.

"Really?"

"Really. And I'm supposed to crank until I can't turn it anymore."

The day was typical for southern Illinois in late August: hot and humid. At least she was sitting on an icy, albeit uncomfortable, seat in the shady pavilion. Doug Buchanan had to be sweltering out in the sun where he manned the deep-fat fryer along with three of his cousins. Wearing a Cardinals cap to keep the sun off his balding head and an apron that said, "Kiss the Cook," Doug looked so friendly and benign that Abby wondered again how she had ever thought of him as The Hulk.

One of Doug's cousins gestured their way and said something that she couldn't make out. Whatever it was made the other men laugh.

A short distance away, under the shade of a maple

tree, Jason and Jackson, Doug's twin teenage sons were practicing their washer-throwing skills in preparation for the tournament to be held tomorrow. The washers clinked and clacked, depending upon how, or whether, they hit the sand-filled wooden boxes. Those sounds along with the rhythm of the turning crank and the hot afternoon made Abby drowsy, and she surveyed the activities going on around her through a sleepy haze.

Next to them, Doug's wife Dora and a dozen other Buchanan women began unpacking coolers and setting out dish after dish onto the groaning picnic tables under Alton City Park Pavilion #1. Abby turned and smiled at the look on John's face as cakes, pies, bowls of watermelon chunks, and dozens of other goodies made their appearance.

"Hey, Dora, is that potato salad?" he asked.

"Yep," she said with a wide smile. "And I brought macaroni salad and deviled eggs."

John sighed blissfully.

"This is nothing. Wait'll tomorrow," Doug called to them. "That's when the ladies go all out. I heard Aunt Hil's making her chocolate chip cake."

Under the second pavilion reserved for the event, Eulah and Beulah played dominoes with several of the other elderly relatives. Fanning themselves with paper plates, they chattered happily while they waited their turns.

Abby smiled and a wave of contentment washed over her, knowing that she had been instrumental in getting the Old Dears in touch with their Buchanan relatives. And now the 85-year-old twins were at their first-ever family reunion.

Eleven-year-old Merri came over, panting and red-faced, but smiling. On each arm clung—as they had from the first half hour there—an adoring little girl. One little blonde looked about four, the other about six.

"What are you doing?" Abby asked.

"We're taking a break from the kiddie games," Merri said. "I'm hot."

Merri was a different girl from the one Abby had met when she had arrived at the beginning of summer to be her tutor. Naturally, she still had her moments of sadness and snarky attitude. After all, her mother was hardly ever around and her father was serving time in Joliet Prison. But Eulah and Beulah had made her their pretend granddaughter and invited her to come along to the Buchanan reunion.

Abby pushed Merri's hair away from her sweaty face and grinned. "It's hard work being an honorary cousin, isn't it?"

Merri frowned, but it was easy to see she loved the little girls' attention. "Yeah, tell me about it," she said. "Is the ice cream about done?"

"Not quite," John said. "I can still turn the crank. Slowly, but still."

"Come on, Mewwi," the smaller girl lisped. "Let's go swing on the swings."

"Okay," Merri said good-naturedly. She turned to look back as she was being dragged away. "But don't forget, John. You're on my team in the water balloon war."

"I won't forget, squirt."

Abby lifted her hair and waited for a breeze to cool her own sweaty neck.

John blew gently and then leaned down to kiss it. "Watch out, girlie. That's what led to the ice incident before."

Earlier John had put a piece of ice down the back of her T-shirt, which had made her leap up from the ice

3

cream churn with a squeal. He had chased her around the pavilion threatening her with more ice until she told him to behave or he'd have to get someone else to help.

John's breath on her neck did anything but cool her off. Abby leaned back and kissed his cheek. "Just stick to your job, ice cream boy."

Doug Buchanan brought a huge platter of fried fish over and handed it to his wife. "Is the ice cream about done, John?"

"I'm still cranking."

Doug laughed and glanced back at his grinning cousins. "You can stop now. Anyone else would have quit a half hour ago. Anyone with normal-sized muscles, anyway."

"Dang it, Doug!" John said. "I think my arm may fall off."

Abby rose from her bumpy perch and rubbed her sore rear. "Yes, and a certain part of my anatomy."

Doug packed the ice cream maker with more ice and covered it with thick blankets. Then, after conferring with the women about the readiness of the food, he put his fingers to his mouth and whistled for everyone to come and eat.

After Reverend Goodson, the Old Dears' pastor, prayed an uncharacteristically short prayer, Merri and a gaggle of other kids converged on the food table. Dora shooed them back and invited the oldest members of the family, including Eulah and Beulah, to fill their plates first. John held Eulah's plate while she made her selections, and Abby held Beulah's, and then they helped the ladies onto the awkward picnic benches near their friends.

Then she and John filled their plates and went to sit by Merri.

"What's that pinky fluffy stuff?" John said, pointing

4

to Merri's plate.

"Dora said it's a salad, but it tastes good enough to be dessert."

"Sounds good to me," he said after he had swallowed what looked to Abby like a mountain-sized bite of potato salad. "I'm going to get some on my next trip."

"This is going to take a while, isn't it?" Abby said.

"Yep," John said.

"Could you try to hurry?" Merri said. "Me and Abby have to—"

"Abby and I," Abby said.

"Whatever," Merri said. "Anyway, we have to get home and get ready for our girls' night with Kate. We're going to make snickerdoodles and—"

"You are?" he said. "Bless you, my child. You know how I love snickerdoodles."

"Well, you're not a girl, John," Merri explained earnestly. "So you know you can't come to our girls' night, right?"

"Yeah, John," Abby said, patting his bicep. "You're definitely not a girl."

"That's okay, Merri," he said. "I'll survive."

"Merri, you're going to love Kate," Abby said. "She's a riot."

"That doesn't sound good."

Abby laughed. "I mean, she's a lot of fun. She always thinks of something crazy to do."

After Abby's disastrous roommate her freshman year at Ambassador College, Kate had been a Godsend. After only a few weeks as sophomores, they had become best friends. They didn't share any classes together since Kate was majoring in art and Abby in elementary education. But together they had explored Chicago's art museums to Kate's delight, and bookstores and coffee shops to Abby's.

While it was true that Kate's personality was so different from her own, Abby knew they each brought balance to the friendship. As for herself, she needed to stop being so serious all the time, to lighten up and go with the flow once in a while. When Kate had decided to wear outdated and mismatched polyester clothes from the thrift store to the dining hall just to see people's faces, Abby had gone along with the joke. Seeing the reactions had been educational, like one of the experiments in her sociology class. And it had been amazingly freeing to do something spontaneous and random.

But sometimes Kate needed Abby to be the voice of reason. When Kate got the idea to paint their dorm room purple suddenly after chapel one day, Abby had reminded her that she had a test to study for and that they'd have to pay a small fortune in primer and paint to convert the walls back to boring white for the next students to occupy 205b Whitaker Hall.

Kate's visit today was another example of her spontaneity. Abby had been trying to get Kate to come visit for weeks, but she had been caught up in a project with her mother and unable to get away. Then, just two hours ago, she'd texted to say she was coming. Now. But instead of spending their time together at Merri's house as they had planned all along, Kate had proposed a "friend-fest weekend in Equality," which according to John was a tiny, Podunk town three hours southeast of Alton.

She would have to talk Kate down from that hare-brained idea when she got there.

"Look at the idiot," John said, gesturing with a thumb.

An electric blue PT Cruiser roared down the gravel road toward them, slowing only minimally before skidding to a stop alongside the pavilions.

White dust coated the windshield, and Abby couldn't see the car's occupants. But she recognized the ARTCRZY license plate and began to disentangle herself from the picnic table. "That idiot would be Kate," she said with a laugh.

"Oh. Sorry." John wiped his hands and rose from the picnic table.

"Come on, both of you," Abby said. "I want to introduce you."

Merri wiggled out of her space at the picnic table and went to stand expectantly at Abby's side. "I thought she wasn't supposed to be here until tonight."

"She wasn't," Abby said. "But that's Kate for you."

The car door opened, and Kate stepped out and rushed toward Abby. She was wearing a pristine white sundress and heeled sandals. Her hair was a shining mahogany mane that fell half way down her back.

Abby threw her arms around her friend. "You look fabulous. How did you find us?"

"We went to the house first, and Merri's mom told us where you were."

"It seems like ages since the beginning of summer break. Wait a minute," Abby said, pulling back to look into Kate's face. "We? We who?" Then, over her shoulder she saw Kate's boyfriend unfolding his tall, lanky frame from the passenger seat. His polo shirt was the same brilliant white of Kate's dress, and he wore charcoal gray tailored slacks.

Abby felt a quick burst of disappointment and shot a look at Kate, but she was looking at Ryan as if he were the best thing since the invention of air conditioning. She must have gone spontaneous again and decided to bring him along. So much for their girls-only weekend.

Abby pasted on a smile and said, "Ryan. You came

7

too. Good. I want you to meet Merri and John. Guys, this is my infamous roommate Kate Greenfield and her boyfriend Ryan Turner."

Ryan and John shook hands, but Kate thrust hers in Abby's face. "Not boyfriend anymore—fiancé! I told you he was going to ask. Isn't it gorgeous?"

The sun glinted off a huge diamond ring on Kate's left hand. "You're engaged? You didn't tell me." Abby shook her head to clear it. "I mean, yes, it's gorgeous."

"I wanted to surprise you. I've been dying to tell you ever since Ryan popped the question last weekend."

Abby hugged her again. "Have you set a date?"

Ryan smiled contentedly. "Next June after Kathryn graduates," he said with an indulgent smile. "One and a half carets of sparkle to hold her until then." He put an arm around Kate's neck and kissed her temple. "But don't worry, Kathryn. I promise to upsize it as soon as I get my law practice."

"Ryan just graduated from the pre-law program at the University of Illinois," Abby explained to John.

"Really? I've never seen you around."

"Chicago campus," Ryan said. "I think Kate said you're at Urbana?"

"That's right. Where will you go to law school?"

"Loyola," Ryan said. "It's really the only choice."

"Do you really think so?" John said. "I have my eye on Kent."

Ryan pushed a strand of silky dark brown hair back from his face. It was similar in color and texture to John's, only freakishly perfect in cut and style.

Kate pulled her to the side and said in what passed for her version of a whisper, "Why didn't you tell me how hot John is? Wow! No wonder you've been going crazy for him. We could have a double wedding, Abby."

8

Abby blinked in panic, but sneaking a look at the guys, she saw that they were still talking about law schools. Hopefully, John hadn't heard Kate's outrageous comment. "Kate! We've only known each other for a few weeks."

Kate just smiled knowingly and then turned and held out a hand to Merri. "You must be Merri," she said. "Abby's told me so much about you."

Merri shook her hand, her expression changing to uncertainty. "Uh, really?"

"Really," Kate said. "About how smart you are, and nice."

Merri's face brightened. "Abby told me about you, too. We're going to my house after this."

"I'm looking forward to it."

"Come on, let's get you guys some food first," Abby said. "Wait until you see the selection."

"How about if John and I go get food so you two can get started gabbing?" Ryan said.

"You're so thoughtful." Kate patted his arm.

When the guys were lost in the crowd, Abby said, "Another imaginary star on Ryan's imaginary chart?"

Kate grinned. "He just keeps on racking them up."

"John, too," Abby said. "I've lost track of how many stars he's collected this week. But, hey, you're the one with stars—in your eyes." She put her arms around Kate and squeezed again. "I'm so glad you're here."

"Do you think I should tell Ryan about his chart— you know, since we're engaged now?"

"No way! Well, at least not here with John around." As far as Abby was concerned, the fact that they had been rating them as possible marriage material was something they never needed to know about.

Merri smiled slyly. "Hmmm. You'd better be nice to me."

"Come on, brat," Abby said, edging her way past a man carrying two heaping plates. "Let's show Kate where we're sitting."

Abby was glad that she'd worn shorts. Hiking first one leg and then the other over the picnic table bench, she managed to sit down halfway gracefully and then glanced doubtfully at Kate's skinny white dress.

Seeing her look, Kate said, "Don't worry. I'm the queen of picnic table sitting. I did a lot of contortions wearing fancy dresses when I ran for Miss Sangamon County. I didn't win the crown, but I did pick up this skill. Watch and learn."

Kate pulled it off gracefully, quickly, and without once flashing her underwear.

"Amazing," Abby said. "I can't imagine why they didn't pick you for queen. So quick, tell me all about it before the guys get back. Did Ryan get down on one knee when he proposed?"

"Yes, he did. Of course, he asked the waiter to bring an extra napkin to kneel on so he wouldn't mess up his pants. He took me to Sixteen in the Trump Tower. It looks out over the lights of downtown Chicago. It was so romantic. I wish you could have been there. Well, not really. But you know what I mean."

"Did they have waiters in tuxedos," Merri asked. "I always thought that'd be cool."

"They did," Kate said, grinning at Merri. "And it *was* cool."

"Did he hide the ring in your dessert," Merri asked.

"No, I don't think that's Ryan's style," Kate said, laughing. "But it was wrapped in beautiful paper and ribbons. I nearly fainted when I opened the box and saw the size of the diamond." She held her ring out for them to admire again.

"Kathryn, you're going to ruin your Manuela sitting on that picnic bench." Ryan was back with two plates. A small frown marred his handsome face for a moment and then was gone.

"It'll be fine," Kate said.

"Hey, Merri Christmas, move over," John said.

When she had scooted over, Merri looked up at Ryan. "What's a Manuela?"

John and Ryan set the plates they carried on the table and then squeezed in at the picnic table.

Kate smiled her thanks and answered the question for Ryan. "Manuela is a designer from New York," she explained. "I'm wearing one of her dresses."

"I bought that dress for Kathryn last weekend in Chicago. It set me back three hundred dollars." He smiled down at Kate. "But she's worth every penny."

Abby concentrated on keeping a pleasant expression on her face. People who dropped price tags into a conversation never impressed her. It was a pretty dress but not Kate's usual casual style. And she wasn't wearing the bright, funky jewelry she usually did—jewelry she had designed, created, and made a small business of selling on campus.

Kate looked from John's plate heaped high with fried fish and various side dishes to the plate of raw broccoli and carrot sticks Ryan had put in front of her. "Where's the food, Ryan?"

"Oh, drat. Is all the good stuff gone?" Abby asked.

"I assumed you wouldn't want any of it, Kathryn. It's all loaded with carbs and fat."

"Well, I do," Merri declared and headed back to the food table with her plate.

Ryan watched Merri leave and muttered something that Abby didn't quite catch. It sounded like, "I rest my case."

Abby blinked. She waited for her roomie to say she loved carbs and fat. That she lived for carbs and fat. That her favorite entertainment was carbs and fat.

But Kate merely smoothed the front of her dress and smiled. "You're right, Ryan."

"We'll get something later in the city." Ryan took a meager bite of fruit salad from his plate. "I was reading online about St. Charles and the downtown St. Louis scene. Sounds like there are a few decent restaurants around."

"Yeah," John said drily, "they have a few."

"We want you to come celebrate with us," Kate said.

Ryan patted his lips with a napkin and took out his phone. "You, too, Roberts, of course. I'll make reservations. Is seven o'clock all right?"

"And then, after dinner," Kate said, "we can zip on down to Equality so that tomorrow we'll have all day to look."

"About that. What made you choose Equality for our little friend-fest weekend," Abby said, using air quotes. "John says it's just a tiny town."

"Tiny town, but a big help with my project. At least I hope so."

"Kate says you have some kind of weird genealogy program." Ryan's voice rose at the end and Abby wasn't sure if he was making a statement or asking a question.

"That's not what *Beautiful Houses* is... not exactly."

"It's all your fault, Abby," Kate said. "I made the mistake of telling Mom about your adventures with the Old Dears' genealogy. Now she is obsessed with tracing our family tree. But we came to a dead end with the Greenfield side of the family. Since you got us hooked, it's only fair you lend us your expertise."

"Genealogy is kind of addictive," Abby said. "And Eulah and Beulah are so happy we found their Buchanan relatives for them."

"Mom wants me to paint a wall mural of our family tree in Dad's den as a surprise. Here, let me show you what I had in mind." Kate took a pen from her purse and began sketching a whimsical tree on a paper napkin. "I thought I'd draw faces on the leaves. And each person will have some sort of item symbolizing them. Like for me, I'll put a paint brush to show my love for art."

In mere seconds, Kate had drawn an amazingly detailed sketch, and as always Abby was astounded by her talent.

"That is so cool," Merri said, returning with a plate of mostly potato chips and pink fluffy salad.

Kate smiled. "Thanks, sweetie. But it won't look very cool if it's all lopsided. And I'm running out of time. The only opportunity I'll have to paint it is next month while Mom and Dad are gone to Colorado on vacation. So that's why I thought if you went with us and we used the program..."

Abby shot a meaningful look at Kate, willing her to stop talking. Fortunately, she seemed to get the message.

"Let's talk about it later," Abby said, tipping her head toward Merri. Whether or not she agreed to go along with them to Equality, it sounded like the girls-only night was off the agenda, and she needed time to figure out how to tell Merri.

Abby glanced at John for his take. He didn't look happy. It was flattering to think he was disappointed that she'd be gone for the weekend. But then he was probably only worried about losing control of the program.

Abby had been telling Kate about *Beautiful House*s and all they'd uncovered with it for the past two and a half months. And for those two and a half months, Kate had steadfastly insisted Abby was joking about the program's abilities. Eventually, she had decided it was just as well Kate didn't believe her because they had begun to realize how dangerous it would be if the program fell into the wrong hands.

But now that Kate had finally come, she couldn't resist setting her straight. "Listen to me," she said, putting her face up to Kate's. "Look at my face. Read my lips. Notice that I'm not kidding around. This is not ordinary genealogy software. It—"

"It no longer works," John said, staring at Abby behind Kate's back. "Not right anyway, not since the Fourth of July."

"But it does still work a little?" Kate said hopefully.

"Yes, but—" John said.

"Great," Ryan said. "Let's go have a look at it."

"Okay," Abby said, shrugging her shoulders at the look John gave her. "But first I want you to meet the Old Dears. There they are at the far end of the pavilion."

The twins, in their identical lavender pants and sequined tops, stood one on either side of Doug Buchanan, as he struggled with a karaoke microphone.

"Aren't they cute," Kate said, laughing. "How do you ever tell them apart?"

"Beaulah's always cheerful and Eulah's...not so much."

The microphone squealed. "Test, test, test," Doug said into it. "Can you hear me in the back?"

A woman behind them called out, "Louder, Dougie."

A man two tables over called out, "Hey, if you're taking requests, I want Proud Mary."

The crowd laughed, and Ryan rolled his eyes. "If they're going to start singing, I'm leaving."

"No, wait," Abby said. "Doug's up to something."

"By now," Doug said, "you've all met these two sweet ladies. Now, it's time to welcome them officially into the Buchanan clan." One of Doug's sons handed each beaming lady a yellow T-shirt.

Grinning happily, the Old Dears held up the shirts so the audience could see that printed on the fronts were the words, *I Survived My First Buchanan Reunion*. The crowd erupted in applause and whistles.

"And we put their names on the back so you can tell them apart," Doug continued.

The cheers turned to laughter when the audience realized the twins had been handed the wrong shirts. After trading, Eulah and Beulah held the shirts up again for everyone to see their names in blue script. Doug went on to remind everyone to be back tomorrow for more great food, the water balloon war, the quilt auction, and the washer tournament.

"Can we leave now?" Kate asked. "I can't wait to try out your program."

"You sure you don't want to stick around?" Ryan said in a fake southern accent. "I have a hankerin' to play worshers. I bet you five dollars I can whup you, too."

"Okay. I guess we can leave now," Abby said. She had looked forward to Kate meeting the ladies, but Eulah and Beulah would have lots of questions that were bound to take more time than Kate—and especially Ryan—would want to spend.

On the way to their cars, John waited until Kate and Ryan were out of earshot. "I thought we agreed not to let anyone else in on this until we could figure out what to do with the program. You know how dangerous it could be if this gets out."

"Yeah," Merri said. "That's the first rule. Besides,

we're the three musketeers. Whoever heard of the five musketeers?"

"I know, I know," Abby said. "I don't know what came over me. Kate's always been so...so...annoying about it, an agnostic, you might say. I don't know what made her change her mind, and I had no idea she had told Ryan about it."

"Speaking of which, how well do you know Turner?"

"I've only met him a few times when he came to campus to visit Kate. He seemed nice enough. Then."

"I think he's a jackass," Merri declared.

John snorted a laugh. "Yeah, you're right about that, squirt. But don't say that word, okay?"

"We just have to give it time," Abby said. "Maybe he'll grow on us."

"Well, until he does," John said, "I think we should stall on showing them the program."

"Why?" Merri said. "Now that it's not working right, all they'll see is a bunch of houses from around the world."

"It won't hurt for them to see that," Abby said, "We just won't mention that the way we helped Eulah and Beulah fill out their family tree was by time-surfing back to meet their ancestors.

Once Again: a Novella

Book 4

**An old house + A new computer program =
The travel opportunity of a lifetime...
...to another century.**

The People

Spending the night in an old attic on Halloween, should have been creepy. But for Merri Randall, it is a night for miracles. When she discovers that the *Beautiful Houses* program is working again after fifteen years, she's given the chance to say goodbye to the "Old Dears" one last time.

Now that she's an adult, Merri realizes the computer program is even more amazing than she had thought when she was eleven. The ability to watch history unfold could be of unimaginable value to her work as a history professor and genealogy consultant.

But would she be able to keep the program safe? The ramifications of such power are terrifying, because if the government ever got its hands on it, Uncle Sam could make Big Brother look like a kindly Wal-Mart greeter in comparison.

But when her colleague Brett Garrison asks her to help his aunt with her genealogy project, Merri decides the opportunity to use the program is just too wonderful to resist. Brett hopes she'll find him too wonderful to resist, too, but Merri has a firm policy against dating fellow faculty members. Even good-looking ones with dimples. Besides, with Abby and John's marriage setting the standard, no man yet has measured up. But what she uncovers about the Garrison family's history may make her change her mind. He's definitely from heroic stock.

The House

The house this time is not actually a house at all, just the ruins of the blockhouse fort the Garrison family built in 1788 as protection from attacking Indians. Only a portion of the stone foundation remains, but it's enough to launch *Beautiful Houses* into what Merri calls "amazing mode."

Watching the fort's history unfold is both heartbreaking and inspiring. Her report to Brett's Aunt Nelda is full of the family's heroic deeds. But to keep the program secret, Merri can't reveal everything she discovered. Like that Nelda inherited her literary talent from her great (x15) grandmother Isabelle. Or that Brett inherited his good looks from his great (x15) grandfather James.

22936871R00162

Made in the USA
San Bernardino, CA
28 July 2015